MW01609980

TO NURSE WITH LOVE

Dahlia Rose

Sugar and Spice Press
North Carolina, USA
www.sugarnspicepress.com

Baby On Board

Chapter One

Major Rafe Steele of the United States Marine Corps slid behind the wheel of his black Escalade with a sigh. For a moment he leaned his head back against the leather headrest and closed his eyes. A big grin crossed his face. It was the start of his four-week leave and it was long overdue. He'd done two back-to-back nine month tours in Afghanistan and then a three-month recon and capture mission in Somali. Leading his unit, they'd managed to take down a terrorist cell and had also taken one of the leaders alive so their mission was a success. Now with all the leave time he had earned and not used, he had four weeks of rest and relaxation. He planned to ride his motorcycle, probably head to Myrtle Beach and sit in the sand and enjoy the cool breeze and waves lapping at his feet. Whatever it was, he intended to be completely and utterly relaxed and enjoy every minute of it. Rafe put the vehicle in drive and drove out of Quantico with a wave to the guards on duty at the gate.

Memorial Day weekend meant one thing: party at his house courtesy of his good friend Lieutenant Brody Gillis. His friend was high on life and could basically find an excuse to have a party at a moment's notice. Usually the party ended up being at his house because he had a pool and, to Brody, that was a prerequisite at any party. Rafe's cell phone rang. Thinking of the devil—it was Brody.

He slipped his wireless bluetooth earpiece in his ear and pressed the button to answer. "Hey, guy, what's going on?"

"Only the best party to end all parties," Brody yelled and whooped.

Rafe winced. "Remember what we said about inside voices, Brody?"

Brody laughed. "I've got the beer coming on Sunday—two kegs—and Giovanni's is going to cater so some of the best Italian food ever will be there. If the food is not to your liking, we've got part of the Swedish volleyball team coming to the party."

Rafe laughed. "How the fuck did you manage that?"

"They were in town visiting our nation's capital and I happened to be in D.C. the same day they were." Rafe could hear the smile in Brody's voice. "I gave them the special invite."

"I'm sure," Rafe said dryly.

"See ya Monday, buddy," Brody said. "Oorah!"

"Oorah," Rafe replied and pressed the disconnect button on his phone.

Leave it to Brody to find the Swedish volleyball team, he thought with a grin. Rafe lived in one of the more expensive subdivisions that had sprung up in the area around Quantico. He joined the Marines when he was eighteen even though his family had a few million dollars. His father was a retired senator who fished constantly since leaving Capitol Hill and his mother came from old southern money. Yet they were two of the most down-to-earth people anyone could meet. The trust fund that he came into when he turned twenty-five bought his house and car and the rest gained interest in the bank. Rafe preferred to live off his military pay. By Saturday, his house would be crawling with women in bikinis and his pool would be full of drunk soldiers.

Rafe gave another long sigh. He actually just wanted time alone in front of his TV doing nothing and napping. But, unfortunately, the party was already planned. Just another reason for his neighbors to think he was some kind of party animal. He saw the looks on their faces sometimes but shrugged it off. It wasn't any of their business anyway. Ten minutes later, he was turning into his neighborhood. His house was at the end of the cul-de-sac—a four-bedroom, three-bathroom red brick home. It was one of the largest on the block. He frowned as he pulled in the driveway. There was something sitting by his front door.

"Is that a car seat? Is that a fucking car seat?" he mumbled to himself.

Rafe parked and quickly hopped out of the Escalade. He jogged up to the front door and hell if it wasn't a baby sleeping on his doorstep. He looked around, hoping that this was some kind of practical joke. He saw no one. It was after seven p.m. and everyone was inside. Anger surged through him. Who leaves a kid outside like this? He tore off the note that was taped to the handle and read the words printed on the paper.

This is Bonnie. She's your daughter. Take care of her. I can't anymore.

What the fuck? My daughter? Rafe looked down at the sleeping baby. Next to the car seat was a baby bag. He picked it up to search through it. There were three cans of baby formula, a few diapers, and some paperwork. The baby moved and made a sound as she opened her eyes. Her gaze met and held his. It seemed like they stared at each other for minutes until her little face scrunched up and a loud wail came from the tiny being.

"Oh, shit. Oh, shit. What do I do?" Rafe looked around, panicked, as the screaming got louder. He saw the little white car in the driveway of his neighbor's house. He'd seen her before. She dressed in nurse scrubs. They'd never really spoken but for a few "good mornings" if he happened to pass her on his way out for a run. A nurse would know what to do. Without a second thought, he put the bag strap over his shoulder and picked up the car seat. Rafe jogged several steps to her door and pressed the doorbell one too many times. The baby's wails were increasing, and when he looked down, her face had turned a bright shade of red. *Oh, no, not good!* He pressed the doorbell harder and then pounded on the door.

"Who's out there trying to break my door down?" a female voice yelled.

"Major Rafe Steele, ma'am," he called. "Um…your neighbor. I'm the house at the end of the street." She opened the door and he held out the baby carrier. "Fix it, please!"

She looked up at him. "Fix what?"

"The crying! The baby is crying. I don't know what to do," he said hastily. "You're a nurse. You can do something, right?"

"Because I'm a nurse you think I can automatically stop a child from crying? Whose baby is it?" she asked.

"Apparently mine. I came home and found her on my doorstep with a note." Rafe took a breath. "I have no clue about babies. Please, please help me fix it so it stops crying."

She stared at him and sighed. "Fine. Come in. Let's see what's going on."

She took the car seat from him and he trailed in behind her. She put the car seat down on the sofa and began to unclip the baby from its confines before lifting the baby into her arms. The crying immediately quieted down to low whimpers as his neighbor crooned and softly patted the baby's back.

"What's the matter with it?" he asked.

She gave him a cool stare. "First, stop calling her it. She's probably hungry and wet. Look in the bag and see if there's a bottle and a diaper."

"Okay," he said and swallowed the lump in his throat. "The note said her name was Bonnie."

"What's the matter, Bonnie? Are you hungry?" she said gently.

"Ma'am, there's a bottle in here and it's still warm." Rafe held it out to her along with a diaper.

"Second thing, my name is Ivy St. Clair, not ma'am," she snapped. "You've been living forty-six steps away from me and haven't seen my name on my mailbox?"

"Ma'am... I mean Ivy, I'm hardly here," he said. "Tours of duty back to back to back."

He watched as she changed the baby's diaper quickly and then popped the bottle in the baby's mouth as she held her in the crook of her arm. He watched the little girl suck hungrily at the nipple. Jesus, what if he had come home later? The child would have been outside alone all that time. Another round of anger flooded him. What kind of mother would do this to her baby?

"Are you going to search the bag and see if you can find any information?" Ivy asked. "Bonnie is well nourished and she has obviously been taken care of. I guess her mother got tired of doing it alone."

He caught the underhanded meaning to her words and gritted his teeth. "Do you think if I knew I had a kid out there I wouldn't have taken care of her and her mother?"

She gave him a bold look. "How do I know? All I

know about you, Major, is that every time you're home there are cars parked up and down the street blocking people in their own driveway, loud music is blasting and a bunch of scantily clad women are running through the neighborhood giggling obnoxiously like airheads."

"My friend throws those parties," he snapped.

"And you're sure reaping the reward, aren't you?" Ivy replied. "Have a seat and check the bag, Major."

"You keep calling me by my rank. Most civilians don't do that," he commented as he sat on her burgundy sofa. He looked around and saw that the rest of the room was decorated in burgundy and blended with hunter green and beiges. It was cozy and welcoming.

"I work at Walter Reed. I deal with you guys all day, everyday," Ivy explained.

Bonnie finished the bottle and Ivy turned her over and rested her against her shoulder and patted the baby's back. The baby burped loudly and they both grinned. He met her gaze and something sparked between them. He knew she felt it too because she looked away quickly.

"Okay, I found her birth certificate. Her name is Bonnie Jaclyn Steele. She gave the baby my last name," he said. "She's six months old."

"What's the mother's name?" Ivy asked.

"Juno Corwin. I don't know that name and can't fix it to a person in my memory," Rafe said truthfully.

"I'm sure you can't," Ivy said dryly. "I don't

7

suppose you keep a file on your conquests—notches on the bedpost must suffice."

"I don't have notches…" Rafe shook his head. "Never mind. Here's Bonnie's immunization record and a list of things she can and cannot have."

Ivy took the papers and scanned them. "She's up to date, has an allergy to amoxicillin, and strawberries give her a rash. All in all, she looks like a healthy six month old."

He sighed. "Good."

"Here. You can take her now." She held the baby out to him.

Rafe felt panic rise in his chest. "Huh?"

"She's your daughter. Did you think I was going to take her off your hands while you continued doing the playboy thing?" Ivy said and rolled her eyes.

He shook his head. "No. I mean, what if she cries again?"

"Then you figure out what's wrong with her," Ivy explained. "She's either hungry, dirty, gassy or just wants to be cuddled."

"I don't have anything in my house for her to sleep in, no baby food, or…" He ran his fingers over his short hair. "I don't have anything."

"Let me ask you, Major, what are you going to do with her?" Ivy asked gently and placed Bonnie in his arms.

The baby looked up at him, and for the first time he noticed she had blue-green eyes. He'd seen those same eyes every time he looked into a mirror. He didn't need a test to tell him this was his baby, and even though he had no clue what to do, Rafe didn't intend for her to be just tossed aside. Her mother might not want the job but he did. This was his little girl.

"I'm going to keep her," he said simply. "I'm her dad."

"Well, then you need to get the playboy mansion in order," Ivy said. "She needs a room, a crib, a changing table, clothes, milk, diapers, baby wipes, toys, gas drops, baby Tylenol if she gets a fever, teething cookies since she is drooling like a faucet…"

As she listed items, Rafe's head began to swim and he lifted his hand to stop her. "Um…can I ask you to go with me and help me get all the things I need?"

"I just came off a twelve-hour shift and it's my first weekend off in like three months…" Ivy began.

Rafe pleaded with his eyes. "Please, you know this stuff, I don't, and I want to be a good dad to my kid. Come on, be a sport. I'll owe you big time. I'll grill you the most amazing steak you've ever had."

She laughed. "Okay. Just let me get changed real quick and then we can go. We'll need that big behemoth of a vehicle you drive." She walked away to head upstairs. "Luckily, she came with the car seat with the base attached, so we can install it in your back seat."

Rafe watched her go and then looked down at the baby who was busy gnawing on her fist. She was amazing, with fair skin and the little soft curls on her head that were dark like his.

"Hi, baby girl," he said gently.

Bonnie smiled and babbled, waving her drool-covered fist in the air. Rafe grinned and for the first time in his life, fell in love. He would call his lawyer in the morning and make sure he had sole custody of his daughter. Juno, whoever she is, could've called him, said something, anything. She didn't have to do it this way. She left his daughter on a doorstep and didn't even wait to see if she would be safe. Bonnie would never have anything like that happen in her life again and he would make sure of it.

His mind turned to Ivy. This was the first time he'd actually seen her up close, and she was a beauty. She had a petite body that held a whole lot of fire yet had fragile features; brown eyes that looked like warm, melted chocolate when she smiled, and ample lips full of sass. Her hair was long and dark as midnight and even though it was pulled into a ponytail, it shimmered in the light. When they shared that look, he felt the spark of desire in the pit of his belly. It seemed not only was he a new dad but he found himself attracted to his neighbor as well. Bonnie grabbed his finger and tried to stick it in her mouth.

"No, sweetie, Daddy's hands aren't clean enough for chewing," he said.

"You're right. Who knows where those fingers have been," Ivy said casually as she descended the stairs.

"You really think I'm some kind of player with a cache of women, don't you?" Rafe said.

"I was thinking man whore, but your way of saying it is much nicer," she replied, slipping her feet in a pair of sandals by the door.

"I'll have to prove you wrong then," he said firmly.

Ivy nodded. "Sure thing, Major."

They gathered up Bonnie and walked outside, and together they figured out how to secure Bonnie's car seat into the back of the Escalade.

"Where to for baby stuff?" he asked as he turned the key in the ignition and Ivy slid into the passenger seat.

"This is going to cost a lot," Ivy hedged. "I don't know how much you make in the military, but maybe we should get what she needs in bits and pieces. She doesn't need everything right now."

"We're getting it all," he said with a wink. "My bank account won't suffer."

Ivy shrugged. "All righty, let's hit a Target."

It was a twenty-minute drive to the super store and then another two hours of buying baby supplies. When they got there, he managed to get Bonnie's car seat situated in the seat of the shopping cart. In the store, they walked back to the baby section and Rafe felt like a fish out of water. He'd never seen so much pink and blue and bright colorful baby items. There were bottles and pacifiers, breasts pumps—which definitely made him uncomfortable looking at—cloth

11

diapers, and so many toys he didn't know where to start first. He stood at the beginning of the first aisle and looked around. He could take apart his service weapon, clean and have it back in working condition in less than thirty minutes. He was trained in hand-to-hand combat and knew how to evade capture in a hostile situation. Rafe didn't think any of that compared to the task at hand.

"Where do we start?" Rafe asked.

Ivy looked around. "Let's go with the basics first—food, diapers and milk."

He looked at row after row of diapers. "How do we pick? What size does she wear? Oh, God, I don't know if I'm cut out for this."

There was a look of pity on her face. "You'll figure it out. Most new dads feel the same way you do. You are just getting started a few months late."

"I wish her mother had contacted me," he murmured and shook his head. "I honestly don't remember her and it's not like I've been with a slew of women." She raised her eyebrow at him but didn't say a word. Rafe shrugged. "I know you have this warped perception of who I am, but I'm not kidding."

"Hey, it's not my concern. I'm just being neighborly in helping you. Having to figure out who you were bumping with sixteen months ago is something I can't help you with," Ivy said and held up her hand when he was about to speak. "I don't want to hear the sordid details. Bonnie's six months old, so I think she would do fine in a size three.

Wouldn't you, sweetie?" Ivy said as she rubbed Bonnie's tummy.

"Sixteen months... Wouldn't it be fifteen? Nine months pregnant, and Bonnie is six months old," he pointed out.

Ivy sighed. "A little medical information for you. When you have sex with a woman, it takes two weeks for the fertilized egg to travel to the womb and implant. Women are not pregnant for just nine months, which is thirty-six weeks. A full term baby is usually born at thirty-eight to forty weeks. So you add two weeks for implantation and two more if she was born at thirty-eight weeks. You have sixteen months."

His mind reeled at the numbers. "Okay, I'll take your word for it."

Ivy grinned. "You should. I'm a professional."

Bonnie gurgled and waved her chubby arms and legs. Rafe trailed along behind as Ivy showed him things he then put in the cart, though his mind was elsewhere, thinking back to the last woman he had been with. It had to have been Vegas and the showgirl party that Brody had put together before they deployed. He had spent that entire weekend in a drunken haze, but he did recall that he and one of the girls had hit it off. She was high maintenance and wanted to live the high life. Even between the drinking and the weekend-long party, she never stopped asking about his military pay and his house. Growing up in a socialite setting, he knew when a woman was gauging his worth. For them to be together, as a couple, was not in the cards. His instincts never lead him wrong, and after the weekend fling, he was off to fight in the war.

He turned his attention back to the process at hand. They were in the clothes aisle now and she was choosing Onesies and little girl outfits. He spied a pink and black tutu and steered toward it. It came with its own top and tiny ballerina slippers.

"What size should I get her?" he called out and held it up for Ivy to see.

She actually grinned and he felt his heart catch. "Six to nine months, and look at you, making Ms. Bonnie into a ballerina."

Rafe grinned. "She gets the best in all things from now on."

At the end of their shopping spree, Rafe pushed three carts one at a time out to the car and loaded up the back of his luxury SUV. That included a massive mahogany crib that he would have to put together. She helped him get everything in the house, showed him how to change diapers and how to make formula.

"Okay, I have to get going," Ivy yawned. "I'm dead on my feet."

Rafe felt a sliver of terror slide into his heart. *Alone with Bonnie?* He'd just found her on his doorstep a few hours ago.

"Um, can't you stay? There's plenty of room," he said. "What if something happens?"

"Then you'll handle it, Dad. Just like women, men have the instinct to protect and nurture their young, so you'll be fine." She pulled out a pen and a small notebook from her purse and scribbled on it quickly. "Here's my number and my cell. If you need anything, give me a ring-a-ding."

Rafe sighed in defeat. He honestly couldn't expect her to give up her sleep and stay at his place to help with a child she barely knew...hell, he barely knew.

"Thanks for all you did today." He smiled at her as he took Bonnie out of the car seat and held her against him. She patted his face with her little chubby hands and he felt his heart melt. "You can check in on us anytime you want. I'm going to spend the weekend getting to know my daughter."

Again, Rafe swore he saw something spark in her eyes at his words—respect and something else.

She cleared her throat and went to the door. "Well, goodnight."

It closed quietly behind her and he was left alone with Bonnie. She began to babble and drool, and then fuss.

"You're probably hungry, huh, baby girl? Let's make you a bottle and then we'll figure out the rest of this stuff," he said.

He went into the kitchen and while holding the baby in his arms, followed the direction's Ivy had given him on how to make her formula. He put a scoop of baby cereal in the milk to make it a bit thicker just like Bonnie had showed him. She told him it was a trick mothers used to help babies stay fuller longer. He sat in his leather recliner and held her in his arms. Bonnie fixed her mouth over the nipple hungrily and began to drink the milk down. She stared up at him with beautiful, clear eyes and smiled around the bottle. Rafe couldn't help but grin. He'd heard fathers on base talk about their children with pride. In the hardest of situations, living on a FOB far away from home, Rafe saw the love shine on faces of hardened soldiers when they looked at pictures of their children. He never thought he would experience it. Yet here he was holding Bonnie and those same sensations coursed through him. Was this what his life had been missing?

"You've got grandparents who will be thrilled to meet you, baby girl," he murmured.

He could picture his mother's face when he showed up at their house. Granted, she would have a bunch of questions about everything, but even so she would welcome Bonnie with open arms. He made a mental note to take Bonnie to a pediatrician to make sure she was okay and to request a paternity test. On Tuesday, he would drive to the base and get her added to his medical benefits and everything else the military gave the children of soldiers. Her mother might not have wanted her, but he did. After he got the baby settled he would get on his computer and research who Juno was. He wanted no problems when he took custody of Bonnie. He was not going to give this woman the opportunity to come back into his daughter's life. If she walked away once, she would probably try to do it again.

Maybe pity was what she needed, but Rafe had none. He'd seen too many young men and women join up just because their family life sucked and they needed a place to belong. If Juno knew how to find his house, she sure as hell could've contacted him. The nipple fell from Bonnie's mouth; she'd fallen asleep while drinking her milk. He lifted her gently and almost immediately she burped on his shoulder and he felt something warm run down his back.

"Eww," Rafe said good-naturedly as he put her back in the car seat. First things first, he would get her room together.

After he had carefully taken off his soiled shirt and threw it in the wash, he took the car seat into the room he felt would be the perfect nursery and put her in a corner and began to assemble the crib. He had purchased the nicest one that Target had to offer. It had two big drawers beneath it to hold her clothes, and there were two shelves in the closet where he could stack diapers and boxes of diapers, and above that was a bar to hang more clothing and her pretty little dresses. Beneath the changing table he had bought was a drawer for baby powder, rash cream, and other things. While she slept soundly in the car seat, he worked tirelessly in making the room a place for his daughter to call her own.

Plans swirled in his head. His mother always liked Disney so he was going to give Bonnie a Disney princess themed room. Rafe shook his head at the way his life had completely turned in a matter of hours. He'd had every intention of coming home and relaxing with a beer. Instead, he was putting a musical Little Mermaid mobile over a crib filled with pink and purple teddy bears. A chuckle escaped his lips at the irony.

Finally, after a couple of hours of work, everything was completed and put away. He gently laid Bonnie in the crib and changed her diaper as she slept. Ivy's milk idea worked because she hardly stirred as he swapped out the wet nappy for a dry one. Rafe covered her with a pink blanket polka-dotted with little brown bears and looked down at his daughter. He picked up the receiver for the baby monitor and walked out of the room. *Just a little longer*, he thought as he found himself going back to the crib to run his fingers over her soft cheek. Rafe stood there, not knowing how long, watching her sleep. But as the time passed, he went from his feet to his knees and then finally to leaning against the crib. He reached his hand in and even in sleep, Bonnie wrapped her soft, tiny hand around his finger as if she knew he would protect her, and that he was her father. Rafe ended up sleeping in that position the rest of the night.

Chapter Two

It seemed that Rafe took to fatherhood like a fish to water. Ivy watched him run down the sidewalk with one of the newest model running strollers. Bonnie was strapped safely within. More than one mother stopped him to peek at the baby. In Strawberry Glen suburbia, he'd become the most eligible single dad overnight. It made her grit her teeth in agitation. Rafe didn't seem to be paying it much attention, however. If he was, he didn't let on. She'd stopped by on Saturday evening to find him on the floor playing with Bonnie, and Donna "Double Ds" from two houses down was in his kitchen making a casserole.

Then again on Sunday afternoon she dropped by to see a plate of cookies on his kitchen counter. She knew the particular pattern immediately. She'd been on the receiving end of those cookies when she moved in. No one but Grace Adams from down the block made salted caramel shortbread cookies. Now it was Monday—Memorial Day—and she planned to sit in her backyard with a good book and relax. There was a knock on the door as she was coming down the stairs, complete with her floppy hat and sunglasses on. Her white cotton shorts and tank top kept her cool and put a smile on her face—she loved dressing down and didn't get to very often. She was always stuck wearing big, frumpy scrubs. When she opened the door, her smile dropped just a little. Rafe stood on her steps looking a bit frazzled, holding Bonnie with the baby bag slung over his shoulder.

"Hi," Ivy said slowly.

"Hey, I need a huge favor," he began. "Can you watch Bonnie for a few hours?"

"Um…why?" She put her hands on her hips and stared at him through the darkened lenses of her sunglasses.

"Well, there's a party at my house and…" he began.

Ivy whipped off her glasses and gave him a direct stare while anger sizzled through her. "Wait. You want to ruin my last day home from work to take care of your daughter while you go party with your friends?"

"It's not the right environment for her, and honestly I forgot about the party until Brody and the caterers showed up. Next thing you know, there is music booming and Bonnie began to fuss." He took a deep breath. "I told Brody yes to the party months ago when we were in Somalia. I reconfirmed when he called just before I came home and found Bonnie on my doorstep."

"And plans change for your child, you moron!" Ivy pointed out.

"This has been in the works long before I was a dad," Rafe argued.

"Why don't you ask Donna 'Double Ds' or Grace or one of the many women who have been in and out of your house to babysit for you?" she demanded to know. He looked down uncomfortably and Ivy narrowed her eyes. "They're all going, aren't they?"

He nodded. "But they kind of invited themselves."

"So, what, I'm such a plain Jane that your friends couldn't see me around your pool?" Ivy sputtered. "Oh, the glam of big, fake boobs and streaked red hair is what they want, and I'm just the woman whose house you came to Friday night. Now you're all Mr. Dad and the women in the neighborhood are baking you cookies and casseroles and you're just eating up the attention, aren't you, while little ol' Ivy is only good for babysitting?"

"You're taking it all wrong, Ivy," he pleaded.

"I'm sure I'm taking it just right," she muttered. "Give me the baby."

He took a step back. "Maybe I should just find another arrangement."

"Listen, I might think you're the biggest slut out there, but Bonnie is cute and just a baby and doesn't know her father's predilection for silicone breasts," Ivy snapped. "I like her. You, on the other hand, not so much right now."

He handed the baby over and Ivy nuzzled Bonnie's neck and inhaled her baby scent. "At least you're bathing her."

Rafe glowered at her. "Say what you want about me, but I would never mistreat my child."

"At least that's in your favor," she said without apology. He opened his mouth to speak and she closed the door in his face, but then she remembered he had the baby bag. She opened the door and snatched it from his hands, then closed the door in his face again. Little Bonnie gurgled and smiled up at her. "I guess we're going to be girl pals today, sweetie. Let's get one of my big old quilts for the yard and we're going to have fun."

Bonnie gurgled and babbled in response, making Ivy smile. She loved children and wanted some of her own. The thought made her frown—with her endometriosis her gynecologist had told her that getting pregnant would be difficult. She put it out of her mind a long time ago because she hadn't been in a serious relationship in years. Her last boyfriend was the type who wanted a family and ten kids. He literally said ten kids and when she told him about her condition, she watched the light die away in his eyes. From there, he got evasive and stopped coming home to the apartment they shared. When she came home from work one day and found all his stuff gone and a note saying that he had told the landlord she would be out in three days, it didn't come as a shock but did teach her to never let a man put only his name on the lease. Luckily, she had savings and Strawberry Glen was a new subdivision looking for buyers. She put down a deposit on the house and was moved in less than a month later.

Baby On Board

Ivy did have a difficult few weeks living out of a hotel and having to put her stuff in storage, but it taught her a valuable lesson: men were dogs. Meeting Rafe had proved that again as well. He was more worried about a party than bonding with his child. Ivy admitted to herself that her feelings were hurt as she set the baby on the spread under the tree in her yard. They'd rather have Donna bouncing around the pool in a tiny bikini—*probably polka dot like her brain*, Ivy thought and it made her chuckle. Not that she wanted to bounce around the pool, but it hurt that Rafe didn't think to invite her. She tried to shrug off the hurt. She was accustomed to being under men's radars. But, God, she wished just once that someone would see her as special. *Just once.* Rafe was handsome—Lord, was he ever, but from today's events she knew, just like all other men, he saw her as just a friend.

He had dark hair that was glossy and slick even though he kept it in the low, high and tight cut of military men. His blue-green eyes held flecks of gold. His jaw was rugged and clean shaven and she'd never seen such kissable lips on a man in her life. He had broad shoulders and was as tall as all get out. Ivy knew she would have to stand on her tiptoes to kiss him. She closed her eyes and gave into the whimsy of dreaming of their lips meeting in passion. She tucked the errant thought away and focused on the baby.

"Okay, little minnow, let's enjoy our Memorial Day," she said firmly and sat down next to Bonnie.

She gave her a Popsicle and watched the orange drip down onto the blanket. Ivy giggled as her little pink tongue licked and smacked at the Popsicle. Afterwards, Ivy cleaned Bonnie up and lay with her in the hammock as the cool breeze blew over them. Ivy dozed as they rocked lazily until Bonnie started to fuss and she took them both inside. While she ate a sandwich, she fed Bonnie a jar of applesauce mixed with oatmeal. She couldn't help but hear the low thrum of music outside her window and voices yelling and laughing. Pushing back at the irritation rising up in her, Ivy closed the window with a slam and turned on the A/C to keep the house cool. Ivy didn't want to think about the kind of fun she was missing out on. Donna and her double Ds were probably topless by now.

When the doorbell rang, Ivy was on the carpet in her living room finally reading her book while Bonnie slept nearby on a blanket. She looked up with a frown. *Ugh, what now?* Ivy got up, grumbling under her breath about rude people ringing her doorbell. She opened the door and Rafe was standing there yet again. This time he was wearing swim shorts, an Army T-shirt and flip-flops. Ivy gave him a cold look, which only intensified when she heard a woman's scream, a splash and then a bunch of whistles.

"Bonnie is fine if you're checking in. Don't let us keep you from your...activities," Ivy said.

"I wanted to hang out here for little bit if I could. I'm not much in a party mood," Rafe said.

"Really? Donna isn't shaking the plastic by now? Maybe she needs another drink," Ivy retorted.

Rafe smirked. "I thought she was a C cup. Anyway, she is not the woman I'm thinking about right now."

He must mean Bonnie, she thought, yet her heart flipped in her chest. Ivy stepped back and ushered him inside. "By all means, come in. Your daughter is asleep."

As he passed, she could smell the sun mixed with his aftershave on his skin. It was a very appealing scent. He walked into the living room just as Bonnie was beginning to stir. When he crouched down in front of her, she smiled and gave a squeal.

Rafe chuckled and picked her up. "How's my baby? How's my sweet baby girl, hmm?"

Ivy watched him, but pushed away the softening feeling she was having as she watched him with Bonnie. "Aren't your guests going to miss you?"

Rafe looked at her as he settled on the floor with Bonnie in his lap. "Please. They really don't care whose house it is as long as the drinks and food are free. I had to lock my bedroom door to keep two couples from trying to use my bed. I then had to lock Bonnie's door because one soldier came out with one of her teddy bears duct taped to his chest."

"Why do you have these parties if they bother you so much?" Ivy asked.

"Seriously, I don't really care. They could party as long as they want and I just sit back and watch the mayhem," Rafe admitted. "Partying has not been my thing for a long time, but my best friend Brody is an immortal college frat boy. I let him have his fun, but in the field he is a stone cold machine. The guys need to blow off steam after being deployed. Who am I to fault them for that?"

"Your house is going to be trashed," she commented. "Do you want some iced tea?"

"Yes, please. I think the only thing drinkable in my house is alcohol right now. I put down my bottled water for only a second and when I came back to get it, it was gone," he said.

Ivy poured him a glass and handed it to him before sitting on the couch. "How long were you guys deployed for?"

"I did six months back to back and then I had a three-month stint in Somalia," he answered.

"That's tough on any soldier. I've seen some guys come back with severe PTSD with less time in than that." Ivy leaned forward and rested her elbows on her thighs and looked at him pointedly. "Are you getting help if you need it?"

Rafe gave her a small smile. "I'm fine, Nurse St. Clair, and I know if the time comes where I need to go for help."

She nodded. "Okay then."

"What area of Walter Reed do you work?" Rafe asked.

"I'm on the rehabilitation floor. I work with the guys who come home with missing arms or legs." Ivy closed her eyes and took a breath before looking at him again. Her job affected her more than anyone knew, but she could see herself doing nothing else. "It's tough, you know, seeing these kids… I mean, a lot of them aren't even twenty-five and they have to deal with the pain and the loss of a limb, plus a slew of other things if they have PTSD on top of everything else. Friday, before you came to my house, was a hard day. One of the boys in my ward couldn't deal with life anymore. His wife left him because she couldn't see herself being with a man missing an arm. He didn't have anyone else and everything felt hopeless to him. He somehow got a razor, though we're not entirely sure where. We found him in the bathroom. The veins in his legs had been cut lengthwise so they couldn't be fixed. By the time we found him it was too late."

"Jesus, Ivy, and then I come running to your house with my problems after you had to deal with that?" Rafe shook his head. "I'm so sorry you had to go through that. I'm sorry for that boy. These kids jump right into marriage thinking their spouse will love them through thick and thin. Most of them don't realize that some of the spouses don't know how to deal with all the deployments and the injuries. Then everyone ends up hurt. We had to watch a kid twenty-four/seven because his wife told him she was leaving him for his best friend who was at home. He wanted to put his gun in his mouth and we had him under suicide watch until he snapped out of it."

"It sucks all the way around. I wish these wars were over so everyone could come home and get the help they need," Ivy said. She slapped her hand on her thigh and sat up. "So why aren't you married? Too many women, so little time?"

He shook his head. "We're back to that, are we? No, it's more like I haven't met the right one yet. And what about you, Nurse St. Clair, why are you single?"

"He was there one day and gone the next," Ivy shrugged. "To be blunt, I have a condition called endometriosis and it might make having kids difficult…well, not might, it will. He left because he wanted to have kids and didn't want to walk the rough road with me."

"Well, he's an ass. When you did get pregnant, that child would have been a blessing, like my Bonnie here," Rafe said. "Men are jerks."

Ivy laughed. "I say the same thing all the time, but you're disparaging your kind."

Bonnie was busy trying to pull Rafe's nose and he was trying to nibble at her hand, making her laugh the sweetest baby laughs Ivy had ever heard. Looking at them together made Ivy's heart ache for a child of her own. She wanted that connection and sense of family. She had no one; she was alone even when she had a mother.

"I'm hungry and I know she has to be as well. I saw there was a jar of peas in her bag," Ivy said.

Rafe grimaced. "That stuff looks awful. She wants pizza."

"She has no teeth. Stop projecting on your kid," Ivy teased. "Do you want some of what I'm having? It's not catered like at your house but it's good."

"I'm in," he said with a grin. "I'll feed baby girl her green goop."

"Aren't you planning to go back over to your house?" Ivy asked as she pulled a covered dish from the fridge. "I hope taco casserole is okay?"

"Works for me, and no I'm not heading back there until I'm ready to kick them out," Rafe replied.

A knock on her door made them both look up. Ivy crossed the room to open it. *Again with the people at my door!* Rafe didn't move, but since her living room, eating area and kitchen was one big open area only separated by a marble kitchen island, he could see the front door clearly. Ivy had to resist the urge to roll her eyes as she opened the door and found Donna and her double Ds on the other side, wearing a polka dot bikini no less. The redhead's bikini top barely covered her breasts and she had on an extremely short pair of cutoffs.

"Well, if it isn't Donna double..." Ivy stopped herself before the entire nickname came out. She looked back and saw Rafe trying hard not to laugh. "It's for you, Rafe."

He stood with Bonnie in his arms and went to the door while Ivy stepped back, but not before she caught the pouty face on Donna.

"You left your own party, naughty boy," Donna said. "I was waiting for you to come back and then I decided to take the bull by the horns and come get you myself."

"I came to check on the baby," Rafe said. "I was meaning to ask where your boys were."

"With their father until Wednesday, so I'm all yours. Come back to your house and play with me, Rafe."

Ivy rolled her eyes at Donna's breathy voice.

"Not right now. I'm feeding Bonnie her dinner," Rafe said.

"Let her do that. She's a nurse and obviously kind of...a bore. You don't need to spend your time over here when there's a party at your place," Donna said on a loud whisper. Ivy had no doubt she meant for her to hear it.

"Excuse me. I'm a what?" Ivy felt her anger rise. "You dare come to my door with those plastic things barely concealed and say what? Say it again to my face."

Ivy was quiet and usually kept to herself, but she would be damned if she would back down and let this woman insult her.

"Ivy," Rafe's voice warned softly. "The baby."

Donna put an innocent expression on her face, but Ivy could see the malice behind it. "Seriously, it seems they are letting anyone get a house in this fine neighborhood anymore."

"Honey, you're not in a mansion in Hollywood, you live in Maryland," Ivy snapped. If this chick wanted fire, well, she was going to get it. "Most people in this neighborhood work for a living. We don't have the luxury of living off our older ex husband's alimony."

Rafe chose that time to interrupt. "Donna, head back to the party. I'll be there soon."

"Okay, darling. Make sure your baby is okay with this one. She doesn't seem to be right in the head," Donna said sweetly.

"I'll show you who's right in the head," Ivy snapped and went to step around Rafe.

Donna seemed to decide that she'd pushed her luck and turned and went down the steps in a hurry. Rafe closed the door before he turned to Ivy.

"What the heck was that?" he asked.

"She was baiting me and I took the bait," Ivy said. "I didn't see you saying anything in my defense when she was openly insulting me."

"Well, hell, you didn't give me a chance," Rafe replied. "Sometimes you have to rise above people like that and let them not see that they make you angry."

"This coming from a man who probably never had to deal with a damn thing in his life," Ivy snapped. "Let me guess. You were a jock in high school and girls like that were just dangling off your arms?"

"I was never mean or cruel to anyone. I was raised better than that," Rafe said. "I'm sure you were too."

Ivy looked at him in amazement. "So I was supposed to let her just come to my door and insult me? You don't know how I was raised, Rafe, don't presume to know me."

"I hear you," Rafe said quietly.

"I'll finish feeding Bonnie. You go back to your friends. They are obviously missing you," Ivy said angrily.

"Ivy…"

She took the baby from him gently. "I promised to watch her so you could play host and I don't break my promises."

"This isn't over," he said quietly.

"No, it is. I see what side of the fence you're on and it isn't mine." Ivy's voice held no emotion. "You're the type that likes to hang out with girls like me for the favors, the babysitting, and for the down time. But when you're having parties or going to dinner on the town, you want girls like Donna on your arm. I refuse to be a second class anything. Go to your party. Pick Bonnie up when it's done."

She took Bonnie to the table and sat with her in her lap, essentially blocking him out. She felt his gaze on her for what seemed like the longest of moments before he opened the door and stepped outside without a word. She sighed and rested her head against Bonnie's for a minute. In response, she got five wet, drool-covered fingers in her face.

"Eww," Ivy laughed. "Well, let's get you fed."

She had felt herself opening up to Rafe, but she promised to never make that mistake again. It was much later when he came for Bonnie, who, by that time, was asleep on the same blanket as before. Ivy opened the door when he knocked and the baby bag was already packed and waiting for him.

She handed it to him. "She had a bottle at nine. If you want to take her in the blanket that's fine because you didn't bring one. Just put it on my steps when I'm at work. I'll grab it when I come home."

Rafe didn't say a word. Instead, he pulled her against him and before she could say a thing, his lips were devouring hers. Ivy struggled for a minute and then warmth flooded her body. Lord, the man had amazing lips and it was just as she imagined it would be. He teased her mouth open with his tongue and when she gave him entry, he delved deeper into her mouth and moaned, pulling her harder against him so she would feel his throbbing manhood. She wanted more, but then reason flooded into her subconscious and pushed away the pleasure of his mouth on hers. Ivy wrenched her mouth away from him and stepped back, eyeing him angrily.

"Why did you do that?" she asked. "What, Donna didn't put out after all? I'm sure there were a few others there who were willing to give you a piece of ass before they left."

"Is it so hard to believe that I wanted to kiss you?" Rafe asked. He walked over to where Bonnie was sleeping and scooped her up in his arms. On his way back to the door his hand snaked out and went behind Ivy's neck. He dragged her to him and he kissed her hard, long and deep.

"I'm not what you think, Ivy. Eventually you'll see that," Rafe said, stepping back again.

She wanted him to leave. She didn't like the feelings coursing through her—feelings he had elicited with just one kiss. Ivy watched as he walked down the street until he opened the door to his house. He looked back and met her gaze for a minute and she forgot how to breathe until he went inside and closed the door. She would blame his kissing her on the fact that he probably had alcohol when he went back to the party or maybe he was just trying to prove a point. He wanted her for just a friend, nothing more. It would do her well to remember that and not expect anything. Ivy refused to be heartbroken again.

* * * *

Tuesday morning came too early in Ivy's opinion. She locked her door and headed to her car, carrying her travel mug of coffee and a chocolate glazed donut between her teeth. As a reflex, she looked up the street and saw Rafe setting Bonnie in the running stroller, and of course Donna and her plastic girls were decked out in a pink sports bra and spandex running shorts standing beside him. Rafe looked up and met Ivy's gaze and she looked away quickly. *Typical*, she thought. She had no doubt that Donna was looking for husband number three in Rafe. Ivy pushed the thought aside nonchalantly, telling herself she didn't care. But then why did it burn in her belly just thinking about it? She got in her car and in the process of backing out her driveway, she watched Donna walk back to her house alone while Rafe turned the stroller to start his run. She didn't want to talk to him, so she pulled away from the curb quickly and headed to work.

Walter Reed was the largest military hospital in the United States. It housed new patients and long-term facilities for the soldier that needed extended rehabilitation and prosthesis for lost limbs. There was also a mental health wing for soldiers who are fractured mentally in the field and had serious anger management problems. PTSD and traumatic brain injuries were some of the top cases there. The entire staff was dedicated to making these soldiers better so they could live a somewhat normal life with their families after what they had been through, entrenched in FOB all over the Middle East. Ivy kept an eye on her patients, diligently looking for signs of mental distress. She didn't want to lose another one on her watch, didn't want to explain to a mother and father that their son just couldn't take the thought of being alone any longer. Sometimes when it got really bad she wished she had taken a job in a normal hospital, but each day she came home satisfied that she helped her patients through another day. That was all that mattered when the day ended. She would never change her job. She put away her lunch and bag before pinning her ID to her chest and walking toward the nurses' station.

"What do we have today, Marie?" Ivy asked the nurse behind the desk.

"Two new patients in from Germany. One lost his foot to the ankle from an IED. The other crushed both legs when the Humvee he was in flipped over. Yes, you guessed it, another IED explosion," Marie answered. "I swear they keep sending these boys in healthy and they are all coming back broken."

"And we patch them up and make them better," Ivy said firmly. "Or as good as we can."

"That's all we can do," Marie sighed. "Sometimes it gets to me. Some days it's all I can do not to burst out crying."

"I feel the same way," Ivy admitted.

"Oh, also, Officer Yummy is here to see his brother and don't you know he asked if you were working today?" Marie grinned.

Ivy rolled her eyes. Marie Watson was thirty five and recently divorced. She had been married to a thirty-year-old soldier. They'd had a great relationship as far as Ivy could tell. When Charles came in to see her, it was like watching two light bulbs light up. Then Charles came back from his first tour a totally changed person and things came to a head when Marie found him in their bed with another woman. Her friend was not about second chances and filed for divorce a week later. It was confusing and sad what had happened, because they had been all about each other. Sometimes the relationship they had made Ivy envious. But now Marie was on the hunt for a new love and she deserved it.

Detective Reese Alvater, a.k.a. Officer Yummy, nicknamed by Marie, came in every other day to see his brother on their floor. He'd lost his arm in Afghanistan and was dealing with a brain injury and shell shock. The combination made him volatile; one minute he was the sweetest kid and the next they had to restrain him and use sedatives to calm him. Specialist Jon Alvater had a long road ahead of him. It was just him and his brother left in the family and the detective was determined to see his brother through it all. Marie also thought that the handsome detective had a thing for Ivy. She couldn't see it. Though Ivy couldn't argue that the man was good looking. He had sexy, sandy brown hair to go with gorgeous blue eyes, and he was around six foot two and built. She was friendly and caring toward him and his brother. That was it.

Ivy picked up a chart and flipped through the pages. "I seriously doubt the man has any interest in me except that I'm the nurse his brother has seemed to imprint on."

"That's still a good thing, Ivy. That boy won't eat, drink or take his meds from anyone but you," Marie said.

"Eventually, the therapists are going to have to break him of that," Ivy said. "I can't be there for him forever and he needs to learn that he can stand on his own two feet and live. Until then, I'll do what I can for him."

Marie patted Ivy's hand on the counter and handed her another chart. "You always do, sweetie. That's why this place would be lost without you. Anyway, he hasn't had his morning meds yet and his brother is in with him now. Perfect time for you to go make sure he eats and takes his pills."

"I'll do the rounds for the other patients after I finish with him," Ivy said. "Time to make the big bucks."

Marie's laugh trailed behind her as she went down the hall to the last room on the left. Ivy knocked on the door and poked her head inside and teased. "Is it safe to come in? Everyone decent?"

"Nurse St. Clair, you're here." Jon beamed a smile to her from his bed. Ivy felt her heart break all over again. This boy was once a vivacious twenty-two-year-old kid with his whole life ahead of him and sometimes he reverted back to a childlike state. Today, at least, he was calm and happy and that was a good thing.

"Hey, Jon. Did you sleep well last night?" Ivy asked with a smile.

"Uh-huh. No bad dreams or anything," Jon said. He held up a box. "Look what Reese brought me. An iPad. I can use it with one hand."

"Well, that looks awesome. I don't have one yet, so you tell me if you like it and I might just have to get one," Ivy said with a smile.

"I don't know why I have to use one hand. Where did my other hand go?" Jon asked quizzically. "And why am I always hurting?"

His brother, Detective Alvater, looked at Ivy with sadness in his big blue eyes. It was one of those days when Jon forgot that he was a soldier. The therapist said it was his way of coping, but each time they had to remind him of who he was, it was like flipping a switch; he'd go from calm to agitated.

"Jon, you were a soldier and you got hurt in Afghanistan four weeks ago," Ivy explained gently. "But we're here to take care of you, okay?"

He nodded with a smile. "Sure. Can I play with my iPad now?"

"In a few minutes. I need to check you over and you need to eat breakfast and take your medicine for me," Ivy said with a smile.

Jon nodded and his brother pushed the hospital table with his breakfast tray on it over the bed so he could eat. While he did, she checked his vitals and looked at his arm for any signs of infection. When Jon was first flown in from Landstuhl Military Hospital in Germany, the wound was jagged. The surgeons at Walter Reed fixed it up so he could be fitted for a prosthesis when he was in a better frame of mind. They had to heal him mentally first before the long task of rehabilitation could begin.

Ivy finished her exam and made notes in the charts, then she smiled at Jon. "Time for your medication, sir."

Jon grinned at her and took the small paper cup. "I like when you call me that."

He swallowed the pills with a sip of water and

finished his breakfast. She was pleased to see he ate it all and pulled a Snickers candy bar from the pocket of her uniform.

"A special treat for later, okay?" she said and put it on the table.

"All right!" Jon said. "You rock, Ivy."

"So you keep telling me," she said with humor in her voice. "I'll let you guys get back to your visit."

"Hey, Jon, why don't you try out that iPad. I need to speak to Ivy for a minute," his brother said.

The injured soldier nodded and started using his fingers to play on the touch screen while his brother followed her to the door. They both stepped outside and she faced him.

"What can I do for you, Detective?" she asked with a smile.

"I've been coming here for months. Don't you think you should call me Reese?" he teased.

"Okay. Reese it is," Ivy said.

Reese grinned. "See, that wasn't so bad. Okay, here goes. Are you seeing anyone? Any toes I might be stepping on if I ask you out?"

Ivy thought of Rafe but pushed him out of her mind quickly. He had his type and she wasn't it apparently. She looked up at the tall, very sexy man who was asking her out and felt a thrill. Why not? Why shouldn't she take the plunge and see where it led.

"No, I'm single," Ivy affirmed.

"How about me, you and some dinner and a little dancing?" Reese asked. "Tonight, maybe? I know this little club that had the greatest calamari and a hardwood dance floor."

"Are you trying to tell me you're smooth on your feet?" Ivy teased.

He winked at her. "Come to dinner and find out what else is smooth about me."

Ivy laughed. "Why, Detective Alvater, I do believe you're being a flirt."

"I am. Is it working?" Reese asked.

"Yes, I think it is," Ivy smiled shyly at him. "I get off at five, maybe six, because I like to check in on Jon before I go."

"How about I pick you up at eight?" Reese suggested.

She nodded and scribbled her address on a note pad she kept in her pocket. She handed it to him. "That sounds perfect. This is my address and I'll see you then."

"Ivy," he called her name as she was walking away.

"Thanks for what you're doing for Jon, and I can't wait to see you tonight," Reese said.

A slow smile spread across her face. She was actually looking forward to it herself. "Me too."

Back up at the desk, she handed Marie the chart and the nurse gave her a raised eyebrow and nothing more.

"Fine. He asked me out, okay?"

Marie chortled with glee. "I need to go to Vegas and use my ESP powers."

"You're a nut," Ivy said as she picked up another chart.

"But I'm a nut with ESP," Marie called behind her as she walked away.

Ivy grinned and sashayed down the hall. She had a date with a really nice guy—the first in a long time. But why was the kiss that she and Rafe shared still at the forefront of her mind? He wanted to prove a point that night and that was it. She would go out and have fun with Reese. He obviously saw something in her besides plain Jane.

Chapter Three

"Mom, I'm bringing a surprise over," Rafe said into the phone. He was packing up Bonnie's baby bag while he held the phone between his shoulder and ear.

"Well, that's nice sweetheart. Is it another potted plant?" his mother asked.

"Better," Rafe said with a grin.

"Thank God, because I was going to go postal if you brought me another piece of vegetation," his mother said.

That was Frieda Steele for you. She never minced words even when his father was on Capitol Hill. If his mother had something to say, she would say it and be damned who didn't like it.

Rafe laughed. "I'm on my way over, Mom. Is dad there?"

"He's in his shed playing with those fishing lures," she replied.

"Okay, just don't let him on that river right now, Mom. He needs to see the surprise too," Rafe explained.

"What in the world are you bringing here, Rafe?" He could tell his mother's interest was piqued.

"You'll see. Bye, Mom."

TO NURSE WITH LOVE

He walked over to where Bonnie was playing in her playpen and he bent to pick her up. They'd already been to a pediatrician and his lawyer that morning. Bonnie was in perfect health and right on schedule in her growth. The doctor took a sample from him and the baby to run in the lab for a paternity test. At the lawyer's they started the process of him gaining full custody of Bonnie. Mr. Sneed would find Bonnie's mother and when they were ready for the court case, all would be well in place.

"Time to go meet your grandparents," Rafe gave her little chubby cheeks a kiss and the baby squealed. It thrilled him at how sweet his daughter was, how she accepted his love and gave it in return. Each day since he found her on his doorstep, he fell more in love with her.

Rafe strapped her into her car seat while she regaled him with a stream of baby talk and giggles. He chuckled. Who knew he could actually make a baby girl laugh? He took her outside to his Escalade and made sure she was secure before he got into the driver's seat and looked at a small bag sitting on the passenger seat. It was an impulse purchase he'd made. He grabbed one of the stickers from the bag and got out of the car. He smoothed the sticker on the rear window and stepped back to look at it. *Baby on Board.* Feeling a sense of satisfaction, he climbed back into the SUV and pulled out of his driveway. He also bought one for the Humvee he drove on base. He was proud and wanted everyone to know he was a dad.

Baby On Board

As he drove to his parents' lake house, his mind shifted to Ivy and the kiss they shared. He did it, and hell, it shook him down to the very fiber of his being. He'd never had a gut reaction of desire for any women like he did for her. Yet nothing seemed to go right when he was around her. She had this impression of him that she would not let go of. It bothered him, yet he couldn't blame her either. He thought back to the various parties at his house and how out of control they sometimes got. He thought about Donna and the way she spoke to Ivy. He should've opened his mouth and given the fake double D's a dressing down. Instead, he scolded Ivy for defending herself. That was a mistake. He would make it up to her tonight when he got home. He made a mental note to grab some steaks and other items from the market on his way home. He and Bonnie would have dinner with Ivy and maybe they could start over. Rafe wanted more with Ivy than just friendship.

It was a forty-five minute drive before he pulled into the driveway. The sun reflected like diamonds off the lake and it was simply gorgeous. It reminded him of when they lived in D.C. and would come up to this house for summer vacations and holidays. At Christmas time when the water froze and it snowed, it looked like a winter wonderland. Bonnie would grow up seeing all of it and her memories would be a mirror image of his. He took her out of the car seat, choosing to leave it in the car and carry her up to the door in his arms. He couldn't reach his keys so he rang the doorbell and waited for his mother to answer. When she opened the door, her eyes widened in surprise and then narrowed.

"Rafe Steele, whose child did you steal? My God, is this the PTSD they keep talking about? Have you flipped out and stolen someone's child?" she demanded.

Rafe couldn't help but laugh. "Mom, seriously? This is Bonnie and she's my daughter and your granddaughter."

"How... Wait, when..." His mother stepped back so he could enter. "Frank, come down here!"

"I came home a few days ago and she was on my doorstep with a note. I think her mom was a girl I met in Vegas," Rafe explained. He never lied to his parents even if the news was not the best for them to hear. "It was a wild weekend and she never contacted me, but look at her eyes, Mom, and her face. Bonnie is mine."

"Give her to me," his mother said gently and reached out to take the baby. She held her close and shut her eyes for a moment before looking at the baby again. "Yes, she is one of us, isn't she?"

"Hey, what's the hubbub?" Rafe looked up at his father coming down the stairs. He was wearing a pair of cargo shorts, a plaid T-shirt and of course his fishing hat. Rafe swore he slept in it and his mother affirmed that she had to take it off his head a few times in bed when he'd fallen asleep.

"We've got a granddaughter, Frank. Look at her." His mother's voice shook and he knew she was on the brink of tears. His parents wouldn't care how Bonnie came into the world. They would love her because she was a part of them.

His father stood next to his mother and looked at the baby in amazement. "Rafe, you've been hiding this little darling from us?"

"I just found out about her a few days ago, Dad," Rafe explained. "But I had to take care of a few things before I could bring her over."

"Let's go into the family room," his mother suggested.

"What kind of things?" his father asked. "Give me that baby, Frieda. Don't make me fight you for her."

"As if you could take me," his mother said with humor in her voice. "Go to Grandpa, Bonnie, let him give you some love too."

Rafe shook his head at their banter. He was accustomed to it, but it never ceased to make him smile. He sat down on the couch while his father lowered himself onto the carpet with the baby.

"I took her to the doctor to make sure she was okay and then went to Richard Sneed to start paperwork so I can have full custody of her," Rafe explained. "The mother—her name is Juno—just left her on my doorstep. She could've called me when she was pregnant. I would have made sure she was taken care of. But to leave the baby on the doorstep like that…"

His mother shook her head. "Honey, young people don't think sometimes. She was probably very scared and must have been in some kind of emotional state to do that. We should be thankful she at least thought to give the baby to you and fate made sure you were home in time that night to find her. It had to be a hard journey to leave Vegas or where ever she lived to drop the baby off at your door. She was bringing Bonnie to safety and that was the right thing. She looks like she was well cared for at least."

"How are you making out as a new daddy?" his father asked. He was holding Bonnie's arms and letting her bounce on his thighs. She squealed and his dad chuckled. "You like that, huh? Is Grandpa's lap a fun horsey?"

"The first night I was out of my depth and panicked as hell," Rafe said. "I ran over to my neighbor's house. She is a nurse at Walter Reed and she helped me get myself together. She even went with me to buy supplies for my house. Bonnie has her own room and everything. I've learned to make bottles, change diapers, give her a bath, and rock her to sleep. I never knew that I could feel so fulfilled from caring for a small child. I love being a dad and it scares me to death her mother could come back and try to take her from me."

"That's not going to happen. Even if she does, the courts look at the father's rights too," his mother said firmly. "I'm sure Richard will take care of everything."

"Yeah, he said he could have temporary custody papers in front of a judge by the end of the week," Rafe answered. "He said the situation is pretty straight forward with the mother abandoning her. We didn't get to base today, but tomorrow I'm taking her there to get her added onto my medical and stuff."

"It sounds like you've got it all covered then," his mother said and then laughed when Bonnie bit his father on the fingers. "I hope you can stay a while so we can get to know our grandbaby."

"I sure can," Rafe said with a smile.

"What will you do now, Son?" his father asked. "You're a single dad with a new baby. Are you still going to leave for deployments?"

"I doubt I will have to go back again, Dad," Rafe answered. "I did my time in Iraq and Afghanistan. Now that I have her I will have to rethink special ops missions. I know I could be killed anywhere, but I'm not going to put myself in danger and leave her unless it's necessary. I have enough rank that I can ask for a new MOS at Quantico. I just have to think about what that is."

"You'll make the right choice," his father said and patted him on the knee. "You always do."

The rest of the afternoon was spent as his parents' house. His dad took Bonnie out to the water so she could see the lake and they had lunch on the deck and then a stroll around the neighborhood. His parents were thrilled with Bonnie and fell in love with her just as he had. When it was time to head home, they kissed her reluctantly, not wanting her to leave. He promised his mother she could stop over any time and take Bonnie for the day. He would have to figure out daycare while on leave because when he started going back to base, Bonnie would need to be taken care of. His parents, of course, promised to help as much as they could; they were going to be hands-on grandparents just as they were parents. He never had a nanny or was left to wonder if his parents cared. Where they went so did he, and that was how close knit they were.

It was after six when he drove back into the Strawberry Glen neighborhood. As he passed Ivy's house, he noticed she was home. Bonnie was asleep in the car seat when he took her out of the vehicle and got her inside. While she napped, he would get the stuff together for dinner and then take it over to Ivy's house when the baby woke up. He was looking forward to spending the evening with her and hopefully he'd have the opportunity to kiss her again. Bonnie slept longer than he expected and it was around seven-thirty when she woke up. He fed and changed her and then packed up the food and supplies in two different bags. It was ten 'til eight when he finally left his house and walked the few feet to Ivy's door.

He rang the doorbell and she took longer than expected to answer. Rafe frowned, hoping she didn't have a long day and was already in bed. He certainly did not want to disturb her if that was the case. But when she opened the door he got a different surprise. Ivy was not in her pajamas but a sleek midnight blue dress and strappy heels. Her hair was curled and pinned up, leaving a few tendrils loose around her face. The dress accentuated her every curve and it was a halter top which meant her back was probably exposed. She left him speechless for a minute and then he frowned. She was dressed up and it obviously was not for him.

"Hey, what's up?" she asked.

"I was going to cook you those steaks I promised. I assumed you'd be home and in for the night," Rafe snapped and winced. *Why did it come out like that? Because she's not dressed up for you, you dolt,* he berated himself.

"You know what they say about assumptions," she replied. "I'm heading out."

"On a date?" Rafe asked.

One cool eyebrow rose in his direction. "Yes, on a date. Aside from what Donna said last night, men do find me attractive and want to spend time in my presence."

"I never said that wasn't the case," Rafe pointed out.

"No, you said nothing at all," Ivy reminded him. "Thanks for the thought of making me dinner. It was nice of you, but I've already got plans."

"Change them," Rafe said.

"Why? Because you said so?" Ivy asked. "I think

not. I'm not here for your beck and call, Rafe, and besides, my date is already here."

Rafe turned around to see a sleek blue car pull into her driveway and as the man stepped out, Rafe grit his teeth. The man was wearing a casual black shirt with the sleeves rolled up and charcoal gray slacks. He walked up to the front door and gave Ivy a smile before casting a curious glance in Rafe's direction.

"You look spectacular, Ivy," he said, running his eyes slowly over her body. "Am I interrupting something?"

Rafe instantly disliked the man.

"Thank you, and no you're not interrupting anything. This is my neighbor, Major Rafe Steele, and his daughter Bonnie," Ivy explained. "Rafe, this is Detective Reese Alvater."

"Nice to meet you," Reese smiled. "I'd shake your hand but it seems you have them all full. My brother lost his arm over in Afghanistan four weeks ago. I don't know how you guys do it, but damn if I'm not proud that we have guys like you out there protecting our country."

"Yeah, thanks," Rafe replied through gritted teeth and then sighed. "It's tough over there. Sorry to hear about your brother. Tell him even though he doesn't know us, we're all pulling for him. That's what brothers in arms do."

"Let me grab my purse and I'm all ready to go," Ivy said and left the doorway.

Baby On Board

The two men were left alone, and a tense silence hung in the air. Bonnie babbled at the detective and Reese smiled. "Cute kid."

"Thanks. Tell Ivy I'll talk to her later." Rafe turned and headed down the steps to the sidewalk. He wanted to punch the detective in the face for asking Ivy out on a date.

"Sure thing, man," Reese called out.

Bonnie patted his cheeks with her tiny hands as if to say, "It's okay, Daddy." Rafe smiled even though he felt jealousy burning through him. He couldn't be angry at Ivy; he held no claim to her. Yet the fact that another man was taking her out and probably going to kiss her before the night was over made him want to rush back to her house and order the detective gone. He stepped inside his own house and put Bonnie in her playpen before putting the food he had carefully prepared away in the fridge. He went to the window that faced her house and looked through the blinds and saw Ivy come out and lock her door. The detective wrapped her into his arms for a hug and lifted her off her feet. Rafe saw red and watched them get into his car and drive away. He vowed not to look outside for the rest of the night. If he saw them come home and kiss, he wouldn't be responsible for what he might do. Rafe spent the rest of the evening taking care of his baby while Ivy, in that fabulous blue dress, was at the forefront of his mind.

* * * *

Ivy sat across from Reese while the music played around them and other patrons ate and laughed. They were drinking their first glass of wine and she was checking out the atmosphere of the place he chose to take her. *Noir* had a sexy, romantic ambiance, with secluded booths made in soft white fabric that contrasted nicely with the black tables. They used the same color scheme for the glasses that held their drinks and they were embossed with gold around the edges. It was an amazing place. The man across from her looked even more handsome by the dimmed lights of the club.

"What do you think of the place?" Reese asked.

"I like it a lot," Ivy admitted. "I didn't know there was a place like this so close to Walter Reed."

"You nurse types never get out to the fun spots?" Reese teased.

Ivy laughed and took a sip of her wine. "Not until a very handsome detective comes in and forces us out from under the fluorescent lights."

"We do what we can," Reese said. "Did I mention you look utterly amazing tonight? I don't know how I'm talking when I'm so damn tongue tied by you."

"You mentioned it, but I don't mind hearing it again," Ivy replied. "You're also a charmer."

"Only when there's an amazing woman to charm," he answered and picked her hand off the table. "I'm amazed such tiny hands can control my brother better than anyone else. The first time I saw you I figured I should put you in my pocket to protect you."

Ivy laughed. "I'm tougher than I look, though I hate being short. It seems everyone is taller than I am."

"I think you're perfect the way you are." Reese kissed the tips of her fingers and her heart fluttered just a bit. "I'm a very lucky man to be sitting across from you tonight."

He's sweet. He's sexy. He's attentive. So then why am I thinking about Rafe right now? Ivy asked herself. She smiled at Reese as the waiter came over to take their order. *Put him out of your head. Focus on the guy who really has feelings for you.*

"I'll have the sea bass with rice pilaf and steamed vegetables," Reese said and handed the waiter the menu. "What about you, Ivy?"

"I'll go with what you recommended and have the calamari with the spicy mayo," Ivy said and the waiter took her menu with a bow.

"You like things spicy, huh?" Reese said.

"Everyone needs some heat now and then, don't we?" Ivy replied.

"Then let's see what we can create on the dance floor while we wait on our food." He stood and held out his hand to her and she took it readily.

He pulled her against him and together they found the rhythm of the music. Ivy had to admit he was a great dancer and being close to him, she could see the muscles of his chest beneath his shirt. She closed her eyes and tried to get lost in the moment, tried not to wish it was Rafe holding her.

"Have you always been a detective here in Maryland?" she asked as they swayed.

"No, I transferred out from Michigan a few years back when Jon was eighteen," Reese explained. "He wanted to be a Marine from the time he was in high school and I'm the only family he has. It was an easy choice for me to move this way when he got stationed in Quantico."

"No girlfriend to beg you to stay?" Ivy looked up at him, and for a moment she swore she saw a spark of hurt in his eyes.

Reese shook his head. "No one worth mentioning."

"Ah. One of those, huh?" she said.

"It wasn't meant to be," he replied. "What about you and Major Dad? Is there something I should know there?"

Ivy laughed even though her heart flipped in her chest with the mention of Rafe. "Nothing there. A party guy turned dad. The real ex-wives of Strawberry Glen keep him occupied. I just babysat for him once."

Reese chuckled. "So it's one of those neighborhoods where you're afraid a heat wave might make some of your neighbors melt away?"

Ivy giggled at the picture in her mind. "Yes, it is. I have some good neighbors and some you just want to go spider monkey on." She threw him a look. "I hope you don't mind I'm one hundred percent real?"

Reese pulled her closer and then gave her a quick dip. When he pulled her back up, she met his eyes. "I like you just the way you are."

He bent his head and kissed her, but she didn't have that surge of pure lust like she had when Rafe kissed her. Still, it was sweet and she tried to sink into the moment with him. The song ended and the couples went back to their seats. Not long after she and Reese sat down, their food was served. He was right, the calamari was amazing. While they ate, the conversation ranged from books to baseball. Reese was a great guy and the date went well. The meal was cleared and they shared more wine and more dancing until it was time for him to take her home. At her door, he kissed her once more and she clung to his arms as he deepened the kiss.

"I'll call you about this weekend," he murmured, looking down at her with desire in his eyes.

Ivy nodded, hoping and praying she could feel something more for him. She watched him leave before unlocking her door and going inside. While she undressed in her room, she wondered why she wanted what she couldn't have. Rafe was not in the cards—not the way she wanted him to be. She would not fight Donna, Grace or anyone for that matter for his attention. She had more self worth than that and, by God, she would make sure things worked with Reese if he wanted to take it further. After her shower, she slid into bed and sleep claimed her quickly. It wasn't Reese that filled her dreams but Rafe. He offered her passion like she'd never known and she accepted it with a pleased whimper as he claimed her as his.

Chapter Four

The week passed by fairly quickly. Ivy had another date with Reese on Saturday night and work at the hospital was routine. Jon was doing better. He didn't have one episode all week where he had to be restrained. She hoped it stayed that way because the doctors wanted to move him to the secure mental health ward. She doubted very much he would get better there and would probably lose the valuable headway they had made in his care.

When Reese came to see his brother, he brought her flowers. Marie, of course, claimed victory about predicting their hitting it off. All the while Ivy thought about Rafe, but when she saw him around the neighborhood with Bonnie she tried to stay far away. One reason was because she was trying very hard to squash the attraction she felt for him and also because there was always Donna or someone else with him, fawning over him. And it burned her.

By Friday after work, Ivy thought she had a handle on the situation. She pulled into her driveway and got out of her car. There was no one around and she breathed a sigh of relief. Seeing him each day was harder than she expected. The kiss, Lord, the kiss was in her dreams and she wished that Reese's matched the heat that she received from Rafe's kiss. *Put it out of your head, woman,* Ivy ordered herself firmly. *That man is not for you.* Her cell phone rang as she unlocked her front door and went inside. Ivy fished it from the depths of her bag and answered it without checking who it was.

"Hello?" she said as she dropped her bag onto the sofa and went into the kitchen. The heat outside was sweltering and it wasn't even the first day of summer. A cold glass of iced tea with extra ice was calling to her.

"Hey, pretty lady, are we still on for tomorrow night?" It was Reese.

"Unless you are cancelling on me, we sure are," Ivy replied.

"Never," he laughed huskily. "As long as there are no homicides before my shift ends I'll be there on time."

"Then I'll get all dolled up and be waiting for you," Ivy said.

"I was thinking about our kiss today," he said.

"Oh, really?" she teased. *Why don't I feel more?* Ivy demanded of herself. She would give it a little more time to see where this was heading. Ivy didn't want to lead him on. She enjoyed his company and he was an attractive man, but if the feelings weren't there she couldn't force it either.

"Yes, and tomorrow I get to taste those lips again," Reese said. "I'm on a stake out tonight so if you need me shoot me a text, okay?"

"I will. You be careful, Reese," she said worriedly. His job was dangerous and she certainly didn't want to see him hurt in any way.

"I definitely will. I have a date with a hot nurse tomorrow," Reese answered.

She hung up with a smile. He did have a way of charming her to pieces. No, she wouldn't count Reese out quite yet. It was certainly better than pining for what she couldn't have. With her glass of iced tea in hand, she went upstairs and stripped out of her uniform for a shower. Ivy hummed while the cool water flowed over her skin. After the heat of the day and driving home in bumper-to-bumper traffic, she wanted to refresh her heated skin. By eight o'clock, Ivy was settling into a quiet evening at home with some TV and leftovers for dinner. There was even a piece of carrot cake in the fridge she planned to enjoy before bed. That would just have to wait because around nine her phone rang again and this time it was Rafe on the line and his voice was frantic.

"Ivy, please, can you come over?" Rafe asked. "Bonnie has a fever. I think it's a fever, and she's coughing. She almost threw up... Jesus, can you come? She's crying and I can't comfort her."

She could hear the panic in his voice and the baby crying in the background. He'd only been a dad for a short time and even seasoned parents got scared. She could only imagine how he felt.

"I'll be right over," Ivy said without hesitation.

She hung up the phone, stuffed her phone into the pocket of her cargo shorts and slipped into her sandals. Ivy took her house keys off the counter and made sure to lock up before she jogged over to Rafe's place. She pressed the doorbell and he swung the door open. She didn't know a military haircut could look tousled, but his sure did. He held the crying baby, bouncing her in his arms.

Rafe stepped aside and let her in, begging, "Tell me what to do."

"Give her here and get me the thermometer we bought at Target," Ivy said calmly. As he rushed upstairs she sat on the sofa with Bonnie in her arms. The baby rubbed her nose and sniffled. "Okay, sweet girl, what's going on with you tonight, huh? Why are you making Daddy scared?"

Bonnie's whimpers were the only answer and Ivy knew a cranky baby when she saw one. Rafe came back with the digital thermometer and Ivy took it from him. Making sure it was on, she waited for the readout to say zero before she pressed it gently against Bonnie's ear. The beep signaled the reading was complete and she looked at the number.

"She has a slight fever—one hundred point five," Ivy told him.

"Oh, God, Oh, God, I'll get her stuff so we can go to the ER," Rafe said and began to look around. "Where are my keys?"

"Rafe, calm down. She doesn't need to go to the hospital," Ivy said gently. "She probably just has a stuffy nose and look at her gums. They're red and swollen. She's teething."

"Teething?" he repeated the word.

Ivy nodded. "Yes, as in her teeth are coming in and this is all normal. Now, what we'll do first is give her some baby Tylenol to ease her pain because her gums are hurting and it will help lower her slight fever. Then, we're going to give her a cool bath and put the humidifier in her room to clear her nose. She'll get a bottle and we'll sit with her and comfort her until she falls asleep. Then, tomorrow, you're going to buy teething rings that can be cooled in the fridge so she can chew on them."

He nodded. "Okay, I can do that."

"Yes, you can," she said calmly, looking at the tension ease from his shoulders. "First, Tylenol."

They went through the steps that Ivy laid out and soon Bonnie was comfortable and even happily babbling while they bathed her. By the time they got to the bottle, her eyelids were drooping and she fell asleep being rocked in her daddy's arms while he sat in his recliner. He leaned his head back and closed his eyes and soon she heard a soft snore. Ivy grinned as she looked at him. He'd worked himself up just as much as the baby had. She got up and took the sleeping baby from his arms and took her to her room. Making sure the humidifier was on, she tucked the baby in. Ivy clicked on the Disney princess color changing nightlight and turned off the light switch. She looked up and gasped in delight. Rafe had somehow managed to put glow-in-the-dark stars and a moon on the ceiling. That was how much he loved his daughter. He'd just found out he was a dad and he pulled out all the stops to make sure her room was perfect. It was the small things that endeared him to her. Ivy went downstairs and tapped his shoulder gently.

Rafe sat up with a start and looked around. "Where's Bonnie?"

"She's okay. I put her to bed," Ivy answered. "If her fever comes back, she can have one dropper of the Tylenol in four hours."

"I don't know what I would do if you hadn't been home," he said with a sigh and ran his hand over his face. "Thank you."

"It's no problem. I know how hard it is on a parent when their child is in pain. I used to work in the pediatrics ward before Walter Reed," she explained. "Anyway, Bonnie is fine. If her fever climbs to over one hundred and two and does not go down, then you worry. For now, she's just teething, but you can take her to the pediatrician for your own peace of mind."

"Where are you going?" Rafe asked.

Ivy chuckled. "Home. The crisis is over."

He reached out and took her hand. "Stay for a little while. I haven't seen you in days."

"You're taking care of Bonnie, and I have work," Ivy reminded him but sat down on the sofa. "It's two different schedules."

"I figured you'd at least call at some point," Rafe said.

"Why?"

"Because you left on a date after I came over with steaks and... Shit. Never mind." He stopped but then added, "I saw him kiss you when he brought you home."

"Wait. Were you spying on me?" Ivy demanded. "And for your information, I kissed him back. Stuff like that happens after a date."

"I happened to be looking outside when you came home—"

"Spying."

"I wanted to break his face for kissing you," Rafe said harshly.

Ivy looked at him with surprise. "Why ever for? It's not like I'm in the league of women you hang out with or ever will be. Donna and her double Ds are more your style..."

He was out of the chair in an instant and pressing her against the sofa. Nose to nose, she looked up into the dark, intense blue-green of his gaze. Ivy forgot to breathe and her heart pounded against her chest.

"Enough with Donna and her fake ass breasts. There is no league to be in because since I first kissed you, I can't get you out of my head," Rafe murmured.

"That's because you feel I'm unattainable. Trust me, I'll bore you quickly and then you'll move on," Ivy said in a rush.

"Damn it. I'm not some kind of player who

collects women as trophies!" Rafe's eyes narrowed.

Without another word, he took her lips in a kiss and she moaned instantly. The heat and desire that swamped her was unlike anything she could possibly imagine. Rafe pulled her against him and Ivy wrapped her legs around his waist. He moaned in response against her mouth and took the kiss deeper. Ivy felt as if she was melting from the inside out. He was ravenous; Ivy could feel it in his every touch. He cupped her breasts and she arched into his hands, letting the sensations take her away. The cargo shorts she wore were short, and she felt his fingers trace around the edge before slipping between the fabric and her skin.

"Rafe, don't," she whispered against his lips.

He moved his hand and cupped her through her shorts. His eyes met hers and she felt as if she were drowning in the depths of his gaze. "Let me show you how I can please you. You need this."

She pulled away. "Why do I need it, huh? Because it's poor Ivy who needs a pity roll in the sack? Or maybe it's you who needs release and why not give it to my plain Jane neighbor?"

He ran his hand over his head and sighed. "And we're back to that? Can't you see past what you think I am or how I see you? You're not plain, Ivy, you are gorgeous. If you haven't figured out yet how much I want you, it's your damn self-esteem getting in the way. You let people like Donna and Grace play against it. I don't know if you were teased in high school or what, but it's time to get over it and see that a man likes you for who you are."

Ivy narrowed her eyes at him as some of his words rang true and they hurt. "I do have a man who likes me for who I am. Reese does," she lashed back at him.

A look of anger passed over Rafe's face as he pushed away from where he knelt. "Don't bring that man's name into anything having to do with us."

She stood, her hands clenched at her sides. "There is no *us*. You call when you need something and I help you. What the heck do you do for me? Oh, a few kisses, that's right. You feel I should be bowing on the ground in front of you because you kissed me."

"I came over to make you dinner," he pointed out.

"And I had a date," she shot back. "Did you want me to cancel and stay home with you?"

"Yes," he said without hesitation.

Ivy threw her hands wide. "Why, because you kissed me once? You invited Donna and Grace and practically all the other women from the neighborhood to your party, but left me out. Yeah, I know it sounds petty, but I don't care. You ran to me when you found Bonnie on your doorstep, not them. Then Donna comes to my house and instead of standing up for me, you warn me off of bitch slapping her. How am I supposed to know you have any interest in me whatsoever?"

"I didn't invite you because I know it's not your thing," Rafe explained. "Donna and her friends are the kind of girls those guys like. They play it loose and free. If I'd invited you and one of these guys touched you, I would have broken the arm that reached out to you."

"Why are you telling me this now?" Ivy asked. "It's because of Reese, right? You saw him with me and now you think you want me too."

"I don't think. I know. And you want me too," Rafe said. He stepped forward and took her by the shoulders, pulling her against him. "Tell me he makes you feel like this. Tell me the fire in your belly ignites when he kisses you."

"It does and more." She looked up at him and spoke with defiance in her voice.

"Liar," he said huskily.

He kissed her again and this time it was so sweet and gentle it almost ruined her resolve. Rafe lifted his head and ran his thumb across her bottom lip. "I'm throwing my hat in the ring for you, Ivy."

"I'm not some prize to be won," she snapped. "You just want what you can't have."

"I'm going to have you, there is no doubt about it." A slow smile spread across his face. "Get used to it."

"I'm going home." Ivy pushed away in frustration.

"You'll be back," he grinned.

Ivy threw her hands up in the air. "I give up. You're hopeless and so full of yourself. Remember what I said about Bonnie."

"I will. I'll remember how you taste too," he teased.

Ivy didn't comment. She just left and closed the door silently behind her. She was walking back to her house when Donna stepped out onto her porch. She gave Ivy a cool glance.

"You were in there a long time," she commented.

"I didn't know I had a time limit," Ivy replied. "Or that you were spying for that matter."

"You need to know when to back off. Men like Rafe don't go for women like you," Donna said casually. "I mean, look at you, sweetie, you're not that spectacular."

Ivy gave her an evil smile. "If you didn't blow up the fun bags I could say the same about you. I don't think men wonder what's going on in your head. You're accustomed to being a trophy for them."

"At least I'm a prize babe, not a ribbon." By that point, Donna had made her way down the porch and was practically nose to nose with Ivy. "Rafe is out of your league, honey."

"Tell him that...honey," Ivy said. "Now, step back, I need to go home. I've got a date tomorrow night and I need my beauty sleep."

Donna laughed. "No problem. I don't know what good that will do you. Just remember that Rafe is mine. I can make life in this neighborhood really difficult for you."

This time it was Ivy who stepped forward. "Go ahead and try it. Do you really think I'm afraid of you and your band of bimbettes? I own my house, and I don't give a fuck about anyone in this neighborhood that would believe you over me. But I tell you this—mess with me and I will take great delight in taking you down. Let's see how you stand up against this plain Jane. Try me."

Donna's eyes widened and she took a few steps back before turning to go back up her porch. "Yeah, I thought so," Ivy muttered and went on to her house. She'd dealt with women like Donna before. They put on an act but backed down quickly. As soon as Ivy stepped into her house and shut the door behind her, she sighed and turned off the downstairs lights. She would watch TV in her room until she fell asleep. But while she stared at the screen, Ivy didn't really see beyond what was on her mind. All she could think about was Rafe and how it felt to be touched by him. The thought made her nipples tighten and a sweet ache to throb between her legs. She wasn't meant to have him and should put it out of her mind. *I'm throwing my hat in the ring.* His words echoed in her head and thrilled her, even though she believed he saw her as just another conquest.

Chapter Five

Rafe watched as Bonnie ate her oatmeal in her high chair. His mother was coming over to pick her up for the day since he had to go Quantico and set up the childcare situation. His leave would be up in two more weeks and he would be back on schedule. He had an idea about his MOS as well. He was offered a job a few months back that would keep him at Quantico instead of being deployed except in cases where an elite team was needed. He would be in charge of putting the team together as well as in charge of their training.

No matter how he kept himself busy, Rafe couldn't stop his thoughts from straying back to Ivy. He'd watched the detective pick her up on Saturday night and then drop her off late, and the kiss he gave her at the front door lasted way too long in his opinion. He wanted to rush out and lay claim to her to send his competition on the way. He guessed that would make the situation worse so even though ever fiber of his being wanted him to go, he stayed inside.

Rafe was dressed in his uniform and Bonnie's face was a mess. He wiped the dried oatmeal off her face with a wet cloth and she gave him a toothless

70

grin. He looked at her gums curiously before he grinned as well. There were two tiny, very obvious white teeth breaking through.

"Look at you. My baby has her first teeth." Rafe chuckled and held out his hand to her. Bonnie stuck his index finger in her mouth and this time, instead of feeling just gums when she used him as a chew toy, he could feel the hard ridges of teeth. He wondered if it was normal to feel such a sense of pride. She'd hit a milestone while in his care. *Hell yeah!*

"Hello. Where's my son and my gorgeous grandbaby?" his mother's voice called out. He had given his parents a key to his house and she had let herself in.

"Kitchen, Mom," Rafe answered as he gathered up Bonnie's dirty bowl and empty sippy cup.

His mom came around the corner. "There's my pretty girl. How's Grandma's baby?"

"Hello to you too, Mom," Rafe said dryly.

She waved a hand in his direction and made a beeline for Bonnie. "Nice to see you, Son, but you're not as cute as my Bonnie Bunny."

"Bonnie Bunny," he chuckled. "Well, she could be now. Ms. Bunny here has her first two teeth."

The squeal that came from his mother was like that of a teenager. Rafe didn't know his mother could actually make such a noise. He turned to watch while she bent to plant kisses all over Bonnie's cheeks.

"You're growing up too fast," his mother said to the baby. She looked up and her eyes were misty.

"We just got her and already she's trying to leave the nest."

"Mom, she's getting teeth not going off to college," Rafe pointed out as he loaded up the baby bag.

"You won't understand until she's a teen, going out on dates and bringing boys home," his mother replied.

"I own guns, Mom. Boys are a no-no." He walked over with Bonnie's bag and car seat. "Everything you need is in the bag, including the Tylenol drops and her cold rings are in a Ziploc bag with one of those ice pack thingies."

"You sound like such a dad." He watched tears fill his mom's eyes again.

"Okay, Mom, no crying." He walked up to her and rubbed her back.

"All you need now is a woman in your life."

Of course she would go there. Rafe rolled his eyes. His mother was notorious for trying to fix him up with some of her friends' daughters. His personal life was something he tried to keep off her radar, yet he found himself opening up to her.

"There is someone I'm interested in," Rafe admitted.

His mother clapped her hands. "Who is she?"

"The nurse that helped me with Bonnie that first night. Her name is Ivy and she lives three houses down from me," he said.

"Oh, thank God, for a minute I thought you meant

the large chested one outside watering her flower beds," his mother said with a sigh. "Seriously, I don't know why women do that to themselves."

"That would be Donna and one of the reasons Ivy thinks I'm a slut," Rafe explained. "Her, the parties Brody likes to throw at my place, the way Donna keeps trying to throw herself at me... Well, everything, even the fact that I didn't know I had a daughter."

"She doesn't like Bonnie?" his mother asked indignantly.

"No, that's not it. Bonnie has her charmed, but she thinks I'm some kind of playboy and doesn't take me seriously. The fire is there, but Ivy assumes that all I want is the...usual," he said.

"Well, first, Brody is the slut and I've told you those parties would give people the wrong idea," his mother said primly. "But that's beside the point. Boys will be boys and Brody has no intention of growing up. But since when do you let any kind of stigma stop you? I recall when that whole scandal on Capitol Hill almost got the better of us. You stood beside your father and said my dad is innocent of all these charges and we were proved right. Do the same with Ivy and fight for her if you care. Keep the double Ds away from you and all should be well."

Rafe laughed out loud. "That's what Ivy calls her too."

His mother grinned. "I like her already. Maybe I'll have to visit her sometime."

"Mom, don't," Rafe warned. "I don't want you taking muffins and my baby pictures to her house to scope her out."

His mother batted her eyes at him innocently. "Whatever do you mean?"

"Uh-huh." Rafe shook his head. "Come on, let's get Bonnie in your car and you on your way. I have an appointment for the daycare and I don't want to be late."

"Come on, sweet baby girl," his mother crooned and took Bonnie from her high chair. "We're going to go get Grandpa and then go do some shopping and have lunch."

"Mom, don't buy—"

"I'm going to spoil my granddaughter and you can't say a word," she said, interrupting him.

He held up his hands. "I stand corrected. I might be gone all day on base, so I'll pick her up around six."

"It's fine. I'll bring her home." His mother kissed his cheek. "Have a good day, dear."

They walked out together to his driveway. Rafe noticed Donna was still in her front yard. It didn't take a rocket scientist to know she had been waiting for him to come out. It doesn't take that long to water plants and when she saw him she began bending over to tend the plants. Making sure her ass was facing him, Rafe cast a glance at his mother who rolled her eyes.

Donna then straightened up and waved. "Good morning, Rafe. I didn't see you there."

Yeah, sure you didn't, he thought. "Hi, Donna. Enjoy the day."

"Uh-huh, and diamonds are made of glass," his mother murmured.

Rafe grinned at his mother's comment while he got Bonnie's car seat installed safely in her car.

"Are you going to be home for lunch?" Donna called. "I have this amazing chicken salad we could share."

Donna beamed a smile that he knew probably had made many a man fall to their knees. He was not one of them; his sights were set elsewhere. Rafe made a mental note to put her off once and for all. With Donna always trying to work her way into his life, Ivy would never see him differently.

"I'm sorry, but no. You enjoy your lunch though," Rafe said.

He watched his mother pull out of the driveway with Bonnie before getting into his own vehicle and driving out of the subdivision. Driving along, the radio was set to one of his favorite channels and as the music played he thought about Ivy. One of the first things he wanted to do was take her out on a date. His mother wouldn't mind babysitting for an evening. He wanted to romance Ivy and show her there was more than just physical attraction between them. Even though just thinking about her made his cock ache in his pants. Rafe smiled. He was going to show her exactly how it felt to be loved by him in every possible way and very soon. He maneuvered his way through traffic and turned onto the long road that led to Quantico Base. There was a line that moved slowly up to the gates and when he got through the checkpoint it was smooth sailing to the daycare. He was given the grand tour and by the time it was over he felt sure the ladies who ran the daycare would take good care of Bonnie. Even so, he planned to run a check on all their names for his own peace of mind. He left the daycare and drove to his next appointment that would change his military employment status. He found a parking space in front of the building where his commander's office was housed.

Rafe knocked and when he was given the command to enter, he stepped inside and saluted. "Good morning, sir."

Colonel Craig, known in the ranks as "Big C" and one of the toughest leaders in the military, looked up and snorted. "Stop that, Rafe. If I had a dime for every time I've been saluted over the years, I would be a millionaire and retired."

Rafe chuckled. "You know you're not leaving the Army until they carry you out in a box draped with a flag."

Colonel Craig grinned. "Got that right. Now, about this new unit... I actually thought you would say no. You like to be out in the fray with the boys."

"I was planning on it, sir, but plans change. I found out I had a daughter and became a single dad in only a matter of weeks," Rafe explained. "I have to be around for her and with this MOS change, it would be best for her. It's not just about me anymore."

Baby On Board

Colonel Craig nodded. "I understand, Rafe. My wife was home with our three kids through every deployment and stuck with me each move. I saw it was hard on her and our boys having to pick up and start a new life in a new city, trying to make new friends. It was like they were serving their time in the military too. But we stuck it out and now we've been settled down in Maryland for years now. Still, I look back with some regret. Being a single parent has to be worse, so if you want the job leading the elite unit, it's yours. We'll push through the paperwork to brass ASAP. Then you get to pick your team."

Rafe nodded in approval. "Thank you, sir, I won't let you down."

"I know you won't, Rafe." Colonel Craig chuckled. "I've known you for over ten years now. Hell, even when you were wet behind the ears, I could see back then the kind of soldier you would be. Any man who could start the entire platoon calling me 'Big C' has to have some balls." The commander laughed. "You think I didn't know it was you? That name caught on like wildfire. I had to find out who did it."

"I'm sorry, sir," Rafe shrugged and felt his face burn with embarrassment. A joke he had started as a kid grew into a full-fledged nickname.

"Sorry for what?" the commander asked. "You had the gumption to ask questions. You're a leader, not a follower. Besides, I kind of like it. It grew on me. That doesn't mean I didn't want to clock you a few times for it. Get out of my office, Rafe. Don't let me see you again until it's time for you to report for your new duties. Go enjoy your kid."

"Yes, sir." Rafe saluted. "One million and ten cents, sir."

His commander's laughter followed him out the door. He stepped into the sunshine and sighed. His life had taken some interesting turns, but he accepted them wholeheartedly because he knew that life was a constant evolution.

"You look goofy standing in the sun smiling like that." Brody's voice came from his right.

"Be nice to me or you won't get to be part of the new team I'm putting together." Rafe clapped his friend on the back. "You went MIA after the party."

Brody grinned. "Yeah, I hooked up with that chick from your neighborhood. Grace I think is her name."

"You're not sure of her name?" Rafe asked dryly.

"You know my memory is shot, man," Brody replied. "The one with the big... assets seemed to be keen on you."

"Oh, lucky me." Rafe shook his head. "I have my eyes set on someone else. She's not what I'm looking for. Plus, I don't think I want Bonnie turned into a pageant child. Donna strikes me as that kind of role model."

"How is our new little princess?" Brody asked. "I'm her uncle so I should come by and bring her a pony or something."

Rafe laughed. "Please don't buy my child a pony. Other people would say it as a joke, but your crazy ass would actually go buy one. Baby girl is doing great. You can come by, but no parties. I can't disrupt her schedule like that."

"Yeah, yeah, I know. We have to find a new party central," Brody sighed. "To be honest, though, seeing you with Bonnie makes me feel like I want something more, like parties aren't enough anymore, ya know. I think I might be past all the partying and moving on to something more meaningful."

Rafe gaped at his friend. "What? The Brodmeister hanging up his beer goggles and partying ways? I need to find cover. Lightning might strike at any moment."

Brody punched him in the shoulder. "Ha, ha, very funny. Where you off to now?"

"Nowhere in particular. My mom and dad have Bonnie for the day, so I'm free," Rafe said.

"Well, then you should buy me lunch and tell me about the new team and who you're looking at as prospects," Brody announced. "Not the mess hall. I'm not a cheap date."

"Sounds like a plan. Let's go." Rafe gave Brody a friendly shove. "You're the cheapest date around. Who do you think you're fooling?"

"What can I say? I've been misrepresented," Brody replied.

Their friendly banter continued as they walked toward Rafe's Escalade. With Brody in the passenger seat, Rafe pulled out of the parking lot and headed to one of the restaurants close to Quantico so they could eat and talk.

After a lunch with Brody hitting on one too many waitresses, Rafe dropped him back off on base and impulsively took the exit toward Walter Reed in D.C. It wasn't a huge distance to cover from where the base was. Yet he knew that from Strawberry Glen to work Ivy had more than an hour commute each way. She could have been working for one of the local hospitals that was closer and it showed dedication on her part to work with soldiers each day. Once more, he parked his Escalade and made his way to the hospital's entrance. There were soldiers on crutches, some being pushed in wheel chairs through the manicured gardens, and some sat on benches with their families. As Rafe walked by, he saw a toddler put her head on her father's shoulder and kiss his cheek. The man reached around and hugged his daughter close to him with one arm. The other sleeve was empty. Rafe swallowed thickly as emotion clogged his throat. This is the part many people don't see. How war can destroy a body, but as long as a soldier has good family support and people who love and care for them, it will not destroy their soul.

Rafe recalled Ivy mentioning that she worked on the ward that housed soldiers who had lost limbs while they were deployed. He read the floor map in the lobby and crossed the wide expanse of tile toward the elevators. He took an elevator to the third floor and walked up to the front desk. The nurse behind the desk looked at him curiously, waiting for him to speak.

"Good afternoon, ma'am, is Ivy St. Clair on the floor today?" Rafe asked politely.

"Depends on who's asking, soldier," the nurse responded.

"I'm Sergeant Major Rafe Steele, ma'am," he explained. "I'm her neighbor and wanted to take her out for a bit if she was around."

The nurse looked him up and down. "Hmm. She never mentioned you, but this shall be remedied. I'm Marie. Ivy's not here today. She's riding with a soldier going to the White House for his purple heart."

"I thought they usually waited until a soldier was healed before they give him a medal?" Rafe asked.

Marie shook her head sadly. "He's not going to heal. They found out he has leukemia. It took his legs being blown off for the damn doctors to figure out he had stage four cancer. The boy is not even twenty-one yet and they don't see him living more than six months," she sighed. "Anyway, the President decided to do the ceremony while he was still alive so he could see how proud the nation was of him. Ivy rode with him and two doctors to make sure he was comfortable. The motorcade left here this morning. I don't think she's going to be coming back here this afternoon. These kinds of things are hard on her."

Rafe nodded. "I understand. I'll check in on her at home tonight."

Marie smiled. "I bet you will, Sergeant Major. Ivy's been holding out."

Rafe grinned. "You could be my spy and let me know exactly what she thinks of me."

Marie tapped her chin thoughtfully. "What will that get me?"

"What do you want?" Rafe countered.

"I'll have to think about that." Marie smiled wide. "I like keeping favors in my pocket."

"Uh-oh," Rafe said. "That sounds ominous."

Marie batted her eyes at him innocently. "Why is that? Maybe you'd like to know that Mr. Cop also came by today looking for Ivy and plans to go by her house as well."

"Really?" Rafe gritted his teeth.

"Yes, he is, and he has a big thing for Ivy. No pun intended." Marie chuckled at her own joke.

"I think this is the start of a beautiful friendship, Marie," Rafe said and stuck his hand out.

Marie took it and shook firmly. "See you later, Sergeant Major."

Rafe strode back to the elevators and punched the down button with more force than necessary. There was no way he was going to let that cop get the best of him and take Ivy away. Rafe went straight home and planned to be there when Ivy showed up.

It was a little after seven when Rafe finished cleaning up the kitchen and living room and decided to go outside and sit on Ivy's porch to wait until she came home. His mother had called while he was cleaning and said she would be late in bringing Bonnie home. He was sitting on Ivy's steps playing a game on his phone when he saw the sleek sports car the detective drove show up in front of her house. Reese got out from behind the wheel and stretched before looking curiously to where Rafe sat. He closed the door of his car and moved around it easily, making his way toward Rafe. Rafe stood up to his full height and waited.

"Hey. You're Ivy's neighbor with the baby, right?" Reese's voice was friendly.

"Yeah, that's me," Rafe replied. "And you're the cop."

Reese nodded. "Yep. Are you waiting for her to come home?"

"Yeah, and your being here isn't helping," Rafe said bluntly.

A dark look passed over Reese's face. "Excuse me?"

"You're excused. Go home." Rafe shoved his beret into his pocket. "Ivy is mine. She was before you decided to get brave and ask her out."

Reese gave a bark of humorless laughter and stepped closer. "Listen, soldier boy, do you really think you can run me off?"

"It wouldn't be too difficult," Rafe replied. "I'm telling you to stand down, son, before I take you down myself. Ivy and I have a very strong connection and I don't need you in her face making her confused about what she wants."

"She didn't seem too confused when I was kissing her...or touching her for that matter," Reese smirked.

Rafe saw red and grabbed Reese by the collar. "You keep your hands off her."

"Why should I? She likes it when I touch her nice and slo—"

That was as far as he got before Rafe gave in to the impulse and punched Reese square in the face. He vaguely heard the squeal of car tires and a door slam while he and Reese struggled for the upper hand.

"What in the hell is going on here?" Ivy shrieked.

Both men stopped cold and looked at her. Rafe glanced over to see Reese wiping blood from his lip. Rafe straightened his uniform as Ivy stood in front of them with her hands on her hips. Looking around, he saw that their little scrap had gotten the attention of a few neighbors, including Donna and Grace who were watching the show from their patio furniture. The look on Ivy's face made him swallow. *Uh-oh, she is pissed.*

"Ivy, I came to see if you were okay," Rafe began.

"I did too and this fool—"

"Who are you calling a fool, asshole? You should just leave well enough alone and stand down," Rafe yelled.

"What am I, one of your soldiers? Who says stuff like that in the real world?" Reese scoffed.

"Shut it, both of you!" Ivy yelled and took a deep breath. "So you came to check on me and ended up fighting in my front yard for all of the neighbors to see?"

"He threw the first punch," Reese announced, "after telling me you belong to him, and I had to make it known that you are mine."

"I am not your toy truck in a sand box. I belong to myself and no one else." Ivy seethed. "I cannot believe you two grown men are acting like children. I just spent the day with a boy who will not see his freaking twenty-sixth birthday, let alone thirtieth. He accepted a medal with all the honor, strength and pride that I've ever seen in one person. And here the two of you are, staking claim to me like you think this is the old west." She glared at both of them. "I won't have it, I tell you. Go away both of you and leave me alone."

"Ivy…" Reese said softly.

"Baby doll…" Rafe said.

The look she gave them made Rafe shut his mouth with a snap. "I said go or I will be the one kicking your collective asses up and down this street. Now get your car out of my driveway before I, with the mood I'm in, monster truck my little car over its hood in a hot minute."

Reese moved to go back to his car. "This isn't over, soldier boy."

"Bring it, cop," Rafe snarled.

Ivy pulled her own hair in frustration. "Get off my property, both of you."

"He said that you let him touch you and you liked

it," Rafe said harshly. "Is that true? Are you sleeping with him?"

"Reese, how could you say..." Ivy shook her head. "You know what? Never mind. Go home. And you, Rafe, it's none of your damn business who is touching me."

Without looking back at either of them, she stormed into the house and slammed the door. Reese threw Rafe a dirty look as he got into his car and drove away.

Donna came running up with her eyes wide. "Oh, my God, Rafe, are you okay? Come back to my place and I'll get you some ice. I mean, how could Ivy let him try to hurt you like that?"

Rafe held up his hand and gave her a cold look. "Enough with your fake smiles and the pretense of caring. I know you know who I am. You probably Googled every bit of information on me to gauge how much I'm worth outside my military paycheck. I know that if I were just a lowly soldier you wouldn't be fawning over me like you do. I don't want you, Donna, or anything you're offering. Stay away from me, stop being cutesy and stop being a pest. Leave me alone. Go find an older, rich man to bother."

She gasped as he walked away. "Fucking bastard," Rafe heard her say under her breath. He smiled. There was the true Donna in all her glorious venom. He knew women like her well. He unlocked the door and stepped into his house, crossed over to the sofa and threw himself face down with a sigh.

Rafe decided to lay there for a while and contemplate how he could fix things with Ivy. The chasm between them seemed to be growing in leaps and bounds. What would it take to give them that push that ultimately would bring them together before he lost whatever chance he had completely?

Chapter Six

"And then I come home to find them fighting on my front lawn," Ivy told Marie, who was wiping tears of mirth from her eyes.

Marie sighed and hiccupped. "Why don't I live in your neighborhood? I would pay to see that. I wonder if anyone got it on video and put it on YouTube."

Ivy stared at her in horror as she realized that could have happened. "Oh, my God."

"I'm kidding, Ivy." Marie grinned. "You're making a mental note to check later, aren't you?"

She nodded and Marie started laughing all over again. It took a few seconds for her to settle down. "Seriously, you have two hot guys fighting over you. I should bitch slap you for that alone. Yeah, I'm jealous, so sue me."

"I don't want them fighting over me," Ivy moaned. "I don't know what I want. Reese is sweet and caring, and he asked me out right after my feelings had been bruised by Rafe and his lack of consideration. But when he kisses me it's just nice, you know. Rafe is different. I mean, he kissed me on his couch and next thing you know, we're wrapped up in each other's arms and it feels like I swallowed lava because I'm on fire from the inside out."

"Damn, put me down for some of that," Marie said. "So then you made out with Rafe?"

"He's kissed me a few times," Ivy admitted.

"Yeah, but were those kisses just little pecks or were they kisses that say, 'I wanna take your clothes off and take you on the dining room table?'" Marie asked and leaned forward.

"The second one," Ivy said and sat down before blurting out, "it was amazing. Oh, my God, I've never felt like that before."

"While with Reese it's just nice?" Marie said. "In that case, I think you should go with door number two."

Ivy shook her head. "That could purely be a chemical reaction. I can't build a relationship based on that. He's a hound dog. You should see the parties he throws at his house and the girls running around in tiny bikinis…"

"Seems like a damn good foundation to me," Marie said. "And you're crucifying the man for having a good time? Unless he was having sex on the front lawn, it doesn't sound like he's doing anything wrong. Maybe you shouldn't be thinking that all the women you see at his place are for him. You're being prudish. You should've thrown on your bikini and joined in on the fun."

"Ugh, I hate when you're critical and right," Ivy fussed.

"I do my best, darling," Marie said. "You might

be passing up an amazing thing for just feeling okay with someone. I wouldn't want to feel just okay about any relationship I'm in, I'd want fireworks. I want to look at the man I love when I'm sixty and still feel that sexy little tug in my belly. Can you say you'd have that in a long term relationship with Reese?"

"I don't know. I'm going to have to think about it all." Ivy stuck her tongue out at Marie. "I don't like you."

"You love me and you know it," Marie said.

"Excuse me, can you help me?"

They turned to see a young woman standing in front of the nurses' station. Their conversation was forgotten and they went into business mode. The woman was tall and slim and reminded Ivy of a super model. Her hazel-brown eyes were large and doe-like and reminded Ivy of Bambi. Her chin-length hair framed the tiny face perfectly.

"Yes. How can I help you?" Ivy said gently. She'd seen enough young wives come in looking for their husbands to recognize the total shell-shocked look on her face.

"I'm looking for Jon Alvater. My name is Katie DeRichie," she stammered and tears filled her eyes. "You see, I helped raise Jon and then his brother and I broke up. No one told me he'd been injured when he deployed until I heard from a friend in Michigan, and so I got on the first plane here." She gave a shaky laugh. "Why wouldn't Reese tell me? I didn't want to move with him and so I gave him back his engagement ring. Oh, God, why am I telling you this?"

Ivy's gaze flew to Marie and she wore a look of surprise as well. This was Reese's ex girlfriend…well, ex fiancée, really, that Ivy knew nothing about. It seemed the good cop was keeping some secrets of his own. Still, she couldn't help but feel pity for the young woman who stood before them crying.

"I understand this is a bit much." Ivy came from around the nurses' station and led Katie to a chair. "Let me call Reese to come. I can't let you in to see Jon until he gives permission."

"How is he? Jon, I mean," Katie asked.

"Again, I can't disclose that information, but I can tell you he's very fragile in some ways. That's why Reese has to be here," Ivy said gently. "You sit here and I'll get him on the phone. Marie, can you get her a cold glass of water? She needs it."

Marie nodded and went off down the hall while Ivy used her cell phone far enough away from Katie so that she wouldn't hear.

Reese answered on the first ring. "Hey, sexy lady. I guess you're not mad at me anymore?"

"You need to come to the hospital now, Reese," Ivy said.

"Is it Jon? Has something happened?" Reese asked.

"Oh, no, Jon's fine. I'm sorry, I should have thought about how you would take that," Ivy apologized. "Katie DeRichie, your ex fiancée, is here to see him…and you. You need to come and give permission for her to see him."

"Katie's there?" His voice was hoarse and Ivy heard emotion there. Her female instinct kicked into overdrive. He still felt something for Katie.

"Yes, she is. Can you come?" Ivy kept her voice gentle even though it gave her a little ache to know that he had been using her to forget someone else. She couldn't criticize, though, because wasn't she doing the same thing when it came to her feelings for Rafe?

"I'll be right there," Reese said and she hung up the phone.

"He's on his way, Katie." Ivy smiled at the woman who now held a paper cup in her shaking hands. "Don't worry. It will all be okay."

Katie smiled back at her. "I hope so. God, I hope so."

Ivy did, too, for all of them.

Twenty minutes later, Reese came off the elevators in full stride and Katie stood so quickly that she spilled the water from her cup. He was in uniform and he stood staring at Katie and no one spoke. Even though Ivy was behind the desk with Marie, she felt as if they were both intruding on a very personal moment. She could see the look in Reese's eyes. He never looked at her that way.

"Why didn't you tell me Jon was hurt?" Katie asked Reese.

"I thought you wouldn't care," Reese replied.

She looked at him, shock on her face. "I helped you raise him. He is like my own family. How could you think that?"

Reese shook his head and gave a sad smile. "I thought it was implied since you didn't move with us and chose to stay in Michigan."

"That's doesn't mean a damn thing and you know it, Reese. You always let your pride get the best of you," Katie said angrily.

"Well, how do you think it made me feel? I felt like you didn't love me enough to leave your friends," Reese shot back. Katie's eyes filled with tears and Reese said gruffly, "Jesus, don't do that. You know I can't stand it when you cry."

She nodded. "Can we go see Jon, please?"

Ivy met Reese's gaze. She'd watched the exchange between them silently. What was it with men? She could tell he obviously still felt something for Katie but he was willing to date her to forget the woman he truly loved. Ivy didn't want to be second best in any relationship. They were both waiting for her and she moved briskly from behind the desk.

"I'll take you to his room," she said in a businesslike manner. She met Marie's raised eyebrow with a warning look. Her friend looked down to the papers in front of her and began to shuffle them.

She walked down the hall and knocked on the door and poked her head in. Jon looked at her and smiled. "Hi, Ms. Ivy."

"Hi, Jon. Your brother is here to see you and he

brought a friend." She smiled at the injured soldier.

Reese stepped in. "Hey, Bro. Guess who's here to see you."

Katie stepped from behind Reese and teased, "Why are you in bed? Didn't I teach you sleeping in is just for the weekends?"

Ivy watched Jon's face light up like she'd never seen it before. "Katie, Katie, you came to see me!" He held out his arms to her and Katie walked into his hug. "I missed you so much."

"I missed you too, Jon." Katie's voice was muffled with tears.

"Jon, how about I give you your meds so you and Katie can spend time with each other?" Ivy said gently.

Jon shook his head stubbornly. "I want Katie to do it."

She looked at Ivy. "Would it be all right if I do it?"

Ivy nodded. "That would be great. Just make sure he takes everything in the cup and eats, please."

Katie nodded. "I will definitely do that. Thank you so much, Nurse Ivy."

"You're welcome." Ivy smiled at her. She couldn't help but be genuine with the young woman who traveled all that way to see Jon. "I'll be at the front desk if you need anything."

"I'll step out with you for a minute," Reese said.

Ivy said nothing and fought the sliver of jealousy that speared through her. She was accustomed to be being Jon's caretaker. Even though the therapist said they would have to work toward breaking his imprintation on her. She felt cast aside. *Way to have bruised feelings, Ivy. You cannot be the center of his world.*

"Hey, I'm sorry that she showed up like this," Reese said.

"Hmm, why ever for? Maybe it's because I didn't know about her," Ivy snapped. "You obviously still have feelings for her. What I don't understand is why you asked me out in the first place."

"Because she lives in Michigan and my life is here now. I didn't expect her to show up," Reese explained.

"Because you didn't tell her Jon was hurt," Ivy hissed. "That was cold. If you were in a committed relationship and she helped you take care of him when your parents died, you should've called her."

"You're telling *me* about secrets? You had a freaking Marine trying to break my neck at your house!" Reese retorted.

"Excuse me, I'm not the one who has a fiancée—"

"Ex fiancée," Reese interjected.

Ivy glared at him. "It doesn't look like that to me. Either way, you were dating me knowing you still have feelings for someone else."

"I don't have feelings for her," Reese said and Ivy gave him a pointed look. He muttered a curse. "I don't know what I feel."

"I suggest you figure it out," Ivy snapped.

"I can say the same for you, Ivy," Reese ground out. "Maybe you've been dating me while you want someone else."

Ivy couldn't deny it. "We'll both take a step back, dissect our feelings."

He turned and went back into the room while Ivy walked back to the nurses' station where Marie waited. They were both silent for a few moments until Marie broke the silence.

She slapped her hand down on the counter. "That was so intense. I mean, the only thing that could have made it better is if I'd had popcorn."

"Marie." Ivy said the name like a warning and then sighed. "I'm going to go do the rounds. Macy wants me to sit in with her art therapy class later today."

"You're just trying to avoid seeing them again," Marie said knowingly.

"That too," Ivy called over her shoulder as she strode away. "Your rounds will start in thirty minutes. Get on your hustle, woman."

"Slave driver," Marie called back.

Ivy just wanted to get through the rest of the day and go home. It got progressively worse, especially when a soldier with PTSD decided to punch a hole in the wall of the art room and then run through the hospital. They had to put the entire building on lockdown and Walter Reed was a massive facility. It took hours to find him and calm him down enough so the doctors could get him back to his room and sedate him. It was well after eight when she got home. After letting herself in, she made a beeline for her fridge to grab a bottle of wine. After pouring out a glass, she drank half before she sighed and rested her head on the cool counter. The doorbell rang while she was in that position.

"What now?" she moaned and moved wearily to the door.

Rafe stood on the other side holding Bonnie and both of them wore sunglasses. Bonnie's were pink and star shaped while Rafe's were red and shaped like cars. They both looked so cute and were such a surprise to see, that she couldn't help but laugh.

"What's all this?" Ivy asked.

"We come bearing an invitation to dinner. We saw you pull up. The steaks are ready to go on the grill with homemade rosemary potatoes and mac and cheese with fresh bacon bits and chives too. Don't say no. Let us feed our hardworking nurse."

"Is Donna or any of her crew going to jump me from a bush?" Ivy teased.

Even with the ridiculous glasses on his face, Ivy could see that Rafe didn't find it funny.

"Don't bring her up," Rafe said quietly. "This is about you and me, Ivy. If you don't want to spend time with me say so, but don't use anyone else as an excuse."

Damn, he's not playing around, Ivy thought. "Well, since you guys came over here looking so cool, I'll say yes to dinner. Shall I bring my wine?"

"Finish the glass. I've got a bottle already opened on the kitchen counter," Rafe said with a grin. "Just so you know, we weren't going to take no for an answer."

"Really? Well, let me get a shower and I'll come on by," she said.

"Don't fall asleep. You won't want to miss my cooking," Rafe teased.

"I'll be there in ten." Ivy tickled Bonnie's chin and the baby giggled. "You're such a sweetie. I missed seeing your face."

"We'll see you soon. Let yourself in when you're ready," Rafe said and strode down the street holding Bonnie high. The baby's laughter filled the night and Ivy couldn't help but smile. She already felt tons better after such a horrible day. Ivy would give in to the whim—she would let Rafe in. There was no use fighting it. They were drawn to each other. She could throw Reese up as a roadblock, but Rafe would always find a way to get around it. Tonight she wouldn't think or try to evaluate it. Marie was right; why settle when something amazing could be brewing with Rafe? Ivy went upstairs to shower and wash away the day's events. By the time she headed outside, she felt fresh and happy. *Time to let the reigns go and let fate do its work.*

She opened the door to Rafe's house and stepped inside. The aroma of grilled meat and a home cooked meal filled the air. Ivy loved to cook, but usually eating alone didn't warrant putting together a big meal. Half the time she made a dish and would be eating it all week until she didn't want to see it anymore. Having a man do the cooking was a nice change. She walked straight through his living room and kitchen to the back sliding doors. The first thing she saw was black and blue tile bordering an L-shaped pool. Rafe was standing in front of a large stainless steel grill. Rafe had taken the role of being a father to a new high. Bonnie was in a bouncy seat that had every colorful little toy you could imagine to capture her eye. The seat was on a mat that was made up of colorful foam puzzle pieces and there was even an umbrella to keep the sun off her. It was still open even thought it was late evening and the sun was setting.

"You're going to have to get a gate installed around the pool when she starts walking," Ivy commented as she walked up behind him.

Rafe turned and snapped the stainless steel tongs he was holding. "They come next Friday for that."

Ivy chuckled. "That's great, but you don't have to do it right away. Suppose you have another party or whatever. Your guests won't be able to jump in the pool."

He turned back and flipped a steak. "The only parties I'll be having anymore are Bonnie's birthday parties. I also got her signed up for daycare when I go back to work. Did you grab a glass of wine?"

"No, I'll get it when we go inside. Do you want me to do anything?" Ivy asked.

He pointed to where Bonnie sat. "Nope. Sit, have a conversation with Bonnie. I'm doing it all tonight."

Ivy shrugged playfully. "Hey, I can go for that. How was your day on the job, Bonnie?" She sat down on the foam puzzle pieces and Bonnie jiggled in her bouncy seat and babbled a long stream of incoherent words. "Wow. It seems like you had a rough day too."

Rafe chuckled. "She should have no complaints. She gets to hang out with Grandma who buys her frilly dresses and fills her room with Build-A-Bears. She can poop in her pants and have other people take care of it and always has an ample supply of teething cookies."

Ivy gave him a look. "You tasted the cookies, haven't you?"

He made a face. "Those things are awful. Do the people who make this stuff know how bad their product tastes? She is going to love Oreos when she can have them."

"Her little palate is sensitive. She can't have overly spiced foods yet," Ivy crooned and took her from the bouncy seat. Bonnie was heavier and she looked healthy and definitely happy. He was a perfect father and she was a lucky little girl. Ivy nuzzled the baby and felt her own biological clock ticking. She hoped and prayed that when the time came she could have a child of her own and find a man who wanted to work with her toward that goal. Not every woman was born with fertile soil to plant a seed; some had to work at it. She thought of her ex and how he had looked at her after she told him it would be hard for her to conceive. It made her sad and she pushed the thought out of her head. Tonight was for relaxing. She would eat, enjoy herself, and play with Bonnie.

"You look pensive," Rafe said, coming over with a platter in his hands. "Ready to go inside and eat?"

Ivy smiled. "Yup. I'm excited to taste your culinary skills."

"I've got many other skills I would be happy to show you," he said under his breath, but Ivy heard him loud and clear.

"I'm sure you would." She winked as she passed by him holding Bonnie. It was a brazen move to let him know she had heard his words.

Inside was cool compared to the warmth of the evening. It was already in the eighties and it was just a few weeks into June. It was going to be a long, hot summer. She put Bonnie in her high chair next to the table while Rafe spooned some different colored baby foods onto her pink princess plate.

He used a haughty French accent while he worked. "For the little madam, we have green goop, a.k.a. peas, orange goop, a.k.a. sweet potatoes, and some yellowish beige gunk for dessert—"

"Let me guess, apple sauce?" Ivy laughed.

Rafe inclined his head. "Quite true, madam. And for you, a glass of sparkling white wine and a plate of delicious fare."

She shook her head and smiled. "You're a nut."

He sat down across from her. "I just know how to enjoy life."

"Is there any word on her mother?" Ivy asked and then frowned. "I'm sorry if you feel it's not my place to ask…"

Rafe stopped her by covering her hand with his own. "I made it your business when I showed up at your house asking for help. My lawyer has filed the petitions with the court. I've got temporary custody and he's hired a detective to find her. Then she can sign the papers giving over her parental rights to Bonnie. That's the easy way. The hard way would be if she decides to fight, which my lawyer assures me would go my way since she abandoned her on my doorstep. The final court case is in a month, either way. I don't intend Bonnie to ever go back to a situation where she can't be safe."

"She was well cared for," Ivy interjected. "I don't know her mother's issues but sometimes things get tough for a single mother. I don't think she could manage being a single mother anymore."

"That gives her no right to just leave my daughter on the doorstep. She found where I live. She could have waited with her," Rafe pointed out. "Would you have done it, Ivy? Left your child without knowing she was safe?"

"Of course not," Ivy said quickly. She looked down at the meal in front of her, thinking how blessed she would be to even be a mother.

"Do you want kids, Ivy?" Rafe asked suddenly as if sensing her thoughts.

She looked at the little angel to her right as Rafe

spooned some of the peas into her mouth. Her hair was dark like her father's and had already begun to curl at the edges. Her light blue-green eyes seemed to sparkle when she smiled and showed those two perfect little teeth. Oh, yes, she ached to be a mom.

"I want them very much," Ivy said quietly, feeling emotion clog her throat so she cleared it gently. "Wanting and having are two different things, though."

He looked at her curiously before giving Bonnie another spoonful of orange goop this time. "Care to explain or none of my business?"

Ivy sighed and picked at her potatoes. "Remember, I told you I have endometriosis, which makes actually having a child more difficult."

"But not impossible," Rafe said.

She smiled sadly. "No, not impossible, but to my ex it was a deal breaker. He left soon after he found out."

"I remember you telling me that and I still say he was a fool. A child conceived after both parents support each other through a difficult time would be a treasure."

"It's more than likely I have so much scar tissue…" Ivy shook her head. "Never mind. It's not something we should be discussing anyway."

"Why not?" Rafe demanded. He used a damp washcloth and wiped Bonnie's face. "I want to be with you. I'm not hiding that fact. And if I'm lucky enough to be able to hold you and keep you, you can be sure as hell I won't run because we might have difficulty having a child."

Ivy stared at him with her mouth agape. She certainly wasn't expecting that announcement. "You've been thinking about a future with...um ...me?"

Rafe grinned. "Tied your tongue, have I? I don't sound like the playboy you think I am if I'm craving to spend forever with you, do I? Don't worry about that now. Eat your dinner before it gets cold. Maybe if you're good, I'll let you watch cartoons with Bonnie before her bedtime."

"Well, then, I'll be a good girl and eat." Ivy dug her fork into her mac and cheese and took a bite. "Delicious."

Rafe gave her a wink and used his haughty French voice. "I told you, madam, I'm a culinary genius."

Ivy ate and contemplated what Rafe said—more than Reese ever said. More than she got after five years with her ex even. Still, she couldn't be naïve. Sweet words were one of the many tools men used when they wanted a woman. Yes, of course, Rafe wanted her but what comes after? Ivy hated doubt, especially in herself, in her heart. She knew that she was inextricably drawn toward Rafe and could not fight it. It was the *after* that worried her. Would her heart be broken again if the fire between them ever went out?

After dinner and an hour of watching cartoons, Ivy helped him put Bonnie to bed. She watched the baby sleep under the pink velvet blanket that had become her favorite. The pacifier had fallen from her mouth as sleep took her deeper and her tiny hands spread flat against the soft sheets. Ivy felt as though she could watch the baby sleep forever but she went back into the living room where Rafe waited. He handed her a glass of wine and sat down with a loud sigh.

"Being a single parent is hard work," he said.

"There are tons of mothers who do it every day," Ivy pointed out.

"I admire them and now that I'm part of their ranks, I wouldn't change a thing. It's very fulfilling," Rafe said. "Can I kiss you, Ivy?"

She couldn't help but laugh out loud. "That was a complete one eighty."

He shrugged. "I figured I'd put it out there since it's not far from my mind."

"Only a kiss," she teased.

"Oh, but there is so much more I want to do, yet I don't want to make you run away," Rafe said and took a sip of his wine.

"Is it so awful that I'd run?"

"No, it's so good."

Ivy put her glass down and without thinking, moved across the sofa and straddled his waist. They'd been on the sofa once before like this, but this time she had no intention of stopping. She watched his blue-green eyes darken with desire and she could feel his cock hardening where their bodies were pressed together.

"Then show me," she whispered and bent her head to nip at his lips. "Show me how good you can make me feel."

He groaned and said huskily against her lips, "I was planning to take it slow and give you as much time as you needed."

Ivy gave a soft laugh. "Yes, but now that I'm here, I don't want to take it slow. I want you inside me so deep that I won't remember us being apart. I want to scream your name as I shatter in your arms. Can you do that, Rafe? Can you make me feel like that?"

"Fuck yes," Rafe said as he got off the sofa with his arms wrapped around her. She locked her legs around his waist as he carried her up the stairs. His eyes found hers as he put her down on her feet in his bedroom and then he swooped down and she was lost in his kiss. Tonight she would feel passion so hot it would burn her to the core. Ivy gave in with a soft moan as his hands roamed down her body. Oh, yes, this was what she wanted.

"God, Ivy, I dreamt of you being with me like this," he whispered as he lifted the edge of her shirt. Ivy lifted her arms and he stripped it off her body and he chuckled softly. "Maybe I'm still dreaming."

Ivy cupped his cheeks in her hands and kissed him gently. "No, you're not."

Their lips met with growing passion. His fingers were strong at the base of her neck and she moaned as his fingers massaged her scalp. The man had a touch that made her purr like a kitten. Ivy's fingers nimbly unbuttoned his short-sleeved white cotton shirt before she smoothed her hands over his hard muscled chest. *He feels so good, so damn good.* She worked at his pants until she was able to push them down over his hips, and his erection tented his boxers. Rafe slid her hips up and brought her body hard against his. He ground his hips against hers, alluding to the pleasure that was to come. Ivy gasped as he, in one deft movement, took off her bra and cupped her breasts while playing with her hardening nipples. An ache shot to her core and she felt her pussy throb at the sensations that filled her. Ivy arched, pressing herself more firmly into strong fingers and moaned softly against his lips. She grabbed his boxers and pulled them down, revealing a long, thick cock.

"No more teasing," she demanded, pushing away and working the snap of her shorts before pushing them and her panties down her legs. "Take me hard."

Rafe growled, a low predatory sound that stripped her just as quickly as she had stripped herself. He tackled her and took her off her feet before they landed on the bed. Lips touched and hands roamed each other's skin. Not an inch of her skin didn't feel his lips and she burned hotter because of it. He rolled quickly until she was on top of him and she felt his hardness between them. Ivy shifted so she could take him inside her, but Rafe stopped her.

"No, I want more than just to be inside you. I need to feel you." He looked at her with a deep longing in his eyes and practically lifted her until she was sitting on his chest and her legs straddled his head. "I need to taste you."

The first touch of his hot lips against her pussy had her clutching the dark cherry wood headboard. Ivy whimpered as he sucked her clit and she spread her thighs wider. Rafe speared her with his tongue and she threw her head back in pleasure as his tongue fucked her. A guttural moan escaped him and he pulled her harder against his seeking mouth. Unable to help herself, Ivy began grinding against the source of her pleasure. His tongue seemed to be everywhere. Her body was infused with such heat she never thought possible. He then moved her so that she straddled his face and her knees were on each side of his head and she was facing his feet.

Ivy moved on instinct and grasped his hard cock and wrapped her mouth around the hard steel in her hands. His hips jerked as she ran her tongue around his shaft. Ivy removed her mouth and stroked him firmly, watching his pre-come pearl at the head and she licked it in delight. She cried out around his cock when she felt his fingers slip into her and begin an assault on her senses by fucking her hard and deep, while still feeling his tongue lathe her clit and lips. Ivy came hard, so hard she forgot to breathe and just strained against the source of her pleasure until she felt limp against his body. Rafe took control and moved her to rest on the soft sheets and she watched as he stood and walked away.

"Where are you going?" she asked breathlessly.

He looked at her and chuckled. "I'll be back, don't worry I'm not done with you yet."

She lay there as her body hummed with pleasure. He was back with the bottle of wine and he held it up. "Never let a good bottle of wine go to waste."

"We're having wine now?" she asked with a laugh.

"Lay back," he ordered. Rafe poured a glass of the white wine and swirled his finger in the glass. "I was thinking about this from the first sip I took tonight— how would it taste on your skin."

He dripped the wine on her breast and he sucked her nipple deep into his mouth. Ivy cried out and Rafe moved on to the next breast and gave it the same ministrations. She got exactly what she wanted—his hot mouth against her skin. Ivy clutched at the sheets as pleasure again swept through her body. He worked his way down, cool drops of wine against heated skin. His mouth was drinking the wine, but tasting her at the same time. When he poured some in her navel and sucked it out, she drew in her breath. When he dribbled it between the lips of her sex and licked it up, Ivy begged for release, to feel his mouth and tongue on her pussy again. Rafe gave her what she desired and she muffled her scream with a pillow. He moved and this time positioned himself over her, lifting her leg over his shoulder before he penetrated her. Her pussy swallowed him to the hilt and Ivy arched into his thrusts and watched as his muscles tensed and rippled.

"Oh, God, oh, Jesus, you feel so damn good, Ivy," Rafe muttered.

"More. Please more, Rafe." Ivy begged as she pulled his head down to kiss him.

The movement sent him deeper inside her and he clutched the pillows on either side of her head and pistoned in and out of her. She didn't know she could feel like the world was falling off its axis. She had never felt such pleasure before in her life or such heat that she felt as if she was melting from the inside out. Each thrust rubbed against nerve endings she didn't know she had. Her pleasure spiraled higher and higher until she couldn't help but call out his name over and over again. His body was damp with sweat, but Rafe didn't stop. He moved and in one smooth motion she was on top of him, riding his cock. His neck was arched and his abdominal muscles were tight and tense. He was the most beautiful sight she'd ever seen and Ivy let go and rode him with abandon.

"Let go, Rafe. Fall with me. I need you to come with me!" she cried out.

He grabbed her hips and pumped into her fiercely. "Yes, yes," he growled loudly.

She gave in to the pleasure and fell over the precipice while his hot come filled her. His warmth inside her felt so good it made her pussy throb hard and tightly clench his cock, making her come again. Ivy fell and they rolled until she was lying next to him. Their bodies heaved as they tried to catch their breath.

"Damn, woman, you are amazing." Rafe turned and kissed her gently.

"I can definitely say the same about you." Ivy laughed softly. "I feel like you melted all of my bones."

"That's just the beginning. You're mine now, Ivy. I'm not planning on letting you go," Rafe murmured. "You tell that cop that you're spoken for."

"You don't have to worry about Reese. We would never have worked out. I was doing my best not to think about you," she admitted. "Besides, I think his heart was elsewhere. We could never have made it work if both of us had other people on our minds."

"You were thinking about me, huh?" Rafe pulled her close. "I'm glad to hear it."

"Do you want me to go?" Ivy asked. "I know you probably get up with Bonnie—"

He cupped her face and kissed her hard. "First, you're not leaving this bed and second, Bonnie usually sleeps through the night and if she wakes up, the baby monitor will let me know." Rafe's tone got serious. "I don't want to sleep another night without you in my arms."

"I have to eventually go home. Plus, I have work," Ivy teased. "But I can see myself sleeping with you as long as you promise to hold me all night."

"Like it was going to happen any other way." Rafe snuggled her close to him.

Ivy loved the feel of him. His big frame surrounded her and made her feel so secure. This felt so right. She was glad she gave in to temptation. This was what it felt like to be wanted, cherished and needed. Ivy closed her eyes and let his scent carry her off to sleep.

Chapter Seven

It's amazing how things change so quickly. Ivy found herself spending more time at Rafe's house rather than her own, and now her schedule blended with Rafe's and Bonnie's. He was back on base and each morning he left with his daughter strapped into the car seat to head to Quantico for the day while she went farther into D.C. to Walter Reed. She'd been moved for a few weeks from her usual job in the hospital to working on the fifth floor. Those were the cases of severe injuries, both physical and mental. Two nurses had quit because they were unable to handle the stress of dealing with soldiers who not only had been seriously injured while deployed but came back with PTSD and traumatic brain injuries, which then made them even more difficult to handle.

Walter Reed was about healing the entire body before they sent brave men and women back out into the world. The suicide rate for soldiers who didn't have the right mental care was high. Everyone wanted to see this decrease and all Veterans hospitals as well as Walter Reed had excellent mental care doctors striving to minimize the problem. Jon had started out in the very same ward but they were able to move him from the high security area to the third floor for his care. Things had seemed to get much better for him now that Katie was back in the picture. He no longer needed Ivy to be there for his medication and his almost childlike personality was barely seen anymore. You could now talk to the young man who donned a uniform and went off to fight in a war.

Ivy was glad to see him getting better. Things still needed to be settled with Reese, but her schedule was completely different than when she had been on the third floor and the few times she tried to call him, she got no answer and he didn't return her calls. One afternoon when she was visiting with Marie back on the third floor during her lunch break, Katie and Reese walked in holding hands. Yup, they were back together. Ivy was not upset. She had Rafe and knew that she and Reese were never meant to be. Though it didn't stop Reese from looking guilty as hell when he sent Katie on to see Jon and called Ivy over.

"Ivy, I was meaning to call you. . . ." he began.

"No, you weren't. I left you three messages," Ivy replied. "Reese, it's fine. I'm glad you and Katie found your way back to each other."

"I didn't want a big scene." Reese smiled. "I should've known that's not you, Ivy."

She punched him lightly on the shoulder. "Yes, you should've. Rafe and I have been...well, we're together now. But I'd still like to be friends."

"You and the soldier boy, huh?" Reese shook his head and shrugged. "Even when he tried to choke me that night in front of your house I could tell. But anyway, the doctors said we can take Jon home in a few weeks as long as he keeps going the way he is now. Katie is going to relocate here and we're getting married."

Ivy smiled. She was genuinely happy for all three of them. "Well, congrats on all the great news. I hope I get an invite to the wedding."

Reese nodded. "You will, and you do the same for us."

"I don't know if… We're taking it slow." Ivy felt her face redden in embarrassment. It was too soon to talk about marriage. The thought of Rafe proposing thrilled her though. Was it even in the cards for them?

Reese laughed. "Yeah, he's not letting you go, Ivy. I won't be surprised when I see an invitation in the mail. I'm going to head in to see Jon now. You take care of yourself."

"You too," Ivy replied. "And tell Katie I said congratulations."

"Will do," Reese said and walked down the hall to Jon's room.

Ivy stepped back toward the nurses' station and Marie gave her a thumbs up. "That went very well. No fist throwing or anything. You people bore me."

"I'm sorry there wasn't an episode of Jerry Springer playing out on the floor for you," Ivy said casually. "Next time I'll pep it up."

"You don't have to do that, just tell me about your rigorous sex life with your hunky soldier and that will

115

suffice. I have to live vicariously through you." Marie sighed. "I need sexual healing."

"You need mental health meds," Ivy teased. "You're crazy. I've seen at least two doctors eyeing you. All you actually need to do is date."

Marie shook her head. "Nope, not dating another doctor. You saw how it ended with Dr. Feel Good. He had his hands on me and four other nurses, man whore that he was. Tell Rafe he owes me a soldier and I want to collect, damn it. Someone tall, hunky, and muscular that can lift me while he licks—"

"Whoa, whoa, too much information there." Ivy covered her ears with her hands. "I'm slowly backing away to the elevators and going back upstairs. You keep that mouth zipped until I'm gone."

Marie batted her eyes sweetly. "Then I guess you don't want me to tell you how I want to be upside down and—"

"Must scrub mental picture from my mind," Ivy interrupted her and moved toward the elevators. She pointed at Marie. "You're a sick woman, Marie, a sick, sick woman."

"Try it with Rafe. You might like it!" she heard Marie call before the elevator door closed.

Who says I haven't? Ivy thought with a grin. When it came to Rafe in the bedroom, nothing was off limits and that was how she liked it. Her phone buzzed in her pocket as she walked back onto the fifth floor. She smiled when she saw it was Rafe's number.

"Hey, I was just thinking about you," Ivy said.

"Good things, I hope," he replied and his deep sexy laugh made her shiver.

"All good things," she practically purred. "What can I do for you?"

"Oh, I could think of quite a few things, but I'd rather show you," Rafe chuckled. "I'm going to be late coming home and my mom has agreed to pick up Bonnie from daycare and bring her to you at my house. Is that okay?"

"Um, yeah, sure," Ivy said hesitantly. "Does your mom know we're seeing each other?"

"Yes, she does, and you'd have to meet her eventually, darling," Rafe replied. "Don't worry. She doesn't bite. She'll just drop Bonnie off and ask three million questions."

"Oh, that's so much better," Ivy said dryly. "I have to stop by Target to pick up some diapers and milk. Is six-thirty okay for her to drop her off?"

"I'll let her know," Rafe answered. "And while you're there, can you pick her up a nice dress, please, and this weekend you need to go shopping for something pretty to wear."

"Why are we getting dressed up?" Ivy asked, her heart jumped as she thought, *proposal.*

"We're going to Washington. The President is pinning me with my bronze star and the entire platoon with the bronze star," Rafe replied.

No proposal. She pushed back her disappointment, but still felt pride and happiness at his news. "That's so amazing, honey. Congratulations! I'll make sure to pick the best, frilliest dress a baby girl could have."

Rafe laughed. "You do that. I'll see you tonight when I get home. Bye, doll."

"Bye." Ivy pressed the disconnect button on her phone.

She was truly happy for him, and wonderfully satisfied with their relationship, but since hearing Reese's news, she wondered where her and Rafe's relationship was going. Did he want to be with her for the rest of his life? Did he want to get married at some point or was that not something that interested him? *Ugh, stop this silliness,* she berated herself. Everything was fine with Rafe. She picked up her charts and went about getting ready to give out the afternoon medications. The future would unfold as fate intended and there was no sense in worrying.

She was clocked out by five and in Target by five-twenty. Super Target carried everything from clothes to meat. Ivy roamed through the grocery aisles and picked up some chicken breasts, onions, spinach and a few other items to make enchiladas for dinner before heading to the baby aisles. She was looking at size four diapers, thinking Bonnie might need to go up a size when she heard a familiar voice behind her.

"Ivy, is that you?"

She gritted her teeth, recognizing the voice of her ex instantly. She turned and pasted a fake smile on her face. "Hi, Ben, how are you?"

"Doing good. I had to stop by and pick up some

stuff for Margie and the twins before going home. She's pregnant again." He laughed loudly and Ivy wanted to punch him. "That woman only has to think about a baby and she's pregnant. She's that fertile."

"Good for her…and you. Congratulations," Ivy said, her voice laced with saccharine.

"You're buying diapers. Did you have a baby?" Ben asked curiously as she put the package in her cart.

"No, this is for my boyfriend's daughter. He's a single dad," Ivy responded. *You should've said yes*, but Ivy couldn't lie.

Ben made a sympathetic sound. "Well, with your issue, I'm not surprised you have to pretend to be someone's mother. I hope it satisfies you, Ivy."

"You're a dick, Ben. Just because you practically knock up Margie right after she's given birth does not make you a good dad. Rafe is a soldier and I'm glad to be a part of his and his daughter's life," Ivy snapped. "I hope to God you're not teaching your kids that the only worth a woman has is to bear children."

"What I teach my kids is none of your business," Ben said coldly.

"Yeah, just like what I do is none of yours," Ivy said. "Bite me and have a good evening."

Ivy pushed her cart down the aisle and made her way to the registers, still steaming. She even forgot to pick out a dress for Bonnie and only remembered when she was on her way home. *Fuck.* She would have to get it tomorrow on the way home. Matters didn't get any better when she pulled her car into Rafe's driveway. Donna and Grace were nearby and since Donna had an audience, she probably thought it was the perfect time to try and rub Ivy the wrong way.

"Is Rafe working late?" Donna asked as she and Grace walked over.

"What do you think?" Ivy pulled the grocery bags from the back of her car.

Donna tsked softly. "You know when they start working late it usually means they are bored at home, Ivy. You should have known you wouldn't be able to please that man."

"Oh, and you could?" Ivy retorted and turned to face her.

"You know what they say, those who can, do..." Donna said sweetly.

"And those who can't have three ex-husbands." Ivy was tired and in no mood for playing nice. She dropped her bags where she stood and walked over until she was nose to nose with Donna. "I wonder why Rafe never took you up on that offer? Maybe because he likes real women instead of fake plastic Barbies. Or, maybe he heard from your exes about how dried up and used you are? Looks like gravity is starting to take hold. Those bags you have for breasts are looking a bit tight around the edges where your skin is starting to sag and can't hold up the weight. I wonder if anyone took you up on your offer the night of the party? From what I hear you went home because no one wanted you." Ivy flicked a glance at Grace. "While Grace got lucky with more than one of them that night."

"Shut up," Donna hissed while Grace gasped and turned red.

"You called down the thunder and now you got it. Rafe told you he wasn't interested and you can't handle it. So you think you can pick on me. This isn't high school, sweetie. My self worth is not based on being popular or your lack thereof. You want to feel special and you're not." Ivy sighed. "Did you ever wonder why your kids spend more time at their dad's? It's because they want a parent, but while they're here, it's all about Mommy. Don't step foot on this property again. If you need to hear it from Rafe one more time, I can make sure he tells you loud and clear. You come up to me again, I'll punch you in the face. But don't worry, it will be an excuse for you to get more plastic surgery. So, actually, I would be doing you a favor. Go away, fly, don't bother me anymore."

Ivy turned and picked up her bags. She used the key that Rafe gave her to get into his house. She needed to check on her own place and water her plants. *You spend so much time over here, but what about him spending time with you?* Her mood was sour and Ivy tried to push the negative thoughts away. She wasn't losing herself in this relationship. She was happy and be damned if assholes like Ben or Donna would make her pick a fight with Rafe. She put the food away and found a mallet to start preparations for her chicken enchiladas. She cut the chicken breasts in thin slices and put them between Saran Wrap before she vented her frustration on the meat by pounding it mercilessly. That's how Rafe's mother found her when she stepped into the house with Bonnie in her arms.

"Ivy?" Rafe's mother said.

Ivy smiled and put down the mallet. "I'm sorry. I didn't hear your car pull up."

"I'm not surprised, dear. You were beating the hell out of that chicken. I'm sure it's sufficiently sorry for whatever wrong it did to you," Mrs. Steele said with humor in her voice.

Ivy blew out a breath. "It's been a long day. I'm sure you didn't want to meet me holding a heavy kitchen utensil in my hand."

Mrs. Steele laughed. "Don't worry, dear. Rafe and his father got the best and most tender beef when I was in a mood. It's very nice to meet you."

"You too, Mrs. Steele," Ivy replied. Bonnie was holding out her hands to Ivy. "Let me wash my hands and take Bonnie."

"What are you making? And please call me Frieda," his mother replied.

"It's a spin on enchiladas except instead of using flour tortillas, I use thin slices of chicken and bake it in the oven. You can stuff it with whatever you like, but I like to use healthy stuff like veggies and spinach," Ivy explained. She washed and dried her hands before taking Bonnie and nuzzling the baby. "How's my pretty girl? Would you like some Cheerios?"

"I see she has the top two teeth coming in. Most, though not all, babies get their bottom two teeth in first," Frieda commented. "I think I'll have to get that recipe from you. I'm trying to have Frank eat healthier and he's rebelling, but this recipe could just do the trick."

"It could," Ivy said. "Rafe would eat steaks off the grill every day if I let him."

Frieda shook her head. "Just like his father. The apple doesn't fall far from the tree. You fix him before he's Frank's age. By then, almost all hope is lost."

"Do you think we'll be together that long?" Ivy asked.

Rafe's mother smiled. "Honey, I knew about you even before Rafe actually stopped sticking his foot in his mouth and you got together. Trust me, I've never heard of another woman in his life before now, not even Bonnie's mother. I think you have his heart and that's a very precious thing. Please don't hurt my son, okay?"

Ivy swallowed the emotion in her throat. "Yes, ma'am."

"Now, how about we give this Little Miss some Cheerios and then you can show me how to make your dish?" Frieda said with a smile.

"Sure." Ivy hesitated before putting Bonnie in the high chair. "I thought you might not like me."

"Why ever would you think that?" Frieda looked at her with curiosity written all over her face.

"You know, I'm African American—" Ivy began, but Frieda's laughter cut her off.

"Oh, I'm sorry, dear. I thought you were just covered in chocolate," Frieda said with mirth in her voice. "You see that woman outside, the one with the rather large chest? She is the kind of person I wouldn't approve of. She would use Rafe and twist his love and emotions to her advantage. She would see Bonnie as a tool to hold on to him, but then when he's not around she would see her as a nuisance. I don't want that for my family. You're kind and caring, and you work with the wonderful men and women that serve our country. You could be hot pink with black zebra stripes and I wouldn't care as long as you loved my son and he loved you. I can see how much Bonnie loves you already."

"I might not be able to have children," Ivy blurted out. "I have a condition."

"And that makes you less of a woman?" Frieda asked. "It took me five years to bring Rafe into this world. He was the first and the last. My doctor said I couldn't even risk having any more. If there are children between you and Rafe they will be a gift, and Bonnie is a treasure for us all. Have faith, Ivy. They said I would never have kids and look at the big strapping man my husband and I raised."

"You're remarkable," Ivy said. "I wish I had a mother like you."

"Where's your family, dear?" Frieda asked.

Ivy put some Cheerios on the tray of Bonnie's high chair. She had never told anyone about her family, not even Rafe. Somehow, though, she felt as if she could tell Mrs. Steele anything and so she opened up about her past. "My mom ran off with my stepfather. I have no idea where they are. I have one brother who blames me for everything so we don't talk. I haven't seen him since I was sixteen and became an emancipated minor. My stepfather used to abuse me and I spoke up about it, so we were taken into foster care and my mother convinced my brother I was lying. My stepfather said I seduced him." Ivy laughed softly. "I was only fourteen years old. Every night I was incredibly scared to go to bed because that is when he'd come into my room, after my mother had passed out from the alcohol. Anyway, they had the proof and he was sent away for years. I refused to go back to my mother and my social worker had a lawyer friend who helped me get emancipated. I worked and got my GED early and then went on to nursing school using the Job Corps. That's my story—not fun and definitely not what teenage girls expect growing up."

"You overcame it all, Ivy. I won't say sorry because that would mean I pity you," Frieda said, "and I don't. You fought your way out and you're stronger for it. They can never take that away from you. We dealt with a scandal when Rafe's father was on Capitol Hill. Our family has flaws, every family does, but we stuck together and that's what counts."

Ivy nodded. "You're right, and I swear I would never hurt Rafe or Bonnie. I love them both too much."

It was the first time she ever said she loved Rafe openly and she announced it to his mother. It didn't feel strange, it felt right, and when Rafe came home and Bonnie was down for the night she planned to say it again and again. Life was for living and she was going to live her life to the fullest with Rafe if he would have her.

"I know you won't." Frieda smiled.

"So, how about that recipe? We have to make sure you can fool Mr. Steele," Ivy said.

"Quite right. Let's get to it," Frieda clapped her hands in delight.

With Bonnie in her high chair, babbling happily, Ivy and Rafe's mother stepped into the kitchen to start dinner. They laughed and chatted while keeping an eye on Bonnie as she gnawed her Cheerios. Ivy put the miserable afternoon out of her mind and made a special meal for her man. Frieda made her feel great about her relationship and she couldn't wait until Rafe came home.

Later that evening, Frieda went home armed with the recipe and planned to make it for her and Mr. Steele's dinner. Rafe came home a half hour later, looking rugged and handsome in his uniform. Ivy doubted any other man looked as good as he did in uniform. He kissed her like he hadn't seen her in a week and it made her melt. They had dinner and gave Bonnie a bath before sitting down to an hour of cartoons until the baby fell asleep and then they were alone in the living room, and Ivy lost all the words she had planned to say. Everything she had rehearsed in her head was gone.

"How was your day?" Rafe asked, kissing her temple. She was resting against him while they watched the news.

"Okay, I guess. I saw Reese. He and Katie are getting married. We are still friends," Ivy replied. The rest of it came tumbling out. "I saw my ex, Ben, in Target while I was getting Bonnie's diapers. His wife Margie has twins and she's pregnant again. He acted like I was nothing. He said I was just pretending to be a mom to Bonnie since he thinks I can't have kids."

"I will find him and beat the crap out of him," Rafe growled. "You *are* a mother to Bonnie. She loves you. He can go fuck himself."

Ivy turned and gave him a shaky smile. "I'm glad you feel that way, but it makes me sad sometimes that I may never get to feel a life growing inside me or feel a kick… And then Donna and Grace were the icing on the cake. They came up to me while I was unloading the car. I just snapped and told Donna how used she was and how gravity has not been kind to her because her boobs seemed to be swinging awfully low lately."

Rafe burst out laughing. "Oh, sweetheart, I would have loved to have seen that."

"I was kind of mean," Ivy admitted, "but I was so mad."

"She deserved it. Don't lose any sleep over it, but trust me, if I ever see your ex or you point him out to me, he's going to eat my fist," Rafe said. "By the way, I got a text from my mom. She loves you."

"I like her too," Ivy replied and then took his hands in hers. "Where are we going, Rafe? I mean, what's the end game for this relationship?"

He pulled her close and looked into her eyes. "I was thinking you could move in with me, put your house on the market, and we could get married and you could adopt Bonnie. All the while, we'd be working on making baby number two."

A slow smile spread across her face. "All that, huh?"

"Should I get down on bended knee?" he asked.

"A ring would be nice, but, no, bended knee is not necessary," Ivy said.

"I think it is," Rafe said as he got to his knees in front of Ivy and put his hand in his pocket. He pulled out a box and flipped open the lid, revealing a beautiful white gold princess-cut diamond ring. "Marry me, Ivy. Make me the luckiest man in the world. Be the mother of Bonnie and all our future babies, share a bed with me, share your soul with me and I'll do the same."

"You had this all planned," Ivy whispered, overcome with emotion.

"It's the reason why I was late," he confessed. "I had to go to the jeweler to pick it up. My mom was in on it. It's the same ring she wore as well as my grandmother before her. Now it's been sized just for you." Rafe took her hand and slid the ring on her finger. "Be my wife."

"I will. Oh, I definitely will." Ivy threw her arms around his neck and he pulled her with him until they were lying on the floor in front of the sofa.

Their lips met and they clung to each other.

"Two more things," Rafe said between kisses. "One, the final ruling on Bonnie's case is tomorrow. The detective my lawyer hired could not find Juno, so I'm going to get full parental custody of her."

"That's wonderful," Ivy said. "That calls for more kisses."

She proceeded to smother him with kisses as she dug her hand in his pants. Rafe groaned with pleasure. "Oh, baby… Wait, the next thing… Uh, yeah, God, I can't think while you're doing that. I've been given a mission. I'll be leaving in two weeks."

This stopped her cold. *Oh, God, he is leaving and putting himself in danger?* She got off him and sat back. "How long will you be gone?"

"Three weeks at the most. One week will be training with the new unit. We all know our job, but for this we have to be specific," Rafe explained. "The other two weeks I can't tell you about."

"You'll be safe?" she asked as fear clutched her chest. She didn't think she would be dealing with this so very soon.

"I have you and Bonnie to come home to. Of course I'll be safe, but this is my job, Ivy. It's not going to happen often, but it will. Can you handle that?" Rafe asked.

"I love you. I'll deal with it all as long as you come home to me each and every time," Ivy whispered. "Please be careful."

"I love you too. Do you think you can plan a wedding in two weeks?" Rafe asked.

She could see he wasn't kidding. "I guess I can."

"Good. Let's do it. I want you to be Mrs. Steele before I leave." Rafe kissed her and he lingered at her lips. "My mom will help. She loves weddings."

"Okay, let's do it." Ivy giggled. "We're going to be man, wife and baby."

"Good. Now, how about we consummate the marriage early?" Rafe growled as worked at the buttons of her blouse and then her bra.

"Okay," she gasped as his hand closed over her naked breast and he pulled her close so he could take her nipple in his mouth.

The sensation of his hot mouth on her body made her ache between her legs. He moved to the next breast and enveloped it in the heat of his mouth. Ivy couldn't help but tremble as pleasure seared through her. Rafe moaned and pulled her into a deep kiss. Their tongues parried and dueled while she felt his hardness thicken between them. Rafe's arms wrapped around her as he took their kiss deeper. He grazed her teeth before he buried his tongue deep into her mouth. His guttural moan spoke volumes. She could drown in his kisses. She loved how his hot breath blended with hers and he nipped at her lips teasingly. Rafe sat up and pressed her more intimately against him. She wanted to feel the hard length of him inside her, pounding into her until she screamed his name. Ivy had never felt a desire this deep for anyone. She was desperate for Rafe to fill her every need.

His hands worked at the button of her cut off jeans and tugged them down her hips. The lace of her G-string was thin at her waist and she felt it break under his impatient fingers. He pushed her back onto the carpet and finished removing her shorts. He kissed the flat expanse of her stomach while his fingers deftly searched out and found her core. Ivy cried out in pleasure and bucked against his hand as his finger penetrated her with urgency and his thumb rubbed against her clit.

"Damn, you feel so good. Will I ever be able to take it slow with you?" Rafe groaned. "Every time I touch you it feels like I'm going to explode."

"I don't care. Oh, I don't care." Ivy thrashed her head wildly. "Just as long as you take me."

Rafe undressed with haste and covered her body with his, kissing her wildly. He devoured her mouth while his hand went back to caressing her pussy until she writhed beneath him. He buried his face between her luscious full globes. Ivy moaned her disappointment when he moved his hand from between her legs, but a soft cry escaped her lips as Rafe filled his hands with her breasts.

"Oh, Rafe, yes," Ivy moaned.

"More," he growled. "I always want more when it comes to you. Every cry that comes from your lips is like a drug, and I need more until you satisfy me."

He took her lips again in a hot, hard kiss while his touch was making her restless beneath him. *How did I ever say no to this?* Her hand cupped him and she stroked the smooth shaft over and over until Rafe shuddered. His hands traveled up the back of her neck and he sunk his fingers into her hair. He held her head while he feasted on lips swollen from his kisses. Ivy's hands caressed the muscles of his abdominals, his sculpted shoulders and chest. She stopped at his nipples and pinched them. "God," he said through their kisses and ground himself against her. Ivy gasped against his mouth as pleasure sliced through her. He was rock hard velvet over steel. She wanted to feel that power, to feel the restraint he held on to set free. She tore her lips way from his and urged him onto his back. Rafe's muscles tensed beneath her as she trailed tiny kisses and licks down his body. Rafe arched off the carpet as she blew a soft breath on the head of his cock.

"I want to take you deep into my mouth," Ivy said, breathless. "I want to taste your come."

"Do it. Now, Ivy," Rafe ground out.

Ivy continued her foray of his body, moving like a sleek cat as she tasted him. She ran her tongue over his rigid length and heard his breath hiss from between his lips. Ivy took his hard cock in her mouth, sucking with an urgent up down motion while making a fist around the base and stroking him.

"Fuck. You're going to make me come," he said harshly. He lifted his hips in an urgent thrust as she picked up the pace of her mouth on him.

She felt the first taste of his come on her tongue as he gave a long groan and his body shuddered in ecstasy. She swallowed his come as it spurted into her mouth and she lathed his cock with her tongue to clean him off.

"My turn," he said and rolled her beneath him. Rafe kissed her long and deep until her mind began to fog over. His hands were once again all over her body, touching and stoking the fire she felt to new heights.

He lifted his head from her breasts to look at her. "I love you, always."

When she felt his fingers travel over the sensitive skin of the thick lips of her pussy, she whispered his name. Ivy's hands gripped his shoulders as he slipped his fingers inside her. This time, instead of slowly taking her to the edge, it was a mad race to sensual abyss. He pressed the digits inside her deeply, over and over again, bringing her to completion in a matter of seconds. He guided her legs around his waist and plunged inside her while her body still shook from her orgasm. Ivy cried out in pleasure and his voice joined hers as their bodies united.

"I love you too," Ivy said against his neck and bit him gently.

"You're like a vise around my cock," Rafe said breathlessly. "I want you to take all of me until you scream."

Ivy barely had any control left. Being with Rafe took over her mind, body and soul completely. She licked her lips slowly and watched his eyes darken in pleasure. His fingers tightened on her hips and dug into the soft flesh as he thrust deeper and she cried out. She brought her hands up and massaged her breasts silently, pleading for him to taste them. He obliged and sucked one of her pert nipples into his mouth. The combination of both sensations almost sent her over the edge. Her hips bucked under him and Rafe groaned against her breast.

"More, Rafe. All of it. Make me come for you," she panted.

"Yes, oh, God, Ivy," he said between clenched teeth.

He grabbed her hips, pulling her against him so that he was buried completely inside her and she cried out in pleasure. Their pace picked up and soon the sound of their bodies coupling mingled with their harsh breath and cries of pleasure. She felt her pussy tighten like a vise around his throbbing cock and she strived for that place that would cause her to shatter in ecstasy.

Rafe fisted his hand in her hair and kissed her before muttering. "Right now. Now."

His words and the passion in his eyes drove Ivy to her orgasm on a shaky cry of pleasure. With her release, Rafe let himself go, pounding inside her until he groaned and arched above her. His beautiful body tensed in sexual delight. She felt his warm seed spill in the confines of her body and out of her as he continued to move. Rafe dropped down next to her on the carpet, both of them trying to catch their breath. Her body occasionally shook as mini aftershocks flowed through her. She tried to think clearly, but after an experience like that she chose to let everything slide away for a while. They heard a soft cry from Bonnie in her room and Rafe groaned.

"You get cleaned up. I'll throw on my clothes and wash my hands before checking on her and then we'll switch," Ivy said, starting to get up.

"Oh, bless you. You're a wonderful woman. I need to regain use of my legs," Rafe murmured.

Ivy kissed him gently. "You were fabulous, so you deserve it."

"Hey, Ivy?" Rafe rolled over and rested his head on his hands.

She looked back at him while she was picking up her clothes. "Yes, my love?"

"I hope we made a baby tonight. I'd love to see our child growing inside you," Rafe said.

Ivy pressed her hand to her stomach and tears sprang to her eyes. "Oh, Rafe."

She didn't know what else to say. This was one of her biggest fears; not being able to have a child. She rushed upstairs and poked her head into Bonnie's room. "I'm coming, baby, I'm coming." The baby sniffled and smiled. Ivy rushed into the hallway bathroom and began to quickly clean up. She stopped and looked at herself in the mirror and rubbed her hand against the flatness of her stomach. *Maybe, just maybe*. Because of Rafe, she could dream again and love with all her heart. Because of him, she had a family.

Chapter Eight

Everything was a flurry of activity for the next two weeks. A wedding plus preparations for Rafe to leave for three weeks took up most of her time. Ivy went with Rafe to court the next day and through an expedited hearing, and all the hard work from his lawyer, he now had sole custody of Bonnie. After that victory, his lawyer was now filing papers so she could legally adopt the baby. She had quite a bit of vacation time she never used that had accumulated, so she put in the request with human resources at Walter Reed to take off eight weeks. It would start the week that Rafe left on his mission. It was going to be hard for both her and Bonnie not seeing him. She wanted to spend as much time with Bonnie as possible and have her at home instead of daycare while he was gone. The day before Rafe's award presentation in D.C., she bought Bonnie her dress and she got something new for herself. It wasn't every day you got to enter the White House for a ceremony. She felt a sense of pride when she saw Rafe in uniform standing at attention and being pinned by the President himself.

"Thank you for your service to this country and protecting us all," the President said loud and clear.

"It's my honor, sir, to serve my country." Rafe saluted after the medals were secured to his chest and did a quick turn before marching away. Ivy heard his mother sniffing beside her and she looked over to see pride on both his parents' faces. She felt it too in her heart and wanted to jump up and cheer for him. Later, after the ceremony, the President greeted them all and even held Bonnie. Ivy made sure she got a picture because as Bonnie grew they would tell her about the day she met the leader of their country. They had a celebratory lunch in an exclusive restaurant near Capitol Hill and it was there that they decided that the wedding would be held at his parents' lake house. She loved his parents and they accepted her like family, and for that Ivy was thrilled. They were the family she never had, the one she dreamt about when she was a child and sat terrified in her bed, afraid of her stepfather coming into her room. There weren't too many people she wanted to invite to her wedding. What she knew of her family was scattered and after the incident, no one really spoke to each other. Ivy knew she had an aunt and uncle somewhere, but neither cared enough when the trouble started to even offer her a home. There was no need for them to be there for her special occasion.

Marie accepted her invitation to be her maid of honor and that Sunday they had a girl's day to find dresses and accessories. They bought Bonnie a frilly pink and white dress and Marie got misty eyed as Ivy tried on wedding dresses. After trying on at least a dozen dresses, she finally found the one. It was a simple cream, knee-length sheath dress that had a long train in the back. There was a shiny satin bow high under her chest and delicate straps holding up the dress on either shoulder. It was perfect.

"I can't believe you're getting married." Marie sniffed into a tissue and dabbed her eyes. "I'm jealous and happy all at the same time. Where's my soldier, I ask you?"

Ivy laughed. "I'm sure he's waiting. All you have to do is find him."

"Maybe it's Rafe's best man Brody." Marie sighed. "That boy is fine."

Marie and Brody had been invited for dinner the day after their trip to D.C. They instantly took a liking to one another.

"You know his reputation. Rafe warned you," Ivy said.

"Which makes him all the more appealing. You know a woman loves a man she thinks she can change. Plus, the guy looks like he could do my body good—like milk," Marie said with a laugh.

"You're awful. Do what you want to do, but I'm just saying don't get hurt because then I'll have to fillet him alive if he hurts you," Ivy warned.

"Aw, you're sweet trying to defend my honor," Marie said. "Now, let's buy this dress and get to the flower shop before it closes."

All the plans were in place and the days leading up to the wedding flew by between work and going to the lake house in the evening to help set up. The night before the wedding, Ivy took her suitcase and the baby bag she had packed for Bonnie out to the car. When she came back in, Rafe was strapping Bonnie into the car seat. He stood and pulled Ivy into his arms, rocking back and forth gently while they held each other.

"I don't like this," he murmured. "Sleeping without you is unfair."

"It's tradition. You can't see the bride before the wedding. Besides, you'll have fun with Brody and your father," Ivy said and then warned, "No strippers or women of loose morals…or any women at all, for that matter."

"I nixed that plan before Brody could even mention it. I don't need anyone but you to start my fire. Plus, Mom would kill me if I gave Dad a heart attack." Rafe gave her a slow smile. "Are you sure I can't interest you in a little pre-wedding romp?"

"How about you keep that thought in your head until tomorrow night? Your parents will have Bonnie and we'll be all alone in D.C." Ivy kissed him and Rafe took it deeper until they were both panting. Bonnie let out a loud squeal of displeasure at being strapped into her seat and not going anywhere. Ivy pulled away reluctantly. "That's my cue to leave. Little Miss wants to go to Grandma's."

"Tomorrow you're going to be Mrs. Steele," Rafe said. "Are you ready?"

"I'm already Mrs. Steele. This is just a formality.

You've had my heart for a long time," Ivy pointed out. "See you tomorrow."

"I love you, baby…both my babies," Rafe said.

"We love you too. Goodnight," Ivy replied as she shut the door behind her. She secured Bonnie in the car and they set out to the lake house where tomorrow she and Rafe would take their vows. Ivy was looking forward to the night she would spend with Bonnie, Marie and Frieda. Nervous anticipation filled her as well. She would soon be marrying the man she loved.

* * * *

Even though rain had been forecast, the day was clear and bright. The sky was a pristine blue backdrop that held only a few wispy white clouds. Rafe, his father and Brody showed up early in the morning looking no worse for wear, Frieda assured Ivy. She got the boys settled and came back to Ivy with a message. "Rafe said he loves you madly, so hurry up and meet him at the altar." Frieda grinned. "That child of mine was always impatient."

The guests had begun to arrive and upstairs Rafe's father bounced Bonnie on his knee and the little girl was wearing her new dress and her little white patent leather shoes. Marie was helping Ivy get dressed when they put the last touch, the satin corded elbow-length veil, on her head.

Frieda sniffed behind them. "Oh, dear, I said I wouldn't cry."

"Don't you start, Mrs. Steele. If you do, I'm going to as well." Marie turned around with a beaming smile and watery eyes. "You look so perfect, Ivy."

"It feels like butterflies have taken up residence in my stomach." Ivy laughed nervously.

There was a knock on the door and Frieda went to answer. She came back with a smile. "The hostess said everyone is seated and they are ready to begin the music you chose. Rafe is waiting by the gazebo. It's time."

Through the open window, Ivy heard the beginning notes of *I Need You Now*. Frieda went out first and Marie followed. Ivy took a deep breath and stepped out of the room. She slowly made her way down the stairs and outside to the garden where the gazebo was decorated in white organza, pink lilies and red roses. Her bouquet held the same flowers with baby's breath scattered through it. No matter how beautiful it all was, nothing compared to the sight of Rafe standing there in his Marine dress blues. He looked so handsome, it took her breath away. Each step brought her closer to the future she saw in his eyes. When she took his hand the world melted away and it was just her and him. The pastor spoke but Ivy did not hear most of what he said. Her thoughts were solely on Rafe. Rafe's gaze never left hers, even as he spoke his vows. When the pastor said, "I now pronounce you man and wife, you make kiss the bride," Rafe gave her a wicked grin and swooped in for the kiss. She barely heard the cheers and whistles as they kissed. The reception was glorious and everyone had a good time and they left later that evening in a limousine to D.C. where they stayed in the honeymoon suite at the Marriott. The night was filled with passion and love. She woke up that morning as Ms. Ivy St. Clair and fell asleep in the arms of Rafe as Mrs. Ivy Steele. Her body was languid and satisfied with sexual gratification, while Rafe's hand gently caressed her thigh. Ivy knew now completely what bliss was.

* * * *

Rafe left with his duffel over one shoulder and a picture of his two favorite girls tucked securely in the pocket of his uniform. He would make sure that when they finally got to the carrier that would take them out to sea, they would be with him in the field. He wished he'd had longer at home with them to enjoy the newness of being a permanent family. When he saw Ivy walking down the aisle toward him on their wedding day, his heart tripped. There was no one more beautiful than she was on that day and every day since then—with makeup or without it, dressed in old, baggy clothes or dressed to the nines. No one and nothing compared to the way he felt for Ivy. He saw the looks Donna gave them as they moved back and forth, cleaning out and emptying Ivy's house. He was not on her favorite list anymore and Rafe didn't give a fat rat's ass. He had his wife and his daughter and that's all he would ever need.

When he left for his mission, he promised to call when or if he could. He tried his best to push the ache of missing them from his mind. For this he had to be focused. If not, his life and the lives of his team could be put in danger. Rafe was going to do his very best to bring them all home in one piece.

It was many hours on a C-5 to get them out to the aircraft carrier in the Persian Gulf. From there, the mission would be charted and planned down to the second. They would have one night to rest and prepare, ask questions, and acquire the target location. While he lay on the thin mattress on the top bunk, he pulled the picture of his girls out of his pocket. He caressed their faces and closed his eyes holding the picture to his chest. In his head he heard Bonnie's baby babble and the squeal of her laughter. He heard Ivy's voice like a caress, telling him she loved him and to come home soon. *Yes, baby, I will*, he thought and let sleep take him. Tomorrow, the soldier in him had to be on point.

* * * *

It had been two weeks, three days and seven hours since Rafe left. Ivy wasn't one to brood and ache over a man but she missed Rafe like crazy. Bonnie did too. She woke up looking for her daddy and whimpered at night when it was time for bed. She was accustomed to Rafe holding her and feeding her her last bottle while cartoons were on. Ivy didn't seem to compare because she still fussed every night and missed her routine. She woke up at night crying and Ivy decided to take her to bed with her. She gave her another bottle and caressed the silky black curls on her head. She kissed her cheek and whispered, "Don't worry, sweet pea, Daddy will be home soon." Ivy felt like crying herself. She missed him so much. He hadn't called and she understood he might not have been able to, but still she wished she could hear his voice.

She was feeding Bonnie at the kitchen table a day or so later with still no word from Rafe. The doorbell rang and she wiped Bonnie's face quickly and went to the door. It was probably the postman with a package. Rafe told her he had ordered a few things online and that they would be coming in the mail. It wasn't the postman. It was a petite woman with brown hair and a blotchy face. A man in a leather jacket with greasy black hair stood beside her. They definitely weren't the types that Rafe would associate with, so Ivy was instantly on alert.

"Yes, may I help you?" Ivy said politely.

"I'm here to pick up Bonnie. I'm her momma," the woman sniffed. Ivy knew the signs. She was hooked on something, that's for sure.

"You're Juno," Ivy said carefully.

"Yeah. Is my kid here?" Juno asked angrily and went to push past her.

Ivy stopped her. "Yes, she is here, but you will not be taking her anywhere. Rafe has full custody of her now since you dropped her off like waste at his doorstep."

"Watch your mouth, lady," the man snarled.

"No, you watch yours. You're on *my* doorstep," Ivy replied angrily. "Now you better leave before I call the police."

"Listen, you tell that soldier we want ten thousand for the kid," the man shouted. "If not, we're going to take her."

"Over my dead body and trust me, you'll have a fight on your hands," Ivy replied coldly. "You two need help. You're strung out and Bonnie is not going anywhere with you. Rafe has custody. I have the paperwork right here. I suggest you leave before I call the cops and they will not be on your side. Rafe is a decorated soldier and if we see you back here there will be trouble."

The man with Juno moved until he was up in her face. His breath was soured with smoke and alcohol. "Ten thousand, lady, or you're going to be sorry."

"Get out of my face before I kick your balls into your throat," Ivy said through gritted teeth.

He made a little move, but Ivy refused to flinch.

"Is there a problem, Ivy?" It was Donna's voice and Ivy glanced behind them to where Donna stood holding a gardening trowel. Ivy never thought she'd be so happy to see her.

"Yes, they are threatening to kidnap Bonnie and trying to extort money from me," Ivy said calmly.

"I guess I should call the police then," Donna said as she pulled her Blackberry out of her pocket. "We can't have this sort in the neighborhood."

"Bobby, come on," Juno said urgently, taking the man by the arm and pulling him away.

"You'll be seeing me again, bitch." He gave Ivy an evil smile.

"If I do you'll have a one way ticket to jail...Bobby," Ivy retorted.

They stepped away and got into the most beat up car she'd ever seen and headed out of the cul-de-sac, while Donna came across the lawn to her quickly.

"That was a nasty looking dude. Maybe you should call Rafe," Donna suggested.

"He's out of the country on a mission," Ivy explained.

"You could always...um...stay with me... You and Bonnie, I mean, until he comes home," Donna suggested. When Ivy's mouth dropped open, she rolled her eyes. "Please, I'm over that. So you married Rafe? Good for you. We're still neighbors and I don't want to see you or the baby hurt. I know I can be a mean bitch but don't question it until you've walked in my shoes. I'm not saying we're going to be BFFs but you'll be safe at my place."

Ivy pushed her shock aside. "Thank you so much, but I'm sure we'll be safe. If not, we'll run right over to your house."

"Still, you better call your cop friend and make a complaint." Donna walked away. "I'll leave a key under the flower pot. Use it in an emergency."

Ivy stepped back from the front door and closed it. She was amazed. Wow, Donna "Double Ds" being generous and caring. Who knew that could happen? Ivy tried to shake off the terror she felt from the confrontation with Juno and Bobby. She took Donna's advice and called Reese who came to the house with a set of patrol officers. They took a statement and Reese promised that they would patrol the neighborhood every few hours to check for anything suspicious. She then called Frieda and Frank to let them know what was going on. They wanted her to pack up Bonnie and come out to the lake house to stay until Rafe came home. She promised if anything else happened she would, but she didn't want to disrupt Bonnie's schedule any more than it already had been.

Later that night, with the baby in bed, Ivy checked and rechecked the locks on the doors and windows. A month or two prior, Rafe had installed security lights in the front and back of the home, but Ivy doubted that flooding the area with light would deter Bobby if he really wanted to get in. She'd already put Bonnie to bed but was so nervous she brought the baby into the bed with her to sleep. Ivy made sure her phone was on the charger on the bedside table. It was at that very moment that missing Rafe was almost unbearable and she felt tears fill her eyes. Ivy took a deep breath and told herself to be strong. Rafe didn't marry a weakling. He didn't marry someone who would give in to fear. She would protect Bonnie with her life if she had to.

Later that night, the sound of breaking glass made

her sit up in bed. Not that she had really been sleeping anyway. Ivy scrambled from the bed, locked the bedroom door, and grabbed her phone and the sleeping baby and went into the master bathroom and locked the door and jammed the door security bar she had snagged from downstairs under the lock. She pressed nine-one-one as she heard things being broken downstairs and heavy footsteps on the stairs.

She heard the operator come on and spoke quickly. "This is Ivy Steele at 4124 Strawberry Glen. Someone broke into my house. Two officers were patrolling because of an incident that happened earlier and Detective Reese Alvater took the statement. They're trying to take my baby. They want to kidnap her."

"Who's trying to take your baby, ma'am?" the operator asked.

"The baby's biological mother and her boyfriend. My husband has custody, and I'm in the process of adopting her," Ivy said quickly.

"We're coming to get you, bitch!" she heard Bobby yell.

"They're coming upstairs. He's yelling, saying he's going to get me. Please hurry, please!" Ivy felt fear clutch at her heart. Bonnie was being amazing. She was not crying. Instead, just looking up at Ivy.

"They are on their way, ma'am. You should hear the sirens very soon," the operator said. "Do you know what kind of car they're driving?"

Loud bangs sounded on the bedroom door and

that's when Bonnie began to scream. Ivy searched her mind for the answer. "An old beat up green Cadillac with rust spots on the roof!" She screamed out to Bobby, "Get out of here. Leave us alone! The cops are on the way!"

She gently laid the crying baby on a towel in the tub. She put the phone on speaker and sat it on the closed lid of the toilet and opened the vanity drawer to find something that would work as a weapon. If he got in, she would protect Bonnie the best she could. "Shh, baby, shh. It's okay," Ivy tried to croon through her tears. She found a pair of scissors in the drawer and held them up. If he got in, she was going to take him down. She stood there holding the scissors, waiting, when she realized there was no more pounding, nothing, only silence. All she could hear was Bonnie crying and her own harsh breathing. After a few more minutes, she heard the sirens and the screeching of tires outside. She put the scissors down and picked up the baby, hugging her close. She didn't open the door until she heard the police on the other side of the bedroom door. Reese rushed in with four other officers, and they helped her to the bed to sit with the baby.

"Are you two okay?" Reese asked urgently.

Ivy only nodded and held on to Bonnie all the more. The baby was the only thing that was keeping her from falling apart at that point. They'd caught Bobby and Juno trying to escape in their beat up car and both were arrested. Ivy indentified them in the back of the police car. Bobby glowered at her while Juno sobbed and shook. *It serves them right*, she thought unsympathetically. Any sympathy she had for Juno was completely erased after that. Ivy managed to call Rafe's parents and while the police were still there, they showed up. Donna and a lot of the neighbors had come outside, and it was Donna who stood with her arm around Ivy's shoulder in comfort on the lawn. Frank took the baby and Ivy helped Frieda pack up what they would need to go to the lake house. The sliding door and whatever else had been broken would be fixed and/or replaced before Rafe came home, but right now they could not stay there. Frank made sure that the sliding door was boarded up before they left.

It was late when they got to the lake house and Frieda made sure Ivy felt safe and comfortable in one of the guest rooms. It was when she was in bed that Ivy let go all of the emotion and cried. Bonnie slept beside her and she pushed her face into the pillow to muffle her sobs so as not to wake the baby. The door opened silently and Frieda came in and sat on the bed. She rubbed Ivy's shoulders and in instinct, Ivy turned into her mother-in-law's arms to accept her comfort.

"You were very brave, Ivy. Now you just let it all go," Frieda crooned.

Ivy couldn't stop, even if she wanted to. She was crying not only from fear but from missing Rafe. She just wanted him home.

Chapter Nine

Rafe had been frantic to get back to his family. His father pulled in a favor or two to get an emergency call through to him to let him know what had happened. He was livid. Juno and Bobby were lucky he was in the middle of the ocean because if he was on United States soil, he probably would have been arrested for killing the bastard who broke into his house and put Bonnie and Ivy in danger. That was four days ago and since then Rafe had been antsy to get home. The mission was over, but of course they had to wait for transport to get them back home. So by the time the C-5 landed in Quantico, the tires had barely touched the tarmac before he was rushing off the plane. He did the debriefing on the aircraft carrier in the middle of the Persian Gulf. The brass liked a good outcome and the mission was a success. Paperwork could be dealt with later. Right now, he wanted to be home with his family.

Rafe pulled his SUV onto the dark street and rolled the window down so the warm night air could hit his face. His fingers were clenched around the steering wheel and he willed himself to loosen them. He'd already called the police station where Reese worked and was going to stop by there before going to the house. He recalled when he first met the man and the scuffle they'd had on Ivy's front lawn. Now, he owed the man for taking care of the situation that arose while he was gone. He pulled into the precinct parking lot and parked his car before walking up the steps of the red brick building.

A female officer was at the front desk and she smiled. "What can I help you with?"

"Sergeant Major Rafe Steele to see Detective Alvater," Rafe said.

She picked up a phone and pressed a button and waited for a moment. "Reese, you've got a soldier up here to see you. Okay, yeah."

She hung up the phone and smiled at Rafe. "Head down the hall, turn left, and then take the stairs up to the second floor. That's the detective bullpen," she explained.

"Thank you, ma'am," Rafe said and followed her directions.

Reese was waiting for him and Rafe stuck out his hand as they stood face to face.

"Thanks for looking after my girls. I know we got off on the wrong foot, but I appreciate what you did more than you can know," Rafe said.

Reese grinned. "You probably never thought you'd be saying anything like this to me, huh?"

Rafe smiled in return. "No, but all the same, I'm grateful. Ivy and the baby have been staying at my parents' place. They just went home yesterday after my dad got a security system installed."

"That's a good thing, but that scum won't be back," Reese said.

"I wish he were still here so I could have a few minutes alone with him to show him my displeasure at what took place," Rafe said grimly.

"I'd probably agree to that if it wouldn't mean my job. The fucker was asking for it," Reese replied. "Both he and the chick had outstanding warrants in Vegas along with these charges on top of that. Both of them are going up on felonies."

"That's good. Are they going to go to trial here?" Rafe asked.

"Yeah, and then they will be extradited to Vegas for the charges there. You'll get to testify. Ivy too," Reese answered.

"Juno is still here, in jail, right? Can I see her?" Rafe asked.

"You'll have to talk to her through the bars. I don't think I can trust you to not throttle her," Reese teased.

"I just want to see the woman who thought kidnapping Bonnie was a good idea, even after she gave her up in the first place. She's not a mother, Ivy is," he explained.

Reese nodded. "I'll take you down. She'll be transferred to the women's prison to await trial tomorrow. We didn't have transport for the last few days."

They went downstairs to where the holding cells

were located. The entire area was painted in a drab white that carried dirt and graffiti. The walls wore the mess like a badge of all the years the building was in service. Juno Corwin sat on a lone bunk, her hair lackluster and limp and her face, without makeup, showed acne scars. Rafe barely recognized the woman he had met in Vegas and it certainly was not how she looked now—in less that two years she looked like a totally different person. Back when Rafe had met her, she was a dancer and had a decent job in one of the casino's hotels. Now, she looked like a junkie and it only went to prove that drugs could destroy a person inside and out. She stood when he walked in front of her cell. She obviously recognized him.

She tried to smile. "Bonnie is a beautiful girl, isn't she?"

"Yes, she is," Rafe answered. "Thank you for her. If you hadn't left her, I might never have known I had a daughter."

"I think I deserve something for that, right?" Juno said. "Maybe you could talk to the cops or something. Get me sprung?"

"That's not going to happen. You and your deadbeat boyfriend tried to kidnap Bonnie and hurt my wife," Rafe said coldly. "You should be grateful I wasn't there, otherwise he'd be dead. Consider *that* a gift."

"We're just messed up...the drugs, you know." She grabbed the bars and implored, "Please, get me out—for what we had, for our daughter. I can't survive jail."

"We had nothing. One night and that was it." Rafe shook his head. "Maybe if you'd come to me when you were pregnant I would've helped you, but you left my child on a doorstep. Suppose I'd moved? You didn't even wait to find out if she would be safe or in the right hands, you just left her. Jail is the best place for you. Maybe you'll get cleaned up and fly straight. But you don't ever come back to my home. You lost Bonnie twice—once when you left her and again when you let that scumbag try to take her. I just wanted to see your face to see if you had any remorse. Even now, you're only thinking about yourself. Goodbye, Juno. I hope you get the help that you need."

He walked out and she called his name and it echoed off the dirty walls. He followed Reese back up the stairs and into the florescent lights of the precinct.

"Thanks for that," Rafe said and shook Reese's hand again.

"Don't worry about Ivy or the baby. Those two won't be seeing freedom for a few years and even then I doubt they would be stupid enough to come back here," Reese explained. "If they ever come up for parole you and Ivy will be notified as the victim of the crime."

"Okay, good. That's good." Rafe sighed. "I'm heading home."

"Is Ivy's place on the market?" Reese asked suddenly. "I only ask because we're going to be bringing Jon home soon and all three of us in my apartment won't work. Do you think she'd let me buy it?"

"In this real estate market, a sure buy is better than it sitting empty for months on end. I'll tell her to call you." Rafe grinned. "You sure you won't be uncomfortable living a few houses away from us?"

"You got your girl, I got mine. Everything else is water under the bridge." Reese chuckled. "Though I'm pretty sure you still owe me for that choke hold."

"I'll let you get a punch in," Rafe teased. "Anyway, gotta go. Thanks again, and I'll tell Ivy to call you tomorrow about the house."

"Great. See you around, Major," Reese said and turned back to go to his office.

Rafe stepped out into the night once more and took a deep breath. Everything was going to be okay. He got into his car and took to the streets again heading home to his girls—the sexy woman he was in love with and the beautiful baby girl who could melt his heart with a smile. When he opened the door to his house, Ivy rushed into his arms. He pressed his face into her hair and inhaled her scent deeply. Rafe lifted her off her feet and she wrapped her legs around his waist. Rafe kissed her senseless, until his breath was labored and his cock throbbed between his legs.

"God, I missed you so much," he said huskily.

"We missed you more," Ivy replied and turned her head toward the living room. "Bonnie is waiting up for you."

He followed Ivy's gaze and saw his little girl on her hands and knees rocking back and forth. She made two attempts to crawl and then scooted on her belly toward him.

"Look at you. I've been gone three weeks and you decide to get mobile." Rafe chuckled and swung her high. Bonnie gave a high shriek of happiness and he kissed her over and over again. He preferred her baby powder scent over the smell of gun oil and the acrid smoke of explosions any day.

"She's almost eight months old. She was bound to get mobile sooner rather than later," Ivy said. "She started at your parents' place."

Rafe turned to Ivy, concern in his eyes. "How are you, baby? Are you scared to be here? Do we need to sell the house? We can if it has bad memories for you and you don't feel safe here anymore."

"I'm fine. Rafe, this is *our* home. They don't get to chase us away." Ivy cupped his cheek. "You won't believe it, but even Donna is being…well, nice. She has come to check on us a few times, and even asked if I wanted to come by for coffee. That day when they came to the house, she was there ready to throw down with a garden trowel if she had to. And then when they broke in, she was actually here comforting me."

Rafe looked around. "Am I in some kind of alternate universe? You and Donna 'Double Ds' are actually…friends?"

"I wouldn't say that exactly, but we came to a mutual understanding, I think." Ivy laughed and hugged him tight. "I'm so glad you're home."

"Me too, and I'm starved. I haven't eaten since yesterday," Rafe admitted.

"Go sit with our daughter and let her show you all the new toys she got while you were away. I'll bring dinner to the living room," Ivy said.

Rafe sat on the floor beside Bonnie while he took his boots off. He lay down on the soft carpet and let her climb all over him. She got baby drool on his face as she tried to bite his chin. At the moment, nothing was more perfect than to listen to baby babble and be covered in her drool. He had been a bit of a loner for such a long time that now he couldn't see past a time before he had Bonnie in his life. She showed him what he was missing. Ivy brought him a plate of chicken cacciatore and put it on the coffee table along with a glass of sweet iced tea.

"Come on, munchkin. Let's let Daddy eat." She lifted Bonnie off him and Rafe sat up. "We'll get your bath when he's done and then we can watch your shows on TV."

Rafe took the plate and began to devour the food while Ivy bounced Bonnie on her knees. Then it was bath time with lots of splashing and giggling while Rafe imitated Daffy Duck. Ivy got her bottle warmed up while Rafe sat with her in his arms and turned the TV on. Bonnie snuggled against his chest and instead of watching the television, she kept her eyes on her daddy. Rafe looked down and bent to kiss her head as she drank her milk sleepily. The simplest moments were the best—the ones where Ivy sat next to him while their daughter fell asleep in his arms.

Later, when Bonnie was in her crib and the house was quiet, it was their time to be together. Rafe came out of the shower with a towel wrapped around his waist. Ivy was lying in bed completely nude and looked at him with desire in her eyes. Need raced through him like a punch to the gut and his cock instantly hardened between his legs. He'd dreamt of her every night for the past three weeks.

"Did I mention how much I missed you? I ached right here." Ivy ran her hand down her stomach to the mound of her pussy. She slipped her finger between the slit and she spread her legs wide. Rafe saw that she was already moist and ready for him. His knees almost buckled with the desire he felt for her. "You're not going to make me beg, are you?"

He went to his knees on the bed in front of her spread legs. Rafe ran one lone finger down the line of her pussy and slipped it inside. "So hot. Damn, you make me just want to take you hard. Were you naughty and touched yourself while I was gone?"

"Maybe. Did that make you hard, thinking about me touching myself while you were gone?" Ivy gasped and writhed under his touch. Rafe moved his fingers faster and watched her hips rise and fall to meet his finger's movement. "Oh, God, Rafe."

He rubbed her clit with his thumb and she gasped out his name. Ivy spread her legs even wider in a silent plea. "You want more, don't you?" he asked as he continued to fuck her with his finger and manipulate her clit. "Say it. Tell me what you want," Rafe encouraged.

"Yes, please, more," Ivy panted. She made a soft growl of frustration in her throat and he smiled. "Do it, baby, please."

"I'm going to make you come," he said with arousal in his voice, and he felt his control waver as he bent to suck her clit into his mouth. He buried his fingers to the hilt inside her. It caused him to groan when he felt the hot walls of her pussy contract around the digit and her hips pump against his hands. He pushed deeper and sucked her clit harder and Ivy cried out in pleasure. Her hands clenched the thick duvet on the bed.

"Oh, don't stop, Rafe. I'm going to come hard," Ivy cried out as she bucked on the bed.

"You like how that feels, don't you?" Rafe asked gutturally. "Ah, yes, baby, just like that. Let me see you fall apart."

He watched her body tremble and her feet dig into the bed as she arched into his touch. Ivy reached the summit of her pleasure and cried out his name. He found the spot buried inside her pussy and he fucked her with his fingers hard until she came again. Watching her was like watching living art. Rafe took a mental picture of her and vowed that any other time he went away he would close his eyes and see her just like this. Her body shuddered and released its juice, coating his finger. Her cries of completion were driving him mad with desire. Rafe wasn't done yet; he had to taste her fully. He craved it like a drowning man would crave air. Ivy was his center and he wanted to immerse himself in her completely.

He replaced his fingers with his mouth and she moaned a long sultry sound that filled the air. He licked at her velvet sex and buried his tongue inside her. Rafe closed his eyes and groaned as her flavor filled his mouth. He spread the lips of her pussy and sucked her clit with fervor until she ground her hips against his face and came again under his passionate onslaught. It was as much as he could take. The need to be buried inside her became a primal force and he could only follow his instinct to claim her.

Rafe covered Ivy's body with his own hard frame and took her lips. Their kiss was fierce and hot. He dominated her with a smooth thrust of his tongue. He took her mouth just like he was going to take her body. In one smooth thrust, he filled her. His cock was thick and her pussy milked him as he moved slowly inside her. *Jesus, she feels so good!* Rafe bit the inside of his lip to keep his control. He was going to take her high before he let himself go. He slipped his hands beneath her and cupped the smooth cheeks of her ass before thrusting deep once more. Ivy arched and called his name as he picked up the rhythm of his thrusts.

"Don't hold back, Rafe. Come with me," Ivy begged. He felt her fingers bite into his back and the sweet pain of her fingernails in his flesh only enhanced his pleasure.

"Oh, fuck. Fuck yes!" he moaned.

Ivy reared up and bit his neck before she sucked on the sensitive skin. Rafe pounded into her mercilessly. He pushed her back and bent his head to take one of her nipples in his mouth while their bodies moved urgently toward completion. He was rewarded with her low cry of pleasure. Their harsh breathing filled the air and with a smooth roll, Ivy was now on top. His hands pulled her to him, impaling her onto his steel hard cock with a desire filled frenzy. They both went over the edge into an orgasm that left them panting and unable to move. Ivy fell against him and was pliant. She made small sounds of satisfaction and Rafe chuckled as he gently slid her over.

"Don't move me," she moaned. "Let me lay here just like this."

"I'm going to get us cleaned up," Rafe said. "Maybe I'll wait a minute... I think I'm a tad lightheaded."

"That's what you get when all the blood rushes from your head to the little soldier downstairs," Ivy teased.

"Hey, he's not little. Don't insult him." Rafe slapped her on her bottom before he rolled out of bed.

"Oh, honey, I would never do such a thing. Were you not just there with me?" Ivy leaned up on her elbows. "I feel as if I should shoot off fireworks in the backyard for what we just did."

Rafe came back with a washcloth and a towel. He took pleasure in wiping her body down and felt desire burn in him again as he smoothed the wet cloth over her perky breasts. There was no way he would ever get enough of her. He'd never known love like he knew it with Ivy. Her fierce courage amazed him—standing up to Juno and her boyfriend even when they broke into the house. The way she had dealt with Donna and even him when he put his foot in his mouth more than once. Ivy was his love, his life. Fate brought both Ivy and Bonnie to him.

He climbed back into bed and under the covers with her. "This is so much better than a lumpy thin cot on an aircraft carrier."

"You should put in a requisition to have me with you when you go away," Ivy teased.

"I'd do it if they let me," Rafe said huskily. "I hated every moment of being away from you and Bonnie."

"And I would go with you if they let me," Ivy said. She kissed him gently. "I love you, my sexy soldier."

"Right back at you, baby. I'm yours forever." Rafe yawned. "The lack of sleep is catching up with me."

"Sleep, love." Ivy pulled his head against her breast and he sighed as her fingers trailed through his hair.

Baby On Board

"If Bonnie wakes up, let me go to her. I didn't think I would miss waking up in the middle of the night with her, but I did," Rafe murmured. He felt himself slipping into slumber.

"I'll wake you, darling. Now let go," Ivy whispered.

He felt her kiss the top of his head as he let all thoughts drift away. In the arms of his wife, he was complete. Knowing that whenever he left she would be waiting for him was the best gift possible. No one in the world could love him like Ivy did.

* * * *

Epilogue...

The fall in Maryland came in just as quickly as the summer had earlier in the year. The brisk wind came across the river and could chill you if you weren't adequately dressed. Bonnie was now at the point where she would hold on to tables and chairs, trying to take her first tentative foray toward walking. Each time she let go, Ivy held her breath, hoping she would take that first brave step. She wasn't ready yet, but when she was, Ivy knew that Bonnie would not only walk but run toward her destination. That was how brave her baby was.

They were visiting Rafe's parents for the weekend at the lake house. After dinner, they had gathered in the family room by the fire. While they were inside playing with Bonnie, Ivy slipped her coat on and went out to sit by the water and reflect on the last few months that had been filled with such happiness she could hardly believe it. She had a home and a family that she loved and cherished. Frieda and Frank Steele had become the parents she never had. Frieda was someone she could talk to about anything and Frank was just the gentlest person she'd ever meet. She liked the way he smoked a pipe by the lake when she came over and they would walk together. He told stories of Rafe growing up and actually convinced her to go fishing with him next year. Rafe shook his head sadly when he heard the news and said simply, "You're doomed." Ivy didn't think so. She could sit with Frank in a boat reading a book while they waited for a fish to bite.

She pressed her hand against her stomach and knew the butterflies that she felt there were more than that now. Another miracle had happened and her doctor confirmed it today, just before they left to come for their weekend visit. She was trying to wrap her head around the news and hadn't even told Rafe yet. *A baby.* There was a baby growing inside her. A new life created by her and Rafe, made with love.

"Hey, it's nippy out here. You should come in by the fire." Rafe came up behind her and put his hands on her shoulders.

She covered his hands with her own. "I was going to in a minute."

He came around and took her hands, blowing on them as he cupped them between his. "Your hands are freezing. Is everything okay?"

Ivy couldn't help it. She beamed a smile at him and tears fell from her eyes. "I'm perfect."

This time, he cupped her cheeks and wiped away her tears with his thumb. "Baby, what's wrong? Why are you crying?"

She took his hands framing her face and pressed them against her belly. "It's here. I'm pregnant. My doctor said I'm about ten weeks along."

"But, but you had a period," Rafe stammered. "The doctor said it would be difficult..."

Ivy nodded. "I know, but he said it was not unusual for women with endometriosis to bleed even though they are pregnant. He said I probably won't again and if I do, we'll be ready. He's set me up for two-week appointments because my pregnancy will most likely be high risk." She nudged him. "I guess your boys are strong swimmers. They soldiered through."

"Uh-huh," Rafe said.

Ivy frowned. "Aren't you happy?"

"Baby, I am. God, I am!" Rafe hastily said. "I'm just worried. You said difficult pregnancy... I don't want to lose you. If a child makes me lose you, I...I won't be able to deal with it."

"I'll be fine, Rafe. We'll be fine together," Ivy assured him. "My doctor says I'm healthy and everything looks good. I heard the little heartbeat." A sob caught in her throat. "It was perfect and strong."

Rafe pulled her in for a hug and then took her by the shoulders and looked into her eyes. "Every appointment, I want to be there with you. Monday, when I go in, I'm handing over command of the team to Brody until you deliver. I can ask for leave of absence or a desk job. I don't care. I'm not leaving you."

Ivy smiled happily. "Anything you say, honey. Rafe, we're going to be parents again."

"Yes, we are love. Yes, we are." Rafe hugged her

tight. "Now, can we go inside and get warm? I have to take care of you."

"Yes, and I can see Frieda peeking through the blinds. She knows something's up," Ivy said with humor in her voice. "We won't be able to keep this from them."

Rafe laughed. "A secret from my mother? She could be an interrogator for the CIA."

"Well, I don't want to keep it a secret anyway." Ivy grinned. "Let's go share our good news with our family."

"I love you. Know that I will for always," Rafe said huskily.

"Even when I'm huge and waddling?" Ivy teased.

"I'll kiss your belly and rub your feet," he replied. "After all, you'll be doing all the hard work for the next nine or ten months."

Rafe held out his hand to her and Ivy took it. Linked together mind, body, and soul they walked up the path from the river to the house to share the gift they had been given, where the warmth of the fireplace beckoned and family would share their joy.

The End

And Baby Makes Three

Chapter One

"I now pronounce you man and wife," the minister said. "You may kiss the bride."

Marie Watson wiped happy tears from her cheek. She watched her best friend Ivy St. Clair kiss the man of her dreams, Major Rafe Steele, to seal their marriage. It was a whirlwind relationship and Marie was thrilled for Ivy who finally got her happily ever after. Love suited her. Marie watched as Ivy looked up at her new husband. She wasn't jealous. In fact, Marie had vowed to never walk down the aisle again. Her previous marriage ended abruptly when she came home and found her soldier husband in bed with another woman. Yeah, she was off that love train for good. All she wanted was a good time and to go home to her own bed alone. *Love 'em and kick 'em out.* A small smile crossed her lips at her thought and she turned her attention toward the very handsome best man, Lieutenant Brody Gillis. Now there was a bronco she wouldn't mind trying to break.

She watched as he stood talking with Rafe. He was a tall drink of water, her grandmother would say. Sandy brown hair and a crooked smile gave him a boyish look that complimented his light blue eyes. He had sensual lips, not too thin or thick. Like baby bear's porridge, he was just right. His shoulders were broad beneath the bronze silk dress shirt he wore and his jaw line was smooth, but she could actually picture him with a little five o'clock shadow. It would feel kind of rough against her skin as he… Brody met her gaze and smiled. *Oh, yeah, we've got fireworks.*

"If you start drooling I am going to have to slap you." Ivy blocked her view of Brody and brought her mind back to the present.

"A girl can look, can't she?" Marie teased and pulled Ivy into a hug. "Congratulations, chick, you guys are awesome together."

Ivy grinned. "Thanks, and now we get to honeymoon for one night before he leaves."

"Make it count. You never know. It may be and baby makes three from tonight…or I guess four." Marie winked.

"You know it will be hard for me to conceive—"

Marie cut her off gently. "They say everything worth having is tough, but honey, trust me, your little bundle is coming. I can feel it in my bones."

Ivy gave a watery chuckle. "And your bones are never wrong, huh?"

Marie laughed. "Never."

"Now, back to Brody. He is a great friend and a good guy, but he is a playboy, so don't go there. You'll just end up one of the strings of broken hearts he has trailing behind him," Ivy said.

"Like I have a heart to give him," Marie said

flippantly. "After what I went through with Knucklehead, I'm all about playtime."

Knucklehead was her favorite way to refer to her ex-husband. He was lucky because she used to call him asshole, douchebag and some even lower words after she found him in their home with some ditz. She'd let herself believe in love, in a future with a man, but not anymore. That ship had sailed out to the middle of the ocean, been swallowed up by a hurricane and then hit by a torpedo and sank to the very bottom of the ocean. And then, while it was down there, the remnants were swallowed by the Loch Ness monster. She grinned at the thought.

"The ship got swallowed by a monster again, didn't it?" Ivy asked ruefully. Her friend was privy to her colorful imagination about what she thought of relationships.

Marie nodded happily. "Yup. Anyway, I may give Brody a go. He's looking at me, I'm looking at him. These trains should meet."

"Oh, Lord, now you're a train," Ivy said. "Okay, woman, I warned you. I'm leaving now for my alone time with my new husband."

"Enjoy the night, sweetie. I'll see you back at work," Marie answered.

"I've taken a month's worth of leave so I can be with Bonnie while Rafe is gone," Ivy reminded her.

"I know. Oh, by the way, I forgot to tell you. Jon may be released to Reese in a few weeks. If you're still on leave I'll give you a call and let you know," Marie said.

Ivy hugged her again. "Great, thanks, Marie. See you in a month."

Marie stood with Brody and Rafe's parents who were holding Bonnie and watched Rafe and Ivy drive away. She said goodbye to Rafe's parents, and walked to her car. She leaned against the driver side and waited. A minute or two later Brody came down to his jeep that was parked directly next to her car.

"Hey," she said casually.

He gave her a slow smile, one that was meant to charm the ladies. She had to admit, it worked because she felt that delicious tumble in her belly.

"Hello, Marie. Are you waiting for something?" Brody asked.

"Yes, I am, and that would be…you." Marie's voice was sultry. "You have any plans for the evening, Lieutenant?"

"None that can't be changed. What're you offering?" Brody asked.

"Dinner. I'm an excellent cook. Then we'll see where the rest of the night takes us," Marie brazenly let her gaze travel up and down his body.

"I could eat," Brody teased.

"Then follow me, cowboy, I'll give you a feast." Marie's meaning was very clear. "I live in the Seneca Highlands subdivision."

"That's pretty close to where I live," Brody said.

"Hmm, then the possibilities are endless," she teased.

She got into her car and pulled out of the driveway and left the luxurious lake house that belonged to Rafe's parents. She looked up occasionally to see if, true to his word, Brody was following her. Ivy may have gotten married, but Marie was intent on having some cake. Dinner was quickly forgotten because as soon as she ushered him through the door, he pulled her into his arms and devoured her lips with a kiss.

"Is it bad that when the preacher said *you may kiss the bride*, I wanted to rush over and taste your lips?" Brody asked huskily. She loved the little Texas twang in his voice. The Lone Star state sure knew how to make them.

"Hell no, I was thinking dirtier things about you." She felt her heart give a tumble and mentally cussed at it harshly, reminding herself she was in this for nothing more than fun. And then gave him access to the buttons of her dress.

They stumbled towards the sofa, all the while struggling with their clothes while their lips were locked in a kiss. Brody gave a low groan and pulled her on top of him as he lay back on the sofa. As the kiss became wild and hot, Brody fisted his hands in her hair as he took over the onslaught of her mouth. Marie accepted his hunger and passion excitedly; she'd never felt need consume her like this before. Brody used his foot to push her coffee table out of the way. Marie gasped and then her laughter mixed with his as they tumbled onto the floor.

"Damn, my pants are caught on my shoes," he mumbled against her mouth.

Marie pulled away, breathing harshly and grinned. "Okay, let's take a time out to get naked."

"I agree."

To Marie, it seemed they got their clothes off in record time, and, like magnets, they connected once more and their mouths fused. They rolled around on the floor, arms and legs entwined. Hands groped and massaged every inch of heated flesh they could find. She felt as if she were infused with heat.

"Oh, fuck, I want to feel you around me," he said roughly.

Marie barely heard him. His hands cupped her breasts and she whimpered into his mouth. His lips traveled down her neck and then took one of her nipples in his mouth. As soon as her fingers dug into his shoulders, he feasted on her even more ravenously.

"Oh, damn, your mouth feels good," she gasped out between unsteady breaths.

She heard the air conditioner kick on and the cold air against her skin made her shiver for just an instant, but soon, even that was forgotten. Brody kissed his way down her body to where she was wet and eager for his touch. He pressed his lips against her pussy and feasted on her essence. Marie drowned in the exquisite torture of it. His tongue licked at her clit, slowly, torturously, then, with an almost savage groan, he penetrated her with his stiff tongue.

"Oh, please!" she cried out.

Brody wasn't going to stop until he'd had his fill and he did so with such tenacity that Marie's orgasm took hold so quickly it rocked her off her axis. She grabbed his hair and held on to his face and grounded herself against his mouth as sensation after sensation rolled though her. He kissed his way back up her body until he reached her lips. She could taste her juice on his lips.

"I want you inside me," Marie said between kisses.

Brody pulled her to him roughly and she wrapped her legs around his waist before he drove himself deep inside her. He sat back on his haunches and pulled her up to sit on his lap. He thrust deep and she rode him with a primal vengeance. His hands were on her waist gripping her tight and pulling her hard against him.

"Damn, you're so hot, so tight, I think I'm melting from just being inside you," he growled against her ear.

"Oh, fuck yes, " she gasped in ecstasy. "Take me harder."

Brody gave a low guttural cry and filled her over and over again. The sound of their carnal coupling filled the room and only enhanced the pleasure. Marie could feel herself going over into the abyss again.

"I'm going to come, oh, God, now!" she cried out.

"Ah, shit, I'm there...with you," he moaned against her shoulder.

The orgasm that hit them both took their breaths away. Marie opened her eyes and watched the corded muscles in his neck strain as he threw his head back and gave in to his release. That sent her reeling once more into another orgasm that rolled through her like waves. They collapsed onto the soft carpet, both of their bodies hot, wet and slick from the intensity of their union.

"Wow," Marie said. It was the only word she could form in her mind to give an accurate description to what she felt.

"Yeah," was his muffled reply.

She turned her head to look at him and he was face down on the floor. And she grinned. "So much better than dinner."

"Definitely, but now I really do feel hungry." Brody sighed.

Marie groaned. "I did promise you a meal. Give me a few minutes to regain the use of my legs."

"This I can do since I can't move right now either." Brody chuckled and turned to face her. "I think this is the start of a beautiful relationship."

"A physical relationship, Brody. I'm not in the market for anything more than that," Marie said honestly.

He stared at her for a moment, then said, "We'll see what happens. Now feed me, wench."

She laughed and then gasped as he moved to her

nipple and bit it gently before sucking the hard tip between his lips.

"You keep that up and we won't be eating anytime soon." She gasped again as desire curled in her belly.

"Okay, that'll work." He covered her with his body, and she felt his hard cock slip inside her again.

"Oh, baby, yes," she moaned and arched into his slow, delicious thrusts.

She pushed the thought of him wanting more than a physical relationship aside. After all, he was like Ivy said, a playboy. She let herself slide into passion once more. It was the perfect way to release her stress. The man knew exactly how to make her body writhe in delight.

* * * *

Six weeks later...

Marie walked off the elevator onto the sixth floor where she worked at Walter Reed Hospital. She loved her job, loved being able to help injured men and women that served the United States proudly and with honor. But right now she felt like crap. The flu bug she'd been trying to fight had her feeling like she would upchuck the tea she drank on the way to work. For the last few days her appetite was nil and she was grumpy as the day was long. She walked behind the nurses' station, shoved her purse into the drawer and put her head on the cool counter with a thump.

"Marie?" Ivy placed her hand on her shoulder.

"Mmm?" That was as much energy as she could muster for an answer.

"Are you okay?" Ivy asked with worry in her voice.

"Dying. Kill me," Marie mumbled. "I think I caught a flu bug or a stomach bug or maybe it's Ebola. I feel like death warmed over. Make that nuked in a microwave and cooked to death."

"Essentially, you don't feel well," Ivy said humorously and pulled Marie up by her shoulders. She moaned as she was forced to move. "Hmm, you don't feel like you have a fever."

"I haven't felt well the last two days. This is full-on ick factor times twenty," Marie moaned. "Let me die."

"You're my best friend. How can I let you die?" Ivy soothed. "Maybe you should go home or I can get you something to eat. How about some tea and breakfast?"

Marie felt her stomach roll and she lurched to her feet. "Bathroom!"

She ran down the hall with her hands clamped over her mouth and barely made it to the women's facilities before she fell to her knees in front of the toilet and brought up the mint tea she drank. There was nothing in her stomach by now, but she kept retching until she was weak from the exertion of it.

And Baby Makes Three

Ivy came in and silently bent over her and she felt the soothing coolness of a cold pack on her forehead.

"Thanks," she mumbled. "I think I'll go home."

"Before you do, you may need to use this," Ivy said.

She opened her eyes and saw Ivy holding a pregnancy test. "Why would I need..." Her eyes widened. "Oh, shit, you don't think... Oh, no!"

Ivy nodded. "You have all the symptoms, honey. This is not the flu."

Marie nodded. She felt numb as she stood and flushed the toilet and then took the test from Ivy and closed the stall door to essentially pee on a stick. Two minutes later the evidence was sitting on the edge of a sink and she paced back and forth, stopping every once in a while to look at the test again. *Two lines, two perfectly visible lines. I'm pregnant. Holy Jesus, I'm going to have a baby.*

"Do you know who the father is?" Ivy was standing close by watching.

"Father?" Marie tried to focus her thoughts. She had not considered that at all. "Yeah, I've only been sleeping with... Oh, God, Brody."

Ivy's eyes widened. "As in Rafe's best friend?"

"Do you know any other soldier with a Southern twang named Brody?" Marie snapped, and then sighed. "Oh, Ivy, I'm so sorry. I'm on overload right now, feeling like crap and Brody and now pregnancy..."

"I know. It's okay," Ivy said gently. "Are you going to keep it?"

Marie was staring at the test and she looked up at Ivy, her hand instantly going to her lower stomach protectively. "I am. I feel strongly that the life of a child begins at conception."

Ivy smiled but tears filled her eyes. "Me too."

"Oh, honey, I'm sorry. This has to be hard for you. Here I am pregnant without even really trying and you—"

"Marie..." Ivy cut her off, "...I'm happy for you. Don't ever doubt that. I will not let my problem affect my being happy for my best friend. So, when are you going to tell Brody?"

"Um, how about never?" Marie replied instantly.

"Marie, you have to tell him. He's the father," Ivy prodded.

She shook her head. "You said it yourself. He's a playboy. To be tied down with a child is certainly not what he wants. After Charlie, it's not really what I want either." Marie sighed. "I never told you, but I miscarried when I was with him."

"Oh, no, why didn't you tell me?" Ivy gasped.

"The same reason you didn't call me when Juno showed up and broke into your house. I didn't want to bother you." Marie smiled. "Besides, he didn't want it. We fought big time and he pushed me and I fell and a few hours later I was in the ER losing a child. He said he was sorry, but that was the beginning of the end. Ditzy Diana just put the final nail in the coffin. So telling Brody is not my plan. I don't want a man to feel obligated to be in my child's life. I can be a good single mom. Hey, I come from a long line of single mothers."

She tried to sound flippant but inside she actually hurt. She thought she would break the mold in her family and be married when the children came along. The apple not falling far from the tree quote came into her head. So she'd be a mother alone, but she'd be a damn good one.

"Marie, you really should tell him," Ivy encouraged. "He'd do the right thing."

Marie shook her head. "I don't want the right thing. I don't want me or this baby to be a burden to his life." She took Ivy's hand and begged. "Please don't tell him. Promise me as my best friend you won't tell him."

"I won't tell him," Ivy promised.

"I'm going to head home. Can you tell admin that I am sick?" Marie asked.

"Already did it." Ivy smiled. "I actually put in for your vacation time. You have a few weeks built up. Take it and come to terms with it all. Plus, by that time, hopefully the morning sickness will have subsided."

"I have to make an appointment with an OBGYN. Will you go with me, whenever the appointment is?" Marie asked.

Ivy hugged her and Marie felt tears threaten. "Of course. I'm with you all the way."

"Thanks, Ivy. I really mean that," she said.

She gathered her things and walked out of Walter Reed into the fall sunlight. Pregnant. She was still in shock when she let herself into her house and went upstairs for a shower. She climbed into bed and tried to forget about everything by falling asleep.

Chapter Two

Ivy pulled the decorative pillows from the bed while Rafe pulled back the blankets.

"You seem quiet tonight," he commented.

"I know. It's just been a long day," Ivy said and sat down on the bed. "Rafe, if you knew something, a secret, and you promised not to tell a certain person, can you somehow get around it by giving the information to someone else who could then pass it on to the person who was not supposed to know in the first place?"

Rafe chuckled and climbed into bed. He patted the space next to him, urging her to come closer. "Honey, I'm a bit confused. How about you explain?"

"I have a secret that I promised Marie I would not tell." She snuggled into Rafe's arms.

"That she and Brody have been sweating up the sheets? Honey, I already know that," Rafe said.

She slapped him on the chest. "You didn't tell me, you rat fink."

"It's the man code. You don't tell your wife about your single friends' love lives," Rafe explained.

"Well, maybe I'll keep my secret then," Ivy said primly. She had an inkling something was going on.

Marie looked a tad too pleased when Ivy had come back to work after her time off when Rafe was gone on mission. Who knew all that time she and Brody were sleeping together?

"Does it help if I say that Brody is really into her, but Marie is the one who keeps pulling back?" Rafe said.

"Kind of, but there is something bigger in the picture now." Ivy took a deep breath and let it out. "Marie is pregnant and she made me promise not to tell Brody," Ivy explained. "But since I told you, you can tell Brody, and then at her first doctor appointment if he happens to show up…"

"I see where you're going with this, you little minx. You're using me as a messenger." Rafe chuckled. "I love it. He is away at Pendleton for training for four weeks. I'll call him and have a talk tomorrow."

"Four weeks is perfect. They won't be able to see a heartbeat till about ten weeks anyway, so it coincides with her first appointment. I knew you'd see it my way, darling Rafe," Ivy replied, pleased with herself. Marie wouldn't be happy, but in the end she hoped her friend would understand. Brody had a right to know and if he stepped aside then he would have her wrath to deal with. Ivy would not allow her friend to be hurt.

"Baby, are you okay?" Rafe asked quietly, his fingers caressing the skin of her shoulder. "Marie being pregnant and all doesn't mean that you won't get pregnant, sweetheart."

And Baby Makes Three

She looked up and kissed his chin. "I know that, and I am honestly happy for her. Yes, I am a little sad it's not my news, but we'll keep trying."

Rafe rolled over and pinned her beneath his large body. "Let's practice right now. This may be the perfect moment to make a baby with the woman I love."

"That sounds great to me," Ivy said with a sigh as he trailed kisses down her neck. "Absolutely perfect."

* * * *

"Say what now?" Brody felt like white noise started in his head. Rafe was on the phone giving him news he never expected to hear.

"Marie is pregnant. She didn't want you to know, but Ivy told me and now I'm telling you," Rafe repeated.

"Okay, um, why didn't she want me to know?" Brody asked. He was trying his best to sound neutral, but inside he was literally jumping with excitement. *A baby. Marie is having my baby!*

"Seems she thinks you're a playboy and something about obligation and not wanting you to be with her because of a child," Rafe answered. "You have to admit, Brody, the party never stops when you're around."

"Didn't you notice that when we left on mission for those three weeks I was not talking about parties?" Brody said. "We came back and I went straight to her place. I'm feeling her, man. She's the one pushing me away." He thought back to when they had about a week together before he left on mission and then he came back for another week or so then he left for Pendleton. "This must have happened that first time."

"Weren't thinking about protection, huh?" Rafe said. "It's truly a blessing it's Marie and not some other woman. Look what happened with Bonnie's mother."

Brody sighed. "Neither of us was thinking about protection. We went after each other like...never mind. The thing is, I'm happy about this. I should call her or I'll try to leave jump school early."

"No," Rafe said. "You need this accreditation. Plus, Ivy tells me she won't get a doctor's appointment until she is around ten to twelve weeks. You'll be back home by then. Don't call her and scare her off right now. She just found out. We will keep you in the loop and tell you when the first appointment is scheduled. Both of you need a few weeks to wrap your minds around being a parent. I almost lost it when I found Bonnie on my doorstep."

Rafe's reasoning seemed on point, though everything in him was screaming to go to Marie. But God knows she looked like she was ready to rabbit if he did something as subtle as bring her flowers. If he just showed up or called with the news that he knew, she might skip town. He had to play it smooth and easy with her. He really liked her, couldn't stop thinking about her. Whatever relationship she had been in in the past really screwed her over. That made him angry as hell, but Brody made a firm decision to breach those walls she'd built up long before he found out she was pregnant. A slow smile spread across his face. Oh, yeah, he was about to start a family.

"You've gone silent, Brody," Rafe said. "What are you thinking?"

"That Ivy is right, Rafe. Please tell her to keep me in the loop," Brody pleaded. These next weeks couldn't go by fast enough in his opinion.

"She will. Focus on the training. We'll be seeing you soon," Rafe replied.

"Bye, dude, and thanks." Brody hung up and the excited feeling in his stomach overtook him. He wanted to scream his impending fatherhood from the rooftops. Impulsively, he dialed a number familiar to him. As the phone rang, he hoped his mother answered and not his father. It amazed him how he could be so close to his mother and yet his father filled him with anger and revulsion. How did she stay married to that evil... He heard someone pick up and then her gentle voice came on the line.

"Hey, Mom, how are you?" he asked.

"Brody! It's so good to hear from you." Susan Gillis was a petite woman of sixty years. She made the best apple pie and cupcakes in Texas. "Are you okay?"

"Yeah, Mom, I'm good. I'm at Pendleton and I'm here for four weeks jump training," Brody explained.

"Oh, baby, be careful." His mother's voice held worry. "I should get your father—"

"No, Mom, don't get him. We have nothing to say to each other. I am always careful, but I called you because I have some news." Brody grinned. "I'm going to be a dad."

His mother screamed. "Oh, honey, that's wonderful."

"Woman, what's the screaming about?"

He heard his father's voice and gritted his teeth in anger.

"Brody has made us grandparents," his mother said with delight.

"'Bout time he pass the line along," his father said. Woodward Gillis was a pompous blowhard preacher with a racist streak a mile long. Brody remembered getting a beating all because he brought his black friend Avery home for a play date when he was ten. His mother, on the other hand, taught him to never see color, only people. His father tried to beat prejudice into him and he certainly didn't win. His father picked up the second line in the house. "Tell me about my new daughter-in-law."

Brody rolled his eyes. "We're not married and trust me, I wouldn't be bringing her home to meet you. Mom can visit, but I want you nowhere near her or my unborn child. I think you leak evil from your pores."

"Brody, don't speak to your father like that," his mother admonished.

And Baby Makes Three

"I'll speak to his racist behind any way I want," Brody said stubbornly. "Get off the line, old man."

"This is my damn house and if you want to speak to your mother then you speak to me," his father roared. That voice had long ago stopped scaring him. By the time he was fifteen he stood a foot taller than dear old dad and was built. His father had come at him one day and Brody pinned him to a wall. Needless to say, after that they stayed out of each other's way until he left to join the Marines.

"Fine," Brody said mildly. "Mom, Marie is the woman who is pregnant with my baby. She is beautiful and a nurse at Walter Reed Hospital."

"She sounds lovely, dear." His mother's voice trembled and anger surged through him. His mother hated being caught in the middle of their feuds. "What does she look like?"

"Probably a blonde. He's like his dad, has a soft spot for tiny blondes, just like me." His father laughed raucously.

Brody wished he could reach through the phone and strangle the man. "You should leave Mom then and go find one since Mom has brown hair. Don't worry, Mom, you can come live with me."

"If you were closer, boy, I'd—" his father began angrily.

"You'd what, be scared? Oh, please, you stopped meaning anything to me long ago. If it weren't for Mom I'd have no reason to call your house," Brody retorted.

"Brody, tell me about Marie," his mother interrupted gently. It was her way of telling him to focus on her and not on him.

"She's great, Mom. She has golden brown eyes to match her chocolate brown skin and a really amazing smile," Brody said. He heard a gasp and then the phone dropped.

"I can't wait to meet her…"

"Hell no, woman, you are not allowed to leave this house to meet no ni…" his father roared.

"Say it, old man, finish the word and see how quickly I can find my way to freaking Springfield and kick your sorry racist ass." Brody's voice was deadly.

"You pollute my blood line and you dare threaten me." His father's voice was filled with rage. "You ain't no son of mine. I would've ripped you from your momma's belly if I knew what a disappointment you'd be."

"Woodward!" his mother gasped.

"Don't worry, Mom, it doesn't hurt my feelings in the least," Brody said gently. "Listen, Mom, I'll keep you informed. You know how to reach me. The day you are ready to leave him, you come to me and live out here. You'll like the seasons and how amazing it is at Christmas."

"She ain't ever leaving me, boy, so save your breath." He heard the sneer in his father voice "Not for some idiot of a boy who don't know how to keep his family's blood pure."

"You polluted it long ago," Brody retorted.

And Baby Makes Three

"Your mother isn't going anywhere, trust me." His father laughed.

It was his mother's words that stopped him cold. "Don't be so sure, Woodward, don't be so sure." She spoke to Brody. "Honey, you go on now and enjoy your good news. Children are a blessing and I'm so happy for both you and Marie. I'll talk to you soon. I love you."

"Yes, Mom, and I love you too."

Brody hung up the phone on his father's stuttering anger. He would never hit or raise a hand to his mother. Brody had no worry of that. If he ever did, he had no doubt that his mom would go upside his father's head with one of her best frying pans. He understood she still lived by the old fashioned way— you stay with the man you married—but he wished she would just pick up and leave that bastard and let him live in his own evil. At least he knew his mother was truly happy for him, regardless of what his father thought. He focused on the task at hand and picked up his pack to head out for yet another day of training. He'd be home soon to Marie and that was all that mattered—her and the baby.

Chapter Three

"How's your morning sickness?" Ivy asked.

"The question should be how is my morning, noon and night sickness." Marie moaned in the passenger side of the car. It was her first appointment with her prenatal doctor and she was thankful Ivy offered to drive. Everything made her feel ill. Her favorite foods were done for. She was surviving on ginger ale and ramen noodles with hot sauce. The kid sure loved sandwiches that were comprised of mayo, tomato, vinegar, and salt and pepper. If she could hold the food in it was a good day, but still the nausea kept her off her feet most of the time.

"How about the lemon remedy?" Ivy asked.

Marie didn't know which lemon remedy she was talking about, but she had tried them all—sucking on lemon candies, keeping a lemon handy to sniff when the nausea came on, putting fresh lemon slices in her drinking water, but they were all iffy at best.

Marie shrugged. "It's hit or miss. Sometimes it works and sometimes it doesn't. The books say I should start feeling relief at about thirteen to fourteen weeks. When that happens, I'm doing cartwheels."

And Baby Makes Three

Ivy laughed. "How about we hold off on the acrobatics until after the peanut is born?"

Marie rubbed the lower part of her tummy and smiled. They'd taken up calling her unborn passenger peanut and, between the two of them, had been voraciously reading baby books. Who knew a rendezvous after Ivy's wedding in September would lead to this? They had done the math. Calculating from the date of conception and deducting two weeks for gestation she would be due near the end of June or early July. She decided on a midwife center instead of a traditional doctor's office because she wanted a more home-like environment when she gave birth. There were doctors on staff, for epidurals and in cases of emergencies, but she was really happy with her decision and was anxiously looking forward to seeing her baby for the first time.

"Um, any word from Brody?" Ivy asked casually.

"Nope, not a word for four weeks. I think our happy bedmate days are over," Marie said with as much nonchalance as she could muster. She wanted to pretend that it didn't hurt, but at night when she was alone, oh, it did, and she cried. She had his cell number and almost called a few times, but each time she could never bring herself to hit send to connect the call. She didn't want him to feel indebted to her.

Ivy maneuvered into the parking lot of the midwife center. "Well, maybe you should call him."

"Ivy, we've already had that discussion," Marie said firmly.

"Okay, okay," Ivy said and turned off the SUV. "Let's go in and see the peanut."

Inside, Marie filled out all the forms and understood why people were so frustrated when any nurse at the hospital showed up with a clipboard. There were so many papers to deal with and a lot of repetition, so Ivy helped fill some out as she was getting weighed and her blood pressure was being taken. She came back out to sit in the waiting room with Ivy and the other pregnant women. The center felt homey. There were wonderful vibrant colors and comfy chairs for the patients and even a kiddie center for women who had to bring small children. Ivy kept looking at the door and at her watch, and Marie furrowed her brow in curiosity.

"Ivy, what's up? Do you have somewhere to be?" Marie asked.

Ivy looked at her with innocence written across her face. "No, why?"

"You keep looking at the door like…" Warning bells sounded in her head. Marie glared at Ivy. "You promised you wouldn't tell him."

"And I didn't," Ivy protested. The door swung open just then and Brody strode inside wearing his uniform. "I kept my promise, but Rafe told him."

"All of you are rat finks," Marie said angrily using her favorite term.

"Honey, don't be mad. He's been calling me every day to check on you." Ivy took Marie's hand. "Give him a chance."

And Baby Makes Three

Brody came forward and got down on his haunches in front of her. "Naughty Marie, didn't you think I'd want to be in your life, in the life of our child?"

She shrugged and looked away, trying to ignore the happiness that was bubbling up inside of her. "Who knows? A playboy like you doesn't need a baby carrier strapped to the front of him while playing beer pong."

"That's bullshit and you know it. I've been chasing you like a hound dog chasing a bone and you keep pushing me away," Brody retorted. "You can't push me out of this child's life."

"I don't want him or her to not know a father, but I don't want you feeling like you owe us anything either. I was in that bed enjoying what we did just as much as you and it's half my responsibility," Marie stated in a matter of fact way.

"So you want me to be a dad, but there is no chance for us?" Brody asked quietly. "I'd like there to be a Marie, Brody and Baby Makes Three, a family. Let's start over and see where it goes, but for the record, you were never a booty call for me. I never thought that at any time. I'll be there when you get a food craving at 3:00 a.m. I'll make you tuna with extra pickles—"

"Tuna with extra pickles?" Marie asked.

"Yeah, one of my buddies in training said his wife loved them when she was pregnant, plus I've been reading books on being a dad and what to expect when

197

you're expecting. I fully intend to have sympathy pains when you're in labor," Brody announced.

Ivy started laughing and a woman close by said, "Aww," completely moved by his gesture. Marie had to admit everything he was saying sounded good.

"Well, I do like tuna and pickles. In fact, that sounds good right about now," she admitted.

"I'll make you some tonight, and look what I have." He pulled open the utility pocket on his brown digical uniform and brought two small bears out. One in pink and one in blue and each bear wore a tiny Marine hat with the Marine emblem on the front. "Either boy or girl, we're covered."

"Marie Watson, exam room three, please." A nurse with a friendly smile stood by the open door to usher them in.

Marie held out her hand to Brody and then to Ivy. "Let's go see our peanut."

They waited outside while she changed into a gown and then came into the room while she was lying on the table.

Her midwife came into the room and introduced herself. "I'm Jenny Macey, and I will be taking this journey with you as the months go by. Is this the proud papa?"

"This is Lieutenant Brody Gillis and my best friend Ivy. Yes, he is the father," Marie said.

"Nice to meet you, ma'am." Brody shook her hand.

"No ma'am here, Marine. We're going to be on a

first name basis so when it's labor time, Momma's room is filled with positive energy," Jenny said. "Are you both going to be in the labor room when the time comes?"

Ivy looked at them both. "If you want me to, I'll be there."

Marie took her hand. "Yes, I'd like that."

Jenny smiled. "You have a great support group. Now, let's take a look at this little miracle. Some cold goop for your belly. The gel will help us see the baby better."

They all watched silently as midwife Jenny used the ultrasound on her belly. She moved it around for a few minutes checking things and using the computer graph to chart growth and size. Marie and Ivy both gasped. As nurses, they knew exactly what they were seeing. The little gray image was a little grainy but the most beautiful thing Marie had ever seen. Tears trailed down her face and Ivy was tearing up as well.

Brody looked at them in alarm. "What's wrong? What's going on?"

"They're happy, nothing is wrong. Everything looks good. You're ten weeks on the nose," Jenny said. She used her finger to point out the area for Brody. "There's your baby." She pressed a button and a tiny fast paced rhythm filled the room. "Here, the heartbeat is strong and perfect."

"Doesn't that beat all," Brody said softly. Marie could hear the amazement in his voice. "Can I get a picture of that, Ms. Jenny?"

She laughed. "You can have as many as you want. We'll see you for your next appointment in a month, Marie, but we need your labs done today, so take this slip to the door down the hall to your left and they'll draw your blood."

Jenny handed her a towel to wipe the gel from her stomach and soon they were walking down the hall. Brody held her hand proudly while showing off the three sonogram pictures he held in his hand.

"You know he is going to be at Quantico showing those to anyone that will stop long enough to see it," Ivy said. "He's sent it to Rafe already via camera phone."

"I know. Let him have his moment," Marie said. "Give me my hand, Brody, I'm going to get my blood drawn."

"You need me to go with you, babe?" Brody asked instantly.

"No, you sit here and, um, send the picture to someone else on your phone," she teased.

He grinned. "That's a good idea. I think I missed the commander in the first round."

She shook her head as she walked away and Ivy laughed next to her. "Am I still a rat fink for spilling to Rafe?"

Marie put her arm around Ivy's shoulder. "No, I was wrong. I should've told him myself. I think he is going to make a great dad."

"What about Marie and Brody the couple?" her best friend asked.

And Baby Makes Three

"Like he said, we'll take that day by day and see where it goes, but I hope it sticks, I really do," Marie admitted. "After Charlie, I swore off anything close to a relationship, but this baby changes everything, doesn't it?"

"I think you two are cute together," Ivy said with a smile.

Marie sat to have her blood drawn all the while thinking about Brody. And Baby Makes Three, he'd said, and somehow the child inside her helped form a bond to something that scared the crap out of her. She would try, but she prayed this time it wouldn't fail, not twice, not with her child involved.

* * * *

Later that night she lay on her couch with a cool cloth on her head. She rubbed the tiny hard mound of her lower torso and smiled even though she felt like death. You couldn't tell she was pregnant yet, but because of her profession she could tell exactly where her little bun in the oven was. It was all going to be worth it when forty-two weeks were over and she had a beautiful baby in her arms. *Boy or girl*, she wondered already. Her family had the propensity to have more girls, but what about Brody's family? They never had much time for conversations.

As soon as he entered the room they were in each other's arms before the door was closed. Naked, hot sweaty sexual interactions that left her gasping whenever their culmination hit. Against the wall, on the floor, on the dining room table, once they didn't make it past the front door. In the midst of her sickness, desire made her sex warm. Lord Almighty, he even had the power to make her horny while she felt like she was on the good ship nausea. There was a knock on the door and she groaned. *Just go away*, she thought miserably and the knock came again. She moved off the couch with a groan and her stomach rolled in objection to the movement. She opened the door to reveal Brody standing there holding a large Tupperware bowl and a smaller square one.

"Well, you look chipper," Brody teased.

Marie rolled her eyes and stepped back so he could come in. "You try throwing up everything you've had for the past few weeks."

"This is why I come bearing gifts," he replied. He pulled the cover off the large Tupperware bowl and the smell filled the room. "Hot and sour soup with tofu and chives."

She wrinkled her nose. "That does not sound pleasant."

"My mom said that it's the fats in meats and all that good stuff that makes you ill." He put the bowl on the counter and helped her sit at the dining room table. "So I made you something that will turn your frown upside down."

"You made this? I didn't know you could cook," Marie said.

Brody pulled a bowl from one of her overhead

cabinets. "There's a lot you don't know about me, and we're going to fix that. Now, let's get you and my boy feeling right."

Marie waved him over. "Okay, skip the Sesame Street monologue and give me what you got."

Brody chuckled, grabbed a spoon, and put the bowl in front of her. "I already did."

She took the first tentative sip and her stomach seemed to say, *ahh*. She looked up at him and smiled. "This is fabulous."

"Try a piece of the tofu," Brody encouraged.

Marie took a chunk from the bowl apprehensively, sniffed it, and expected it to make her feel sick all over again. Instead, for the first time in weeks, her stomach seemed to settle. She deemed it a miracle and Brody her savior.

"Oh, I love you so much right now," she moaned in delight.

Brody pushed the hair back from her forehead and smiled. "You'll love me even more when I say no more dry crackers for you and instead you should have homemade gingersnaps with mint. Mom's secret recipe for all the pregnant women in my hometown in Texas."

"I think I love your mom. Can she come live with me?" Marie asked.

"I wish," Brody muttered before commanding softly, "Eat your soup first and then you can have a cookie."

There was something there, the happiness and

light left his eyes for an instant and dark clouds seem to overtake him. Marie sipped her soup silently before saying, "Tell me about your mom and dad."

Brody gave a sarcastic laugh. "Now there's a story meant for cable."

Marie downed the last spoonful of her soup and picked up the square-covered Tupperware that held the cookies. She reached out her hand to him. "Come on to bed and we'll get settled and you tell me all about it."

Brody took her hand and followed her. "I don't think this is a bedtime tale you want to hear."

"If you're going to be in my life and we're going to give this a go, we have to trust each other," Marie said firmly. "Now, I'm going to take a shower and then we're going to bed and there we'll show each other our baggage and get it right out. Understood, Marine?"

Brody grinned. "Ma'am, yes, ma'am."

She smiled. "Good, now get down to your skivvies and I'll meet you in the sack. No hanky-panky because right now I have the energy of a single-cell organism. So for the first time we will talk instead of have sex." Marie placed the Tupperware container full of cookies on the bedside table.

"I really like the sex," Brody teased.

"I do too. It's totally..." Marie pointed her finger at him. "No, bad Marine, we're doing this right."

Brody grinned. "Fine, I'll be waiting."

Marie took a hot shower and the water coursing

down her skin made her feel much better. That, combined with the soup that Brody brought, gave her the sense she may survive the first trimester after all. She came out of the shower wrapped in her fluffy bathrobe and she found a nightshirt in the drawer. She felt Brody's eyes on her and saw his gaze darken as she dropped her bathrobe and slipped into her nightshirt. She opened another drawer and pulled out undies and put them on. It was more for her than him. She usually slept without undies, but with him in her bed she couldn't guarantee she wouldn't try to make love with him. Marie slipped underneath the covers and snuggled into his arms. He was shirtless and his skin was warm beneath her cheek. He leaned over and kissed her gently and then with more passion. Their tongues twined and danced until she pulled away gasping for breath. *No, Marie, no*, she chastised herself. It wasn't fair to set a stipulation on him that she could not follow herself. They had chemistry, of that there was no doubt, but for this to work, their relationship had to be built on something other than the physical.

"Tell me about your mom and dad," Marie encouraged.

"Where to start." Brody sighed. "My mom is a gem. She is strong, hardworking, and doesn't see anything but the person you really are. My father, or the man that created me, doesn't deserve to be called a parent. He is a mean, racist pig who tried to break me from the beginning and when he couldn't, he tried to berate me into submission. But I was a husky lad, and one day he came at me and I'd had enough and I hit back. That was the last of it. I left soon after and joined the Marines and never looked back."

"Don't you see your mother?" Marie asked.

"She comes and visits. My dad won't stop her, and she wouldn't let him," Brody replied. "She is as tough as steel when it comes to seeing her only son. But I cannot understand why she stays with that evil man that thinks he's the second coming. Did I mention he is a minister and preaches fire and brimstone to his very small congregation?"

"He will hate me then, seeing as, in his eyes, I'm the wrong color," Marie said mildly. She'd dealt with hate before especially in an interracial relationship. There was a lot she had kept secret about her life with Charlie, a lot she wasn't willing to share even with Ivy.

"I called my mom to share the news. She is thrilled, and that is all that matters," Brody said. "That man can rot in hell for all I care. There is no love lost between us."

"It must be hard knowing that you can't share with your father." Marie rubbed her hand across his chest comfortingly.

"But that won't happen to me and this baby." He rested his hand on her lower stomach. "My son is in there, all warm and snug."

"You're so sure it's a boy, huh? It could be a girl," Marie said with a smile.

And Baby Makes Three

"A little girl would be great, but then when she becomes a teenager I'll start cleaning my gun at the dinner table," Brody said casually.

"You won't do that if we have a boy?" Marie laughed. "He could be a real heartbreaker and have girls lining up outside our door."

"That's my boy," Brody said proudly.

His words made the smile fall from her lips and sent her careening into the past where men cheated and the feelings of the women who loved them didn't matter. The closeness she was feeling to him fell away and anger rose up.

"Oh, no, you are not raising my child to be a playboy man-whore like you are." Marie felt her irritation rise even higher. "If it's a girl, she's to be protected, yet the boy gets to have no morals and be the slut of his high school?"

"Whoa, who said that? And, by the way, I'm not a playboy, my mom raised me right," Brody retorted.

"Says the man who planned every party at Rafe's house." Marie sat up. "Oh, I heard that your name is on every party roster in Quantico and beyond."

"Jesus, how did we go from having a nice moment to you thinking I've been in every bed on the East Coast?" Brody asked.

"Because you are a leopard who cannot change his spots and proved it by actually saying that if this baby is a boy he could slut around," Marie snapped. "You should go home. This wasn't a good idea."

"Marie, there hasn't been anyone else in my life

since we got together the day of the wedding," Brody said calmly. "And while I may have coordinated those parties, I never slept with any of the girls there. It was all for a good time, a way for our guys to de-stress after all they go through. Me? I run the grill, keep the bar stocked, and handle the music and the clean up. I'm not saying that I haven't had dates, girlfriends, and even a committed relationship once. But for the love of God, my past is not the thing that should dictate my future with you and my child."

"That's what they all say," she muttered.

"Don't let what happened to you with your ex-husband ruin what we could have," Brody insisted.

"You don't know anything about that," Marie said and shook her head while tears started to fall down her cheeks.

"Oh, baby, don't cry," he said in a gentle voice and tried to pull her into his arms.

Marie shook her head again and pushed him away, wiping her tears away furiously. "I'm not crying because I'm hurt. I'm angry. These are tears of anger, and don't you dare blame it on hormones!"

Brody pulled her against him and settled back into bed. "I wouldn't think of it, honey, you have every right to be angry. Do you want a cookie?"

"No," she mumbled.

"All right. Then how about you go to sleep and I'll hold you all night?" he crooned.

"I told you to go home." She yawned.

"I know you did, baby, and I will as soon as you

fall asleep." Brody ran his fingers through her hair and she felt herself drifting off and barely heard him say, "Eventually you'll have to let me in and tell me how he hurt you so very badly."

"Okay," Marie said. She had told herself she would relax just for a minute and then kick him out. That wasn't the case because she ended up sleeping in his arms all night. In the morning he was sitting on the side of the bed with a hot cup of tea and mint gingersnaps for her.

It was the first morning in weeks where she didn't throw up her breakfast, and they ended up watching TV in bed whiling away the Saturday afternoon. She remembered his words as he dozed on the pillow next to her. She wasn't ready to let him in, but she wasn't willing to give him up either. So they would stay the course the best they could and she hoped to hell she was making the right choices.

Chapter Four

"I don't know what to do, Rafe. I'm half scared to go to her house lately," Brody said helplessly. "Yesterday, I show up with all the ingredients ready to make her dinner. She asked for mashed potatoes and Salisbury steak. So I start cooking, and then halfway through she changes her mind and says that the smell is making her sick and she couldn't possibly eat what I was making. Then, she is crying and I go to see why, afraid it is somehow my fault again, but she's sitting in front of the TV, crying at a fabric softener commercial. Why? Because the baby on the commercial put its finger in its mother's mouth and she thought it was cute." Brody looked at Rafe. "Then, wasting all the food that was half made, she ended up wanting cheese pizza. So I order pizza. Then, when the pizza arrives, she tops it with catsup and pickles."

They were sitting in the office they shared. Since Rafe took over command of the new elite unit out of Quantico, the commute was brutal but well worth it for all of them. Ivy and Marie loved their jobs at Walter Reed while Rafe and Brody loved their careers in the Marines. Somehow, they made it all work and that was what mattered in the long run. While people shattered and fell, either on the field or at the hospital, they managed to stay a tight unit. They were friends who were so close they were more like family.

Rafe looked at Brody with sympathy in his eyes. "Ivy said it's Marie's second trimester and her hormones are completely out of whack."

"Did I mention one minute she is rubbing against me like a kitten and the next she shuts down cold and I go to sleep with my boys aching," Brody said. "I don't know if I'm walking into a minefield or into a meadow filled with daffodils."

Rafe was roaring with laughter by the time he was finished speaking and Brody looked at him sullenly. "Hey, remember Ivy is pregnant now and soon you will be sitting here instead of me, buddy."

In December Ivy told Rafe she was pregnant, and then called Marie, crying in joy. Brody recalled it vividly because Marie was then crying and when the foursome finally got together to celebrate their growing families, at least ten minutes was spent with weepy eyes and constant hugs.

"Ivy is so thrilled to be carrying that even while she's feeling crappy she has a smile on her face." Rafe sighed. "Sometimes she thinks I don't see her crying, but I do. She is scared that she may miscarry. She is taking a leave of absence from the hospital. Her doctor wants her to be taking it as easy as possible until the birth."

"I wish Marie would stay home. At night her back

aches and her feet swell and, whatever you do, don't tell her she has started waddling. She has vowed a cruel death to anyone who mentions it." Brody grinned. "In happier news, we can feel the baby move—little tiny rolls of movement. She is twenty-six weeks today and I am supposed to meet her for the appointment at the midwife center. We find out if she's having a boy or girl."

"Well, then you can see how all the suffering is for the best in the end." Rafe drummed his fingers on the desk. "Do you want to know the sex of the baby?"

"Hell yeah. We've got a nursery to prepare," Brody replied. "Speaking of which, what would you think of me asking Marie to move in with me?"

"Don't you mean the other way around? Your bachelor pad of a townhouse is no place to raise a baby," Rafe commented.

"Good point. If she agrees to moving in together, I could sublet it," Brody mused.

"That's certainly better than being in your complex," Rafe said. "Marie wouldn't be too happy with the neighbors you have. You know, the ones with the extra short skirts and the stiletto heels."

Brody rolled his eyes. "Like I knew any of that when I bought the place. Still, you do have a point. Marie has such bad juju about her ex that she won't talk to me about it."

Rafe handed him some papers. "Here sign off on these. I'm requisitioning some equipment for training." He sat back and laced his hands behind his head. "From what I've heard from Ivy, the guy came back pretty screwed up from his tour and cheated on her. But that can't be all there is to it because Marie is as prickly as a pear when she even hears his name. All you can do is wait for her to trust you enough to open up."

"Have you met Marie?" Brody asked skeptically. "Fort Knox has nothing on her."

Rafe laughed. "Get out of here and go watch your baby wiggle around."

Brody handed him the paperwork that he'd signed. "I'll be back in about two hours."

"I'll be on the range if I'm not in here," Rafe said.

The phone rang as Brody got up to leave so he just raised his hand in goodbye to Rafe. He left the building and got into his car and grimaced. He loved the low-slung corvette but every time Marie rode in it she complained. He couldn't blame her since she drove a twenty-twelve Acura. They both needed something bigger that would fit a car seat and baby supplies. Along with baby shopping they definitely needed to vehicle shop or at least he did. At least his corvette was paid off and a family car was now necessary. As he drove he thought of Marie's fears. The main one being that she thought he wouldn't stick around. She didn't say it much, but he saw the skeptical look she had on her face each time he talked about anything permanent.

And then before he could say too much she would

quickly changed the subject. He had no intention of losing interest in her or their child. In fact, the more time he spent with her, the more he loved her. But there was no way he could say those words to her and freak her out. Marie didn't want grand gestures; she had to be coaxed into it slowly. Needless to say, his plan was to be around for a lifetime. He pulled up to the midwife center and went in. Since he'd been going to her prenatal appointments, he'd become a familiar face around the center. They ushered him back to the examination room where Marie was already set up with Jenny. Brody knocked and then stepped quietly inside.

"Hey, Dad, you're just in time." Jenny smiled. She was measuring Marie's burgeoning belly with a tape. "The little peanut is right on schedule with growth." He sat down next to the exam table and took Marie's hand and kissed it gently. "Hear that, baby? You are a wonderful cloning cubicle."

Marie sighed and looked at Jenny's confused expression. "He's convinced that the baby is going to be an exact replica of him. Pay him no attention."

"Well, then we can take a peek and see for ourselves." Jenny beamed. "This time you get pictures in three and four dimension so you'll be able to see what he or she looks like. If you could get the lights, please."

Brody reached up and flicked the light switch. The room went dim except for the glare from the monitor, and while he sat on one side of the table,

And Baby Makes Three

Jenny was on the other moving the ultrasound wand over Marie's belly.

"Here we go," she said gently. "Here is the head, legs and arms, all ten fingers and toes. No abnormalities of the spine or bones that we can see."

Both Brody and Marie were silent as Jenny did her examination. She stopped the screen occasionally and a small graph would appear where she clicked the mouse. Brody had read in the books that that was how they charted development, so he watched every move she made on the screen with interest even though he didn't know exactly what she was doing.

"Okay, peanut, let's see the goods. Show Mommy and Daddy if they should buy pink or blue," Jenny murmured. Brody held his breath as she continued the exam. "And there it is." She pointed at the screen. "You're having a boy."

Brody laughed because right on the screen he could see the quite obvious male genitalia of his son. *My boy*. Now he knew why dads on television wanted to hand out cigars when they found out they were having a boy. Pride filled his chest to the point he felt as if he might burst.

"You were right. We're having a boy," Marie said and he could hear the tears of joy in her voice.

"Our son." Brody leaned over and kissed her, not caring that Jenny was in the room. He had to kiss the woman of his dreams and the mother of his son.

Armed with pictures in three and four D, they left the midwife center after the exam and walked out into the cool air. The March wind was bitterly cold and Brody worried about her catching a cold, so he bundled her up into her car quickly.

"We need to make plans for our peanut," Marie said with a smile. "How about Saturday we go shopping for the nursery?"

"Deal, if you'll go with me to pick out an SUV. I'm thinking the 'vette should be for date night with my favorite girl or something," Brody said.

"Why, Brody Gillis, I may start to believe you are indeed a family man," Marie teased.

He bent down to kiss her. "Believe it, sugar lips. See you later tonight. We've got a lot to discuss."

"I feel like Chinese food and some of those little sugar rolls," Marie said.

"Well, that might change by tonight. So we'll wait and see before making reservations," Brody hinted.

She winked, and then said impulsively, "I'm glad you're with me, Brody. I'm so happy we get to share a child together."

"Me too, babe, me too," he said and kissed her again through the open car window. "Now buckle up and drive safe. Call me when you get back to the hospital so I know you made it okay."

She saluted. "Sir, yes, sir!"

Brody watched her drive away with new determination in his heart. He was going to marry Marie Watson and they were going to be a family. Her words sealed his decision. He loved her with his entire being. He never thought he would feel that way about anyone, but here he was in love and happier than he ever remembered being. Life was grand.

* * * *

Marie got out of her car the best she could. Her growing stomach was starting to make it an uncomfortably tight drive in her Acura. But each day that she felt the movements of her son inside her body and knowing he was healthy made it all worthwhile. Today was Ivy's last day—doctor's orders—until after she gave birth. Marie wanted to work as long as she could, but she knew in another eight weeks she would be out on maternity leave as well. Today an impromptu baby shower had been planned for both of them in the nurses' lounge after their shift was over. They planned it early when they knew that Ivy would be gone for a few months and Marie was leaving the next few weeks. Their co-workers and the doctors thought she and Ivy had no idea, but that cat had been let out of the bag about a week before. They both practiced their surprised faces on each other beforehand and died laughing.

Marie walked through the doors as they whooshed open and the warmth of the air welcomed her. She was waiting for the warmer temperatures to make their way to the East Coast. Marie's dream was to move somewhere where it was warm all year round. She wasn't built for the cold. She walked up to the desk where Ivy was working on a chart. Her baby bump was barely noticeable beneath her scrubs. They would have their babies only a couple months apart—Marie was due near the end of June and Ivy around the beginning of September. It was one of the reasons she thought moving away wasn't a good idea. They wanted their children to grow up together.

"I can see the bump," Marie sing-songed.

"Yeah, like yours isn't noticeable at all," Ivy replied and they grinned at each other. "What's the verdict?"

"Boy," Marie replied and they squealed.

"Oh, my goodness, you guys have to pick a name," Ivy gushed. "Two boys could be best friends or maybe I'll have a girl and they'll get married."

"If they could just hear us now, Rafe and Brody would be rolling their eyes," Marie said.

"Was he excited?" Ivy asked.

"I thought he was going to start roaring and thumping his chest it swelled so much." Marie stowed her thick coat and put her bag away. "I think he is going to be a really good dad... I'm thinking about asking him to move in with me."

Ivy looked at her in surprise. "That's a big step."

"Why? Don't you think I should do it?" Marie asked in alarm. She trusted Ivy's judgment and she was already feeling insecure about the whole thing as soon as the idea popped into her head.

"Oh, no, no!" Ivy said hurriedly. "That's not what I meant. As far as this whole situation, I think Brody has been amazing and my thoughts of him being a playboy were obviously wrong. I meant with everything that happened with Charlie, I never thought you would take such a big step."

"I know, I have doubts, believe me, but it feels right to be with him," Marie admitted. "I was going to go by his townhouse and talk to him later."

"Um, is that is good idea? He lives in kind of a bachelor-type complex," Ivy explained.

Marie smiled. "How bad could it be? I've never been there and he's been spending so much time at my place, I feel as if I should go bring up this subject on his turf, to show him I'm willing to meet him half way."

Ivy shrugged. "Well, it is a perfect plan to take your relationship to the next level."

"I'm thinking about sleeping with him again. We made this little one the day of your wedding. And then the sex after they came back from their mission was hot but I was pushing him away," Marie admitted. "But my body is so…well, I'm bigger, rounder I'm not sure he will even be attracted to me anymore."

"You guys already sleep in the same bed when he stays over, right?" Ivy asked.

"Yes, and he rubs my belly and talks to the baby and plays music against my belly so the baby can have a love of music." Marie smiled, recalling how he had read in a book that it makes babies more intelligent to play music for them in the womb. "I'm feeling insecure about the whole thing. I'm not a size eight anymore, that's for sure."

"Trust him and yourself. When it's meant to happen, it will naturally," Ivy encouraged.

"I've been holding myself back. The man is fine and even though I may be carrying his child, a woman has needs." Marie winked.

Just then a code alarm sounded and they looked at each other knowing conversation was over. When that alarm went off, one of the patients was in trouble. "It's room four-twelve, Sergeant Russell," a nurse said worriedly as the doctors moved down the hall. Marie frowned and moved with the others. Sergeant Russell was a soldier wounded in Afghanistan. Well, more than wounded. In Marie's opinion, the man had been blown apart. He had one arm while the rest of his limbs were lost to an IED attack. When he came in, the doctors had worked tirelessly so he wouldn't lose his appendages. But each time he lost circulation to an area and necrosis set in, the only way to save him was to remove the severely injured limb.

Losing limb after limb never kept him down. He fought for his health with the same bravery that he showed in theatre when he was trying to save some of his friends and fighting to protect citizens of his country. While he never gave up, his injured body was slowly wearing out. Everyone had hoped and prayed for a miracle, but it seemed the only one that they would be given was that he would no longer be in such pain.

And Baby Makes Three

"Paddles we're going to shock him again," The doctor ordered. But everyone knew in their heart it was too late.

"Come on, let's go people, let's go!" He yelled.

Another doctor took the paddles from his associate's hand. "No let him have his peace now."

Sergeant Russell lost his fight after months and months of trying. He was finally at rest; the brave man was finally at the end of his tour.

Marie didn't hold back the tears that streaked down her face, nor did anyone else. She saw some of the doctors wipe their eyes on the sleeve of their coats. Each loss felt like the first. No one could ever become desensitized to these men dying. The rest of the day took on a somber tone, and while they worked no one could help but slow down as they passed the now empty room. Another man or woman would occupy that bed, sooner rather than later, and God knows they always wanted it to be later. They would fight hard for his or her life too, like they always did, but for now they would mourn.

Marie was sitting at the desk at the nurses' station rubbing her belly gently when she felt the movement of her son. He would have his father, alive and well, with the help of the big man upstairs. Brody would watch his son grow up. She feared him going off to war and then she would be the one getting the news that he had been killed. It firmed her decision all the more. Marie was going to ask him to move in to her home and take that step toward them being a family.

TO NURSE WITH LOVE

After the baby shower that brought smiles to their faces even though their hearts were still heavy, with help, Marie packed up the trunk and back seat of her car and using the GPS on her phone, headed toward Brody's complex. Turning into the cul-de-sac filled with rows and rows of townhomes, she saw a few women jogging even though it was rather chilly outside. A sign was hanging on the office door for Pilates and yoga classes and when she passed a building with large floor-to-ceiling windows, she could see women inside in tight shorts and tiny tops taking part in the exercises and getting into positions she probably couldn't manage even when she wasn't pregnant. Marie pushed her irritation aside, keeping her eyes straight ahead as she looked for his townhouse. Finally finding it, she parked and got out. She made sure the house number was correct in the dim light before she went up to the door and rang the doorbell. She stood waiting patiently for him to answer the door, and when he finally did, surprise was on his face.

"Marie, honey, what are you doing outside in the cold? I thought you were going right home and I was coming to you?" Brody asked.

"You seem to have a problem with me coming to your house," Marie said stiffly. This wasn't exactly how she thought he would act when she saw her at his door.

Brody sighed. "It's no problem, I just don't like thinking of you out in the dark, alone and the streets

222

may be icy." He pulled her into a hug and into his house, directing her to his leather sofa. "How was your day and lil' man in there?"

"We lost Sergeant Russell today," she said and buried her face against his shoulder. She'd told Brody about him and he always asked how the injured soldier was doing.

"Fuck," he said harshly and kissed her temple. "I thought he was taking a turn for the better."

"He spiked another fever, another infection, and this time his body was too weak to fight it off," Marie said softly. "He's in a better place and not in pain anymore. But damn, we wanted to see him win this battle. Just too many of them lose, you know?"

"Oh, honey, I know only too well." Brody murmured.

"I wanted to talk to you about something." Marie looked up at him. "Seeing Sergeant Russell's family and friends grieve, made me think about us. I don't want our son to ever—"

The insistent ringing of his doorbell stopped her words. Brody frowned at the door. "Hold that thought." He retraced the few steps they'd taken to open the door. "What the—"

"Lieutenant Brody, we've come to visit!"

Marie swore she heard an explosion in her head when three tall, very sexy and totally blonde women tried to all hug Brody at once. He wrapped his hand around one waist to anchor himself, she assumed, or to get closer. But her gaze was firmly affixed on the women who looked like models clamoring all over her baby's father, her man. He must have seen her expression because he quickly extricated himself from the women.

"Marie, um, this is Claire, Elin and Alexa. They are part of the Swedish volleyball team that were here last year for a tournament," he said quickly.

Oh, that makes it so much better. She raised an eyebrow in their direction. And then one of the little Swedish cover models slash volleyball players spoke and her accent was so sexy Marie almost wanted to kiss her herself. That only made her even more furious.

"Yes, Brody invited us to a barbeque and then was kind enough to let us stay here when we couldn't get back to our hotel that night." She smiled warmly.

"Really? That was so nice of him." Marie's voice came out flat and dead sounding. There was no way she was going to go through this again.

"Are you going to have a baby?" another asked.

"Why, yes, I am." Marie smiled sweetly. "I'll get out of your way. Obviously, you were expected and I was not. I'll let you guys get to your fun."

Marie moved past them and Brody put his hand on her arm. "Honey, don't go, don't drive mad... I mean, this is all very innocent and explainable."

She looked at his hand like her arm had grown fungus, then she met his pleading eyes with a cold stare. "Remove your hand from my arm, Lieutenant, before I remove it for you."

And Baby Makes Three

He narrowed his eyes angrily and she walked out without looking back. She was stupid to believe he would be any different. The way he had acted when she showed up was evidence enough that he had other guests coming. Guests who were built like Greek goddesses. *Fine, he can play all he wants,* she thought as she drove away. She would be mother *and* father to her child if she had to be.

But the ache in her chest broke free when she finally pulled into her driveway and let herself into her house. After a shower to warm up and a good cry, because she really needed it after all that had gone on today, she wanted to curl up in her bed and cover her head with her blankets and never come out. Instead, she pulled on her warm pajamas and a pair of thick socks, went into the kitchen and pulled a tub of ice cream from the freezer. She put her favorite DVD on and wished every man was like Patrick Swayze. Life would be simple if men acted as they did in movies. Reality truly sucked. She was mourning her troubled relationships and not going to be bothered with answering the phone ringing off the hook, knowing it would be Brody. When it finally stopped, she thought she was going to be given peace and quiet until the insistent ringing turned to insistent knocking on her door.

"Marie Joy Watson, answer the door before I break it down," he roared. "I have no problem causing a scene in front of your neighbors."

She sighed and got up off the sofa as best she

could and moved toward the door. He'd gone from banging his fists on the door to keeping his finger pressed firmly on the doorbell. Marie's irritation rose to new heights and she swung the door open to reveal his angry face.

"Why in the hell are you acting like a juvenile?" Marie snapped. "Don't you have three bimbos to entertain at your bachelor pad?"

"No, they left right after you did, actually, because I had to get my ass in gear and come over here," Brody retorted. "Why the hell can't you just stop putting me in some kind of prefabricated mold you see all men in and for once see the true me?"

"Hmm, let's see. I come to your house and you act like I caught you with your hand in the cookie jar and then low and behold, the triple threat arrives." Marie went back to the chair at the dining room table and knocked his hand away from helping her as she sat down. "It seems to me the mold you're talking about is the one you put yourself in."

"Well, let me clarify this for you. The night they stayed at my place, I stayed with Rafe." Brody sat across the table from her. "He can verify it because Ivy was mad as hell at him that night because of that Donna chick that lives in their neighborhood."

"Oh, that makes me feel so much better." Marie took a scoop of ice cream and popped it into her mouth while she glowered at him. She shook the now empty spoon at him. "I will not be cheated on and getting hit and experiencing all the pain of losing…

I'm just not doing it again. If I can't trust you, then I don't need to be with you."

She watched his eyes narrow before he said slowly, "You said getting hit. Your ex hit you?"

"It's nothing for you to worry about," Marie said slowly. "It's in the past."

"Not if it affects us and how you see me," Brody replied. "I'll get his name one way or the other. Marie, tell me."

"Charlie Milton. He used to be a sergeant," Marie said.

Brody got on his knees and fit himself between her legs. He rested his head on her belly and the baby kicked. They both laughed. He looked up at her, his eyes pleading. "Marie, I was coming over here as soon as you got home to ask if we could live together. I was surprised to see you at my place because you had never shown any interest at ever coming to my house. Plus, with the pregnancy, I didn't want you driving all the way out there to me."

He met her gaze, and she didn't see lies there. She was pretty good at spotting a liar, having had the experience from living with Charlie. Their gaze shifted and could never stay in one place. "Marie, since that first night we got together, I haven't been able to think about anything else but you. And then I found out you were pregnant and I wanted to rush home from Pendleton. You're my world. This boy growing inside your stomach is my world. I would never put that and what I could have with you in jeopardy. I've always wanted a family, not like I had, but one where I could love my children the right way. Without fear or mental abuse. Let me move in with you and we can work towards being a family."

"Oh, Brody, you know how to say all the right things, and I fell for that before," Marie said softly.

"Darling Marie, what did that man do to you?" Brody asked.

She felt the story falling from her lips even though she told herself she wasn't ready to tell him—or anyone. "I met Charlie at the hospital. He was a patient. I should've known how messed up he was, but he bloomed when I was around and he worked harder when it was just for me, and maybe I let it give me a big head." She closed her eyes and willed herself not to cry. "After he was discharged from the hospital, we got married and everything was fine for a while, but then the problems began. When he hit me, I always told myself it was just because of the PTSD. When he cheated I blamed that on the PTSD as well and he told me it was because he felt as if he meant nothing to anyone. The more he hurt me, the harder I tried to fix him. I thought he needed more love, more attention. But, actually, he was just plain mean and rotten to the core. I was losing myself to him and then the one time I fought back, it put him in a rage that kept me out of work for a month. I told Ivy and anyone who called that I came down with the Swine Flu, but I was bruised from head to toe."

"I'll kill him," Brody said softly and she saw his hands clench.

And Baby Makes Three

Marie covered his hands with hers and met his gaze. "He's not worth it. The final straw was when he hit me and the next day I came home and found a woman in my bed. Something inside me snapped, I swear, and when I was throwing them out, I swear I saw fear in his eyes. The bed went next and then all his shit." Marie laughed. "I was the Incredible Hulk that night, and the next day I promptly filed for divorce. I wanted nothing from him, just wanted him out of my life."

"Where is he now?" Brody's voice came out a growl. His body was tense with anger but not at her. It was for the man who callously hurt her and for that she felt her heart swell just a little more. Oh, yes, he was hers and she would fight for him if she had to.

"I honestly don't know. I know he's out of the Army. He could be in Timbuktu now for all I care." Marie lifted his hand and kissed his knuckles. "He doesn't mean enough to me to give a damn where he landed."

"Well, he hurt you and it means a damn lot to me. One of these days I will find him and I will hold him accountable," Brody said.

"I came to your townhouse tonight to ask you to move in with me," she admitted. "But God, seeing those girls there, they're all tall and sexy and I'm short, round and dumpy, I could never compare with them even if I wasn't pregnant and having a baby. I was jealous, okay? I admit it. I was jealous as hell to see them there."

Brody grinned. "Yeah?"

"Don't get too cocky. You're my baby's father," she snapped.

He rubbed her belly. "Is that the only reason?"

Marie smiled and felt her anger evaporate. Impulsively, she leaned forward and kissed his forehead. "No, you're my man and if I was taller or had longer nails I would scratch their eyes out. I did consider climbing them like a coconut tree and going for the eyes."

Brody tilted his head back and roared with laughter. "See, this is why I love you. You are so vocal, you say exactly what you're thinking."

His words shocked her and started a warm feeling in her chest that seemed to expand outward. "You said you love me."

Brody kissed her nose. "Because I do, silly."

"You don't have to say that just because I'm having your kid. I mean, we've had sex a few times and—"

"Would you just quit it?" Brody chuckled. "I know you. I can talk to you about anything. Hell, I think you're freaking gorgeous and if it wasn't for the fact that we may hurt the baby, I'd be jumping your bones."

"We wouldn't hurt the baby." She winked. "We can have some goodie-goodie time. You are my Texas bronco but I can't ride you. But we can do it in other ways."

"Are you sure? I don't want to hurt lil' guy in

there," Brody said doubtfully.

"I'm a nurse. Trust me, I'm sure." Marie smiled and then asked, "So, do you want to move in with me?"

He sat back on his haunches and pretended to consider the question. "I don't know because I am not sure how you feel for me."

"You know how I feel about you, nut." She threw a napkin at his head.

He pulled her close and kissed her until her head began to swim. Brody pulled back and stared into her eyes. "No, I want to hear you say it. Let's put it this way. I need to hear it."

"I love you, Brody, and as long as you keep on the straight path and don't hurt me, I won't have to scalp your ass."

A slow grin spread across his face. "That's my girl."

"So, if we're moving in together, we need to make a plan to encompass your stuff and my stuff." Marie yawned. "We can make a list and go from there."

Brody leaned forward and kissed her forehead. "Right now we're going to get you into bed."

"Geez, tell a guy you love him and the first thing he wants to do is get you into bed," she grumbled. "It's not even nine."

"Well, baby boy is sleepy, so mommy needs to go to bed as well," Brody said as he walked her up the stairs. "Is ice cream all you had for dinner?"

"It's all I wanted," she replied.

"Nope, shower and climb into bed. I'll bring you grilled cheese and tomato soup," Brody said.

She turned to look at him when she got to the bedroom door. Marie was suddenly unsure about this, about everything. Lord, she was scared of another relationship failure.

"Are you sure we can do this?" she asked uncertainly.

He covered the small distance between them quickly and pulled her into his arms. "Darlin', there is nothing we can't handle together. Do you hear me, sweetheart?"

"Okay," she whispered.

"Now go shower, put on warm pajamas and get into bed. I'll be up soon," Brody said and kissed her gently.

She stepped inside the bedroom and closed the door, leaning against the cool wood for a moment. The thing she had promised would never happen again after Charlie had—her heart belonged to Brody lock and stock. But then Marie didn't expect she would be sharing her home and a child with him either. As she undressed and got under the hot spray of water, a smile tugged at her lips. Charlie was a mistake. She mistook charm for love and anger for affection. It would be different with Brody. Like he said, together they could conquer anything.

Chapter Five

That weekend they began his move into her house and shopped for baby furniture and clothes. Brody was having way too much fun buying baby clothes. On base, he'd found mini MarPat—Marine pattern—outfits and digical camouflage onesies on the base along with Marine, Army, Navy and Air Force bears for the nursery. In the store, he was even worse. Brody deviated from the list and went a tad crazy. What couldn't fit in his new full-sized suburban was being delivered. Marie gave up trying to curb his spending craze and let him have his fun. He was a proud first time dad.

"Are you hungry?" Brody asked as he crammed the last of the baby supplies in the trunk.

"Do you know what I want?" She grinned as he helped her into the new suburban. "Hot dogs, sliced on grilled sourdough bread with melted cheese all over the top and lots of pickles on top of the cheese."

"That's very specific and yet it sounds disturbingly delicious," Brody said hesitantly.

She slapped him on the shoulder and laughed. "I've made them before and I thought the same thing. Want to try one?"

"I'm game." Brody got behind the wheel and turned the key to start the vehicle.

"Great. We need some fresh coleslaw to go with it," Marie replied. He gave her a sidelong glance as he drove and she smiled serenely. "Blame the baby. He is very particular."

"I see. He's going to be a boy who knows what he wants," Brody teased.

"Just like his mom," she said.

Brody's response was to reach over and hold her hand while he drove. They stopped at the supermarket to get the ingredients for their very unusual dinner before heading back to the house. In the kitchen she got their meal together while Brody brought in their other purchases. Her house was a four bedroom, two story and they decided that the room across the hall from the master would be the baby's room and Brody could actually use another room for his workout equipment. That left one spare bedroom that she'd always kept clean and decorated for guests. They would share the den downstairs for their office space. He'd moved his leather sofa into the den when he brought over some of his furniture. The rest was quickly claimed and taken by some of his single friends for their own places. It all worked out pretty well considering how fast it happened.

Marie smiled as she pulled the hotdogs from beneath the broiler in her oven. Brody had moved everything in so quickly it was like he thought she would change her mind and wasn't giving her the opportunity to do so. She had to admit she was looking forward to putting together the baby's room with him, picking a name for their son, and more. She watched the muscles in his arms bulge as he came in carrying the box that contained the dismantled changing table. Pregnancy did not put a damper on her arousal. In fact, she'd been downright horny for the past few days. But she didn't feel pretty, instead she felt round and unattractive. Brody wouldn't want to be with her in that way while she was carrying the baby. She'd read men found pregnant women unappealing. So she would have to hold off the sex until after the baby came. But God, she wanted him. Her sex throbbed just thinking about the way he touched her.

"Is our special dinner ready?" he asked, bringing her out of her musings.

"Just about. If you can get the coleslaw out of the refrigerator, I'll get the plates on the table."

"What do you want to drink?" he asked. She took the opportunity to appreciate his ass while he bent over, looking in the fridge.

"Grab me a V8, please. I should offset this with something a little bit healthy," she said.

Brody made a face. "That stuff is horrible. I'll have a coke with my dinner."

"That's because you don't have a baby in your stomach that will kick the hell out of your kidneys on a caffeine high." Marie pointed at the plates filled with food she just placed on the table. "Now eat."

She sat and took a bite of her unusual sandwich and moaned in pleasure. Brody took a bite too and she watched as he made a questionable face before taking another bite and shoveling some coleslaw into his mouth.

"It's actually not bad, especially since you broiled the hotdogs and they have kind of a crispy outside," Brody said.

"Right!" Marie grinned. "You're awesome, you know that?"

He gave her a surprised looked. "Why would you say that?"

She finished her mouthful of sandwich and took a sip of her drink before speaking. "Because not many guys would eat the pregnancy food of their expecting girlfriend."

"Well, honey, this is actually something I probably would've made myself growing up," Brody said. "Now there's fast food joints all over the place and it's easy to pick up a hamburger rather than cook."

"Not here. I like making dinner and soup and grilling in the warmer months," Marie said.

"I'll take over the grilling and you can handle the other stuff," he said.

"I can grill a mean steak," she pointed out.

"We'll have a cook-off and whoever wins gets the coveted grilling spot," he teased.

She shook her head. "Nope, you can have it. I don't like being out in the heat anyway."

And Baby Makes Three

"Why do I feel like I've been conned?" Brody raised his eyebrow in her direction.

Marie returned his look with an innocent look of her own. "I don't know what you mean."

"Uh-huh." His tone said he didn't believe her, but his grin told her he was fine with it.

They finished their meal, talking about one subject to the next and then headed to the room intended to be the nursery to start making a dent in all the boxes and bags that were piling up. In the end, they decided to leave the room the same color— beige—and would just use a simple, thick blue dinosaur baby border around the top of the wall. It would be easy to remove when he got older and eliminate the need to repaint. She sat on the floor and folded baby clothes while he put up the borders. When he was done he helped her put away the stacks of burp towels, clothes and tiny baby socks.

Brody stuck his finger into one of the tiny blue socks and wiggled it around. "I can't believe his little feet are going to be this small."

Marie gave him a stern stare. "Stop stretching out his socks with your big fingers."

"I thought you liked my big fingers?" he said with a wink.

She understood the implication perfectly and felt her sex and nipples tighten in response. She changed the subject quickly. "I think he'll be like his daddy and grow up to be a tall handsome man."

Brody beamed with pride. "You think so?"

"Yes, I do," Marie smiled. "I did tell you our Lamaze classes start in two weeks, right? Ivy and Rafe are going to go with us, since they'll both be in the delivery room."

"I don't know if I want Rafe looking at your nether region." Brody frowned.

"Ivy thinks it will help him. After their doctor showed them a birthing video, he panicked and began worrying about her having the baby," Marie chuckled.

"I'm a little worried about you being in labor too," Brody admitted. "I've never seen a birth or experienced anything like this."

"Well, I have the video and we can watch it, and then going to Lamaze will tell you everything you need to know," Marie explained. "Plus, there is a daddy part to this class to teach you how to make bottles, change diapers, and all that good stuff."

He held out his hands to her and pulled her to her feet gently. Brody wrapped her in his arms and pressed a kiss to her lips. "I'm looking forward to all of it as long as it's with you. Now let's get you to bed."

After her shower, she was leaning back against thick throw pillows and Brody sat near the foot of the bed rubbing her feet while they discussed baby names.

"I'd have thought you wanted him to be Brody Junior," Marie said, her eyes closed, enjoying the foot rub. Brody had the earphones on her belly again and this time he was playing classical music from the iPod.

"Good Lord, we won't do that to him. I hate my name, Brody Bartholomew Gillis," he snorted. "Let's give the boy a fighting chance."

"How about Matthew?" she asked.

"Too common," Body said. "How about we make it his middle name?"

"Okay, then what do you suggest for the first?"

Brody was silent for a moment before announcing, "Grayson. We can call him Gray."

"Grayson Matthew Gillis." Marie tested the name and opened her eyes to look at him. "I like it a lot."

"Then we have a name?" he asked with a grin.

"We have a name," Marie replied and moaned as he went back to rubbing her feet. "You do that so well. My feet are in heaven right now."

"You keep making sounds like that and I'll have you naked in the blink of an eye," Brody said.

She met his gaze and saw desire there that instantly enflamed her. But her self-esteem issues about her body stopped her and she frowned. "Don't say things like that when you don't mean it."

"What do you mean I don't mean it?" She heard confusion in his voice.

She made a frustrated sound. "Because look at me, I'm huge and round in the middle and certainly not sexy."

"That's bullshit. To me you are always sexy," Brody retorted. "I've been trying to keep my hands off you because I figured you weren't in the mood."

"Oh, I've been in nothing but the mood, but…"

"But nothing." Brody took the earphones off her belly and whispered to the baby growing there. "Night, buddy, it's mom and dad time."

"What are you doing?" she questioned.

"I'm going to go grab my shower and then I'm making love to my woman," he said firmly. "Do you disagree?"

His eyes said he would take no refusal, not that she could think of a good one anyway.

"No, I don't disagree," she said meekly.

"Good. That's my girl." He leaned over and kissed her hard.

Marie was unsure of what to do. Before she was pregnant, she would have been naked in the shower with him. In the end, she decided to stay in bed and wait for him to make the first move. Pregnancy had made a very sexually aggressive Marie into a tamed kitten. She didn't know if she liked the change. Insecurity was not an emotion she had very often. Brody came out of the shower a few minutes later, walked into the bedroom very naked and his cock erect. Her breath caught looking at him as he dimmed the lights and moved over to the bed. He slid under the covers and pulled her into his arms, kissing her temples, her eyes and finally her lips.

"You're beautiful to me Marie Watson, not just because of your body, but who you are," he murmured. "You try to be so brave all the time and you don't have to be. I'm here, to hold you and catch you when you fall."

And Baby Makes Three

"I have family, but we're not close, so I consider myself alone. I never had any close friends until I met Ivy and then it was even a battle to let myself believe she had good intentions and wasn't trying to get something out of me." Marie sighed and felt tears fill her eyes. "I'm so scared I won't know how to be a good mother or a good woman to you. For a long time I thought that Charlie was the way he was because I wasn't good enough. I put on a good act, but I'm mucking through the world the best way I can, the only way I know how."

He cupped her cheeks and looked into her eyes. "Baby, you don't have to pretend with me, not ever. And Charlie wasn't your fault, he's a fucking defect. He won't be in our lives this night or any night. Put him out of your mind forever."

"Oh, Brody, he couldn't even come close to walking in your footsteps," Marie said. "Through it all you've been so kind and good."

"Because it's you, Marie, damn woman, that has made me this way. Until I met you, I was just a soldier, would do my job, go home, throw mindless parties, but it all felt empty. Damn, I wanted to be the one you loved from that very first night."

"Oh, Brody, I do love you. I'm just so scared at failing at everything," Marie whispered.

"You won't, baby, trust me, a person like you never fails." He smiled gently. "We're going to be great parents and we'll figure it out together."

"Okay," Marie whispered and kissed him.

"You're right. We can do this. Together, we can do this."

Brody kissed her gently at first and then again with more passion. She clung to his shoulders while his tongue penetrated her mouth and his hands roamed up under her night shirt to cup her breasts.

"Let me make love to you like the goddess you are," he whispered. He helped lift the nightshirt from her body and then slowly removed her panties. They weren't her usual lacy things; instead, she was now wearing pregnancy underwear from Target since they were the most comfortable. Yet Brody didn't seem to notice, peeling them away from her skin with a long groan and cupping her sex. She felt his fingers slip between the lips of her pussy and she shuddered in his arms.

"I can smell your scent, you're thick and swollen and wet against my fingers," Brody murmured. "I want to be inside you already."

"Yes," she whispered.

"Not yet, love, not yet." Brody's voice was harsh with desire.

He cupped her breasts and licked each nipple. He squeezed the heavy globes and she watched as tiny beads of a milky white substance beaded at the tip.

This time Brody's groan was filled with awe. "You're making breast milk already?"

"It's not really breast milk, not yet. It's called colostrum. It's what the baby will need for the first few days. It has antibodies…" She laughed. "You probably don't want to hear all about that, a mood killer."

"On the contrary." He licked the tip of her breast taking the beads of liquid with his tongue. "I almost came just thinking about tasting it, tasting you at the same time."

"Suck them harder, please," she whispered.

Brody did as she asked and Marie cried out as his hot mouth closed over the sensitive nub. He pulled the hard beaded tip and his moan was guttural. She knew he got another taste and it turned him on more. His hips moved reflexively and she could feel his cock primed and ready to take her. He moved to the second breast, repeating the action while she held his head to her breast. It felt so good she felt herself grow wet. Brody kissed his way down her stomach and when she felt his hot breath and lips against her core she gripped the sheets as pleasure washed over her in waves. She felt him penetrate her with one digit moving it slowly, almost tortuously, in and out.

"Oh, please, Brody," she whimpered.

"Nice and slow," he said huskily. "We've fucked, now we're going to make love. I'm going to take you to heights you've never been."

He moved from between her legs and lay close to her. She tasted her own essence on his lips as he kissed her and felt his fingers probe and enter her once more. He thrust them slowly into her, each time going a bit deeper, finding that spot that made her body tremble and her pussy tighten around him. Her head fell back against the pillow and she arched as he pleasured her with his hand. She could feel his eyes on her and she reached between their bodies to stroke his cock in rhythm to his fingers thrusting into her snatch. His groan reverberated through her, yet he kept his own pace, not changing it even as her hips rose faster, her silent way of pleading for release, until she finally crested in her orgasm with a cry. It washed over her like a warm blanket and left her panting.

"I love watching your face when you come," he said gruffly.

"I want to feel you inside me."

With his help, she lay on her side and he put one of her legs over his hard muscled thighs. She felt the tip of his cock at the entrance of her sex. He slipped into her slowly and because of her pregnancy, the lips of her pussy seemed thicker and each glide of his cock more erotic. Brody slowly caressed her belly and reached up to cup her breasts, fondling the nipples and massaging the heavy globes until she was panting with renewed arousal.

"Oh, Brody, more," she said and he thrust deeper into her soaking wet snatch.

"Oh, you feel so damn good," he moaned against her neck.

"Come with me," she pleaded as sensations assaulted her. Everything felt so heightened and she could feel herself falling into another orgasm.

He picked up his speed and she could feel his cock

thickening inside her. His breath was harsh in her ear as he called her name. She could hear the agony of his pleasure in his voice as he reached for the pinnacle of completion. Marie closed her eyes and let it overtake her. She cried out as her release rocketed through her body. Brody followed and a harsh guttural sound was ripped from his throat. She felt his seed fill her and complete the union once more. Once before, their coupling made them parents and now it was as if it sealed their connection as a couple.

"That was incredible," he breathed and snuggled up to her kissing her shoulders gently.

"It was. I need to get cleaned up, it's kind of uncomfortable with wet soaking girl parts." She laughed and then winced. "Ouch."

He was instantly alarmed. "Did I hurt you? Shit, do we need to head to the hospital?"

"No, just Braxton Hicks contractions. Grayson probably wants ice cream or a donut," she said.

"Okay, you lie back and I'll get you cleaned up and then I'll run downstairs for both." Brody was up and moving before she could even answer.

She didn't complain as he cleaned her with a warm cloth and helped her back into her undies. Then they lay in bed and shared a bowl of ice cream and a donut before settling down for sleep.

"Marry me." He turned and wrapped his arm around her, lacing his fingers with hers.

"We don't have to get married. We're good the way we are," she murmured.

"Baby, I understand that you have insecurities because of your ex—"

"If you understand, then you won't rush me," she said in a subdued tone.

"How about we get the marriage license and when you're ready we can just do it? If it expires I'll do it over and over again until you finally take the plunge with me," he offered. "I love you and I want to marry you."

"I love you too." Marie gave a thoughtful sigh. "Okay, we can get the license, but I don't think I'm going to be ready anytime soon."

"I understand, but at least I'll have your name next to mine saying you're going to marry me eventually," Brody teased.

"Is that all you need to make you happy?" she murmured.

"No, I need *you* to make me happy. I'll always need you." Brody turned her face and kissed her softly. "I'll just wait until you catch up with the fact that I'm not going anywhere. No, shh, don't answer. Let me get my beauty sleep."

She laughed out loud at that and he pulled her close. Marie fell asleep with his hands caressing her stomach and baby Grayson's gentle kicks as if in answer to his father's touch. She knew he wasn't going anywhere. She already loved him to distraction, but things changed didn't they? Men could be one way and then the other. She wanted to believe him and should believe him, yet something kept her from taking that very important step, one that would change her life completely. Marriage to Brody would mean she would have to actually commit to being happy or commit to having her heart broken again. But she did have hope and excitement about their future together. Did she dare believe that she, Marie Watson, could have a happy ending?

Chapter Six

Her maternity leave officially began when she was eight months along. She was having more Braxton Hicks contractions and the baby was now turned head down which the midwife said was natural and normal. It was Grayson's way of getting ready for birth and Marie was feeling heavier and more uncomfortable. Brody was still working, of course. One couldn't take time off from the military. But something was up, because he and Rafe had loosely mentioned a change may be coming so both she and Ivy were curious and a little worried. It had become one of the topics they spoke of frequently when they were together. Ivy was moving along in her pregnancy and mostly on bed rest because of some spotting she was having. Marie was worried enough that she called Ivy every day and Rafe took Bonnie to daycare instead of leaving her home for Ivy to manage. Rafe's mother and father had become Ivy's guardian, so to speak, and were at the house almost every day. But the lack of anything to do and boredom was driving Ivy crazy, so Marie planned prenatal massages for them at a local spa. When Ivy's doctor signed off that she could go,

And Baby Makes Three

Marie took the big suburban to pick her up.

"This thing is a tank," Ivy said as she climbed into the passenger seat.

"With this belly, I can't sit behind the wheel of the Acura anymore, let alone get down low enough to actually slide into it," Marie said. "And it doesn't have warming seats."

Ivy laughed. "Good point. It feels great on the back. You've got about eight weeks left. You must be excited."

"It's April now. I wish that June would hurry up and get here." Marie maneuvered the suburban toward the exit they needed. "I feel like a beached whale."

"You're telling me, I feel completely useless just lying around." Ivy sighed. "I cannot stand that Rafe and his parents have to take on such a burden."

"They don't consider you or what you're going through a burden, Ivy," Marie said gently.

"Well, the doctor said if I stop spotting for at least a week, he'll let me get back to cooking and other light tasks." Ivy clapped her hands. "I'll be able to get off that darn couch and play with Bonnie."

"That sounds good. I'll come over and hang out with you guys." Marie laughed. "I wish you were going to the midwife clinic with me."

"Me too, but because I'm high risk we couldn't take the chance. But I did sign up for a doula to be with us in the delivery room," Ivy said. "You're still going to be there, right?"

"You know it. Brody will be an old pro at labor and delivery by then and he can keep Rafe from freaking out." Marie laughed.

Ivy chuckled. "Rafe's mom is excited to watch Bonnie and Grayson. But there's more news."

"Oh, do tell," Marie encouraged.

"It's twins. The doctor confirmed yesterday, one of each." Ivy was grinning wide.

"Oh, my god!" Marie squealed. "Wait, how come they didn't see this sooner?"

"They did, but honestly they didn't even know if one would make it let alone two and the girl is smaller," Ivy replied. "We kept it close to the chest because Dr. Stein thought maybe we'd lose one, but they are both thriving."

"How is Rafe taking the news?" Marie asked.

"Well, let's just say he looks panicked when we talk about the babies," Ivy said. "This is going to be my only birth. The doctor thinks it's a miracle enough I got pregnant with all the scarring."

Marie felt her heart ache for her friend. She wanted more children eventually, but Ivy wouldn't have that chance. "At least our kids will be growing up together."

"I hope so. I'm worried that our men may spring something bad on us," Ivy said.

Marie chewed her bottom lip worriedly for a moment before saying, "I believe it will be something good, for all of us."

They pulled into the *Oasis Spa* and soon were

getting onto memory foam covered massage tables that curved around their burgeoning stomachs. Their skin was warmed while the masseuse worked on their bodies. Marie actually fell asleep while she was being worked on. The pressure and tight muscles of her back eased and Grayson seemed content and the false contractions calmed. By the time they came out she felt refreshed and re-energized. The masseuse even rubbed her belly with warm oils and talked to her son while doing do. Marie was sure that he was in bliss, happily snug in the cocoon of her womb. They had an early lunch before she took Ivy back home and went on to her house. She pulled into the driveway and parked the suburban and noticed that Brody's corvette was there.

"Hmm, home for lunch, are you?" she murmured to herself. She opened the door, stepped through and called out, "Come out, come out, where ever you are."

"I'm not hiding. I'm in the living room," he said and she turned. Brody was sitting amidst pieces of green plastic and assorted nuts, screws and bolts.

"What's all this?" Marie asked.

"I saw these at the commissary and had to get them." He held up the boxes. "A baby swing for those nights when he's cranky, and then a vibrating bouncy seat thingy."

"Uh-huh, and you had to rush home and put them together," Marie said amused. The look on his face was priceless, like it was Christmas and his birthday all in one.

"Well, I'm having an extended lunch. Rafe gave the team a few hours downtime before the training exercise tonight," Brody said and stood up. "So I came home to my best girl and my best baby." He rubbed her belly. "How is he doing in there?"

"Trying to take over the world from the womb," Marie teased. She backed up as he stepped forward, giggling as he cornered her against the counter that separated the kitchen from the living and dining area. "What are you doing?"

"I'm about to give my favorite girl a kiss," he murmured. He did so and it became one of those lip locks that make your breath hitch in your chest. He trailed kisses down her neck and made a sound of pleasure. "Hey, you smell good."

She shivered. "We went for massages today. It's probably the oils you smell. They used a lot of lavender."

"So they rubbed it all over you?" he questioned.

"All over," she murmured as desire caused wetness to pool between her legs. "I was very relaxed after."

"Take off your clothes," he ordered softly.

"Right here?" she asked breathlessly.

He nodded and started working on his uniform. "Uh-huh, right here, right now. I swear I can't seem to get enough of you."

Marie pulled her sweater over her head and

shimmied out of her tights, taking her panties with it. "I swear being pregnant has made me hornier than ever."

He stripped off the last of his clothes and was moving toward her with his erect cock jutting out from between his legs. Marie carefully got to her knees and took his rod in her hands.

"Baby, you don't have to do that," he whispered and moaned when she licked the tip.

"I know I don't have to, but I want to taste you," Marie said.

She took him deep in her mouth and began a slow torturous tease with her lips and tongue. She felt the muscles of his thighs flex and tighten beneath her fingers. She picked up the speed, suctioning her lips tightly around his cock and the in and out pace had him bucking in pleasure. He pulled her to her feet carefully, but she could feel the restraint in him. God, she couldn't wait for him to take her hard and furious again after the baby was born. He devoured her lips, penetrated her mouth with his tongue while his hand was between her legs teasing the most sensitive part of her. He slipped his fingers between the sensitive folds of flesh and rubbed her clit. She whimpered into his mouth and he slipped his fingers deep inside her. Her juices ran down his finger and she could feel it coating her thighs. She ground against his fingers, wanting more and feeling the invisible cord of her orgasm begin to tighten.

She tore her mouth away from his and threw her

head back, panting and moaning his name. "Oh, Brody, oh, yes, I'm going to come."

"Damn, yes, let me feel you come, feel your pussy clench around my fingers," he whispered into her ear. "God, I want to taste you while you come."

He got quickly to his knees and sucked hungrily at her clit as he penetrated her faster with his fingers. Her elbows were braced against the counter as she let go and gave into the orgasm that swelled inside her body. His muffled groan came from between her legs. As the last of her release faded, he kissed his way back up her body and sucked at her nipples. He turned her around so that her ass was pressed against his cock. Marie bent over the counter so that her hands instead of her stomach were braced against the marble countertop. She felt him run the tip of his cock up and down the swollen lips of her sex before penetrating her from behind, and she cried out as need lanced through her.

Brody grabbed her hips and began a steady thrust that built the fire in them both. Even in his need he still had a care to her condition and took them both to the edge of reason while showing the upmost restraint. Marie felt herself slipping over into the abyss of passion and embraced it fully. She heard Brody moan and kiss the skin of her bare back as his seed filled her. In the aftermath, he picked her up like she weighed nothing and took her to the bathroom and, in his usual way, carefully cleaned her and helped her get dressed. Back downstairs, she ate lunch and watched as he put together the swing and bouncy chair while every so often she would comment. Later, she kissed him goodbye and watched him drive away for training. Marie leaned against the doorjamb with a smile on her face. Brody was unlike any other man and she fell more in love with him each day. She closed the door and went back to the living room to put her feet up and watch TV. The perfectly assembled baby accessories stood in the designated spot in the living room and anticipation filled her. In a few more weeks, Grayson would be there and they would be able to hold their little boy.

It was much later when her doorbell rang and Marie frowned. She had on flannel pants and one of Brody's T-shirts to sleep in, along with warm socks. She would probably be asleep by the time he came home, so as she made her way downstairs she wondered who was at her door. She left the chain on and opened it a crack to reveal a face that could sour any mood. Charlie stood at her doorstep wearing the puppy dog look of a man who thought he could charm his way into any life.

"What the hell do you want?" she snapped.

"Baby, don't be that way. Let me in so we can talk," Charlie pleaded. He looked the same, but she could see behind the handsome face and green eyes the ugliness hiding beneath.

"First off, I'm not your baby and when we signed those divorce papers, anything we had to say was done," Marie said. "Say what you need to say and get off my property."

"I need a place to stay, until I can get on my feet," Charlie said. "I kind of got kicked out of my place."

"Go to the veteran office at Walter Reed. You're a soldier who served in Iraqi Freedom. They'll take care of you," she said flatly.

"They'll give me a cot for a few days. No home cooking like you could, babe." He tried his charming smile. It failed miserably.

"So you thought you'd come to see good ol' Marie who will take you in because she loves you so damn much?" Marie asked.

"Yeah, we still have that connection. Everything that happened was because I was messed up, baby. Come on, let me in," he encouraged softly.

"My fiancé wouldn't like that so much," Marie said mildly. "I'm due with his baby in a few weeks and we don't like unwanted guests."

His eyes narrowed. "You went and got pregnant by some dude? You cheated on me?"

Marie laughed incredulously. "We're divorced, you fool, and I miscarried after you kicked the shit out of me. Leave now or I'll call the police. I think that restraining order is still in effect."

"You fucking bitch. I should cut that kid out of your stomach," he snarled.

"I'm calling the police now," Marie said coldly. "I don't fear you anymore and if you do anything to me, Brody will hunt you like a dog. I hear Marine Special

Forces like a good hunt, except scum like you wouldn't be much of a challenge for them. Leave my house and do not return."

She closed the door and put the lock on not trusting him in the least. Then everything happened in slow motion. She heard a loud bang and the door frame splintered and felt it hit her in the back. It propelled her forward and she hit her stomach against the coffee table before falling to the ground. Pain radiated through her and she curled up in a ball and wrapped her hand around her belly as he came inside. Charlie grabbed her by the shoulders and pulled her to her feet.

"Do you think I'm scared of some puissant of a man you're fucking?" he snarled in her face and his breath reeked of stale alcohol.

"I installed security—a silent alarm—after we divorced. The cops will be here in a few minutes and you'll be in jail for the rest of your life," she whispered. Charlie wasn't the smartest man and she hoped her bluff worked. She felt her stomach tighten and pain radiated down her back.

She saw him glance around worriedly for a while and then punched her in the face and she fell to the ground again with a cry of pain. "Bring your bastard into the world with a black eye, bitch. Tell your man it is courtesy of me."

She heard him run away and the pain became worse. Marie managed to get to her knees and pull the cordless phone off the table, not caring that the base crashed to the floor. She called the only person she knew would save her. Brody. Brody would come and take care of her. He answered on the second ring and she whimpered in relief as she heard his voice.

"Hey, babe, what's up? You caught me just as Rafe and I were ready to show these guys how it's done," Brody said.

"Help me," she whimpered. "Brody, come home."

His voice instantly took on alarm. "Honey, what's wrong? Shit, are you in labor? It's early, way too early."

"Charlie, he broke down the door...I hit my stomach...he punched me," she managed to say.

"Hold on, baby, I'm coming. Do you hear me? I'm coming. Stay on the phone," Brody yelled, then he spoke to Rafe, "Call nine-one-one. Her fucking ex broke into the goddamn house. She's hurt."

"Marie, are you there, sweetheart? I'm on my way. The ambulance is en route." His breath came faster, panting in and out and she knew he was running.

Pain radiated through her stomach again and she moaned in agony. "Brody, it hurts."

"It's okay, baby. You'll be okay. Grayson will be okay," he said into the phone frantically.

His voice seemed farther away now, shrouded in a cloud of haze and she sank blissfully into a darkness that was swallowing her mind. "Marie!" was the last word she heard Brody shout before she succumbed to unconsciousness. Maybe when she woke he'd be there and it would have all been a dream.

And Baby Makes Three

* * * *

"I'm going to fucking kill that bastard," Brody snarled and paced up and down the room.

"Calm down, Brody, you don't want her to wake up and see you acting like this," Rafe said.

He couldn't even bear to look at her in the bed. She was lying there looking so fragile, a bright purple bruise covering half of her face and her eye was swollen shut. Her stomach...well, baby Grayson was okay. The fast thumping sound that filled the room was his heart beat, steady and strong. The doctors said they had managed to stop the contractions. The good part was both mother and son would be fine and upon hearing that, he'd taken the breath he seemed to have been holding for hours. The bad part was the rage that burned in him was unlike anything he'd felt before. He wanted to kill Charlie. He wanted to see the man dead for what he did to his Marie. For that, he paced like a caged bear, wanting to tear everything apart with his bare hands. Ivy sat beside the bed, silent tears trickling down her cheeks and when she took a breath it hitched and she blew it out slowly, trying to calm herself. Rafe kept looking at her worriedly and he had every right to. The four—almost seven—of them were like their own little family, and no one messed with their family.

Marie moaned from the bed and whimpered, "Brody."

He was by her side instantly and took her hand. "Baby, I'm here. It's okay, everything is just fine."

She slowly opened her good eye, and the other was just a slit because of the swelling. "Grayson, the baby. I can't feel him!"

"Shh, he's fine, you're fine. The doctors just gave you something to make sure you wouldn't have contractions and so you'd sleep," he explained gently.

"Oh, it was all my fault. I was trying to get Charlie to leave. I goaded him and told him I was pregnant and happy." Marie licked her lips. "He didn't like that and kicked the door down. Everything started hurting and he hit me."

Brody kissed her gently. "No, baby, he came to our home and he is the one to blame. He could've walked away, but he didn't. Now I'm going to hurt him."

"Oh, Brody, no," she moaned. "Let the police handle it, don't get in trouble. Please don't go, don't leave me."

"I won't get in trouble and I won't leave you, honey," he wiped the tears that had started trailing down her cheeks and kissed her eyes gently. "You rest, okay, sweetheart? We'll be right here."

"Rafe, watch him. Don't let him get in trouble, not over Charlie, not over him..." Her voice trailed away as she fell asleep again. The medicine in her IV kept her relaxed and calm but didn't affect the baby.

Brody looked over at Ivy. 'Watch over her until I get back, will you?"

And Baby Makes Three

Ivy threw an alarmed look at Rafe and then nodded. "I'll keep my eye on her. From what I remember her saying, Charlie liked to hang out at *Whiskey River Bar*. The one with turtle racing and hacky sack and all that crap. Make him regret what he did to her. Rafe, don't let him get arrested. Marie will have all our asses on a skewer."

Rafe smiled and kissed her. "Ma'am, yes, ma'am."

Brody nodded, half relieved and half surprised that she wasn't going to raise a fuss about him going to find Charlie. Marie was hurt and upset and she didn't understand that as a man he had to defend her. He had to take a piece out of the man who attacked the woman he loved. He and Rafe left the room and he took one look back at Marie in the bed and closed his eyes. Coming to the house and finding her on the kitchen floor was etched in his memory. Her face contorted in pain and even then the swelling of her face was evident. Even then all she thought about was the baby. *Don't worry about me. Take care of Grayson.* A mother's protection was fierce like a mother lion fighting for her cub. Well, he was daddy lion and Charlie was going to feel his rage, every last bit of it as he pounded him into a pulp.

The night air was cool as they strode outside and Brody didn't even pause to take in a deep breath. By the time Rafe got into the passenger seat, he was pulling out of the parking lot with tires squealing.

"Damn, Brody, let me get my seatbelt on," Rafe growled.

"Tell me if that was Ivy you wouldn't be on a rampage trying to tear trees out of the ground," Brody snarled.

"Yes, I would, that's why I'm going to let you get your fight on so you can satisfy that testosterone fueled anger you've got going," Rafe said. "But you're going to do this the right way. He is going to throw the first punch and then you're defending yourself. I don't need you up on a court martial with our move getting ready to happen."

Brody tried to breathe past his anger. "Just stop me before I kill him. I could do it easily without a second thought."

Rafe slapped his hand on his shoulder. "That's why Ivy let me tag along, so I can be the voice of reason. And because if she wasn't pregnant she would be in this backseat with a baseball bat."

The thought of Ivy swinging on men twice her size made Brody smile. The women in their lives were spitfires.

He knew exactly where *Whiskey River* was and soon was pulling into the little dead-end bar in a bad part of town. He'd partied there once and met some women who weren't much to look at or not someone you wanted to take home to mom. Needless to say he went home alone, and wanted to sanitize himself after the experience. *Whiskey River* was a place for cheap beer and women that were loose in morals and body.

And Baby Makes Three

Needless to say, it was one of the reasons he started throwing parties so his guys wouldn't need to be disinfected after a night at the flea-ridden bar. They stepped into the little bar and instantly stood out. The music was a tad too loud and the eyes that stared at them were either interested or wary—or both.

Rafe went up to the bartender who was also the owner and whispered in his ear. He nodded and Brody caught the subtle move as he pointed out Charlie. The bartender was an ex-Marine that tried to run a clean, honest place with no drugs, just didn't have the best clientele. But he was well known for not taking any bullshit and definitely not playing bodyguard to someone like Charlie. Brody assessed the man as he moved forward. Charlie was about two inches shorter than him but broader across the back. He threw a shot of whiskey back and rubbed the back of his neck and shifted his weight. Brody saw the weakness in his right leg and worked it out in his head how he could use that to his advantage. He pulled up a stool next to Charlie and ordered a drink while Rafe stood close by. He took a sip of the whiskey sour and grimaced because it was made with more whiskey than mix. He pushed it aside because he certainly didn't want alcohol on his breath when he went back to the hospital. Marie didn't need that.

"So, you're Charlie?" he said casually.

"Yeah. What's my name got to do with you?" Charlie shot back.

"Just want to make sure I have the right guy, the one

who kicked in the door to my home and punched my very pregnant girlfriend." Brody's voice was deadly.

"You're the sucker who knocked up that whore." Charlie roared with laughter and it took everything out of Brody not to beat his head into the bar. "I'm sorry to tell you, buddy, that chick's been used and abused."

"No, used and abused by you, you mean," Brody said and raised his voice so others could hear. "It takes a big man to use his fists on a woman who is half his size and pregnant. Kind of like stacking the deck in his favor. Am I right or am I right?"

The woman standing beside him and who he was talking with before Brody came over moved away with disgust in her eyes. The bar flies at *Whiskey River* weren't known to be partial, and to have them walk away from you was a new kind of low.

"Where you going, baby?" he said with the charm of a snake.

"Over here where the real men are. I don't drink with abusers. You hit a pregnant woman." She shook her head. "You're a fucking creep."

"Poor Charlie, you're batting zero, but what else could we expect from a pathetic lowlife like you?" Brody chuckled. "Washed out of the Army because you're a bit too unstable in the field. Oh, yeah, I heard about you. Too scared to fight so you pretended to go insane and when you did go out you ended up under a Humvee crying while your platoon was fighting for their lives."

And Baby Makes Three

The bartender laughed. "Oh, if you hear him tell it, he saved them all."

Other people laughed and Charlie snarled at Brody. "Shut your mouth or I'll shut it for you."

"I'm no woman, Charlie, even though I think a few of *these* ladies could take *you* on," Brody said. "I just wanted to see the man who hit my girl before the cops pick him up and take him away. If the Army made you cry, you ain't seen nothing yet. In prison, they'll make you cry and sing a whole different tune when those guys are tagging your ass."

"Fuck you," Charlie shouted. "All you motherfuckers wish you were like me."

Brody shook his head. "A loser? I'd say no to that. I've got a woman and a baby on the way. Even when you hit and beat her, you never got her to feel lower than you. When you cheated, it hurt for a while until she met a real man and, in case you didn't know, I meant me. You're a footnote in her past, something not even worth remembering. She's right. I don't even need to hit you, you're pathetic enough as is. Why waste my time on garbage like you?"

Charlie let out a roar when Brody turned his back on him and then he felt Charlie's hand on his shoulder. *Thank you*, he thought with evil delight and let himself be swung around. He caught Charlie's punch on the chin, but he didn't really feel it with the adrenaline that was rushing through him. The next swing he blocked and had the satisfaction of planting his fist in the center of Charlie's gut. The man gagged, ready to spill the alcohol he consumed on the floor. Brody kicked his injured knee and relished in his scream. He knocked Charlie to the floor and began rearranging his face until Rafe caught his hand. Charlie was moaning in pain on the floor. He dragged his hand away from Rafe, ready to hit him some more when Rafe caught him in a half nelson and dragged him up.

"He's had enough," Rafe said sharply.

"Not nearly, but I'll let the cops finish this piece of garbage," Brody said and turned to the bartender. "I trust you can hold on to him until the police arrive?"

The bartender nodded. "Already been called for starting a bar fight, and lo and behold, it's also the man who committed an assault tonight. Go figure. Get out of here, Marines."

Rafe gave him a mock salute. "Thanks."

Brody let him drive back to the hospital because his hand was actually beginning to ache. He flexed it and thought about getting an X-ray when they got back but decided against it. He'd wrap it when he got back to the house. In the room, Ivy was still sitting there keeping watch and she looked up when they walked in.

"One bruise on your chin. I hope he looks worse," she commented.

Brody smiled. "Yes, he does, and I wish I could have snapped his neck."

Ivy nodded. "Good. Now you watch over her so we can go get some sleep."

"I'll have the house secured and any mess cleaned up before she gets home," Rafe commented. "I already had Monroe finish the exercise with our boys and they did well. They'll be ready. I'll get you cleared on leave for the next few weeks."

"Thanks. I mean it. Both of you are truly great friends," Brody said gratefully.

"No, we're family," Ivy replied and kissed him on the cheek. "I'll be back tomorrow to see how she is."

"You should be resting—"

Ivy cut off his words. "I can rest here just as well as I can at home. I'll be here tomorrow."

He knew better than to argue, so Brody just nodded. "I'll see you guys then."

The door closed silently behind them and he turned, taking Marie's hand in his own and kissing it gently. She murmured and struggled to wake while he crooned words of love softly, trying to settle her. Grayson's heartbeat was steady and strong and he felt more relief than he thought possible in this kind of situation. He almost lost them tonight and Brody had never known fear like that in his life. He'd faced insurgents being pinned down before and had fought for his life, but nothing compared to the thought of losing them.

"You didn't leave," she murmured, her eyes still closed.

"Of course not, baby, I told you I'd be right here,"

he replied. He'd clear up the white lie later. Right now, she was most important. "I love you sweetheart and no one will ever hurt you again."

"Grayson is okay?" she asked. "I feel so numb like I'm wrapped in clouds and I can't tell."

"He's fine, darling, he is perfectly fine." Brody kissed her hand over and over again.

"Okay. I love you, Brody. I'm sorry I'm so much trouble," she said and he could hear tears in her voice. "I should've been smarter. I want to be home in our bed with you."

"No, sweetheart, you're perfect, strong and brave," he replied. "Now you sleep, okay, and we'll see what the doctors say tomorrow about you going home."

"Lay with me," she whispered.

She didn't have to ask twice. He moved to the side of the bed where there were no wires to hamper him and he slid into the hospital bed with her and even though he felt as if he would fall off at any moment, Brody had no intention of moving. He was still wearing his boots as he lay on top of the blankets and kissed her forehead gently. Marie fell asleep in his arms and he kept watch over her and the baby until dawn broke and he finally dozed off. Their fingers were locked together on her stomach over the child they both cherished.

Chapter Seven

Four days later, Marie was home resting on her sofa, being pampered completely by Brody. The incident with Charlie happened on Friday night and the doctor kept her until he made sure her contractions had ceased completely. Jenny, her midwife, came to the hospital as soon as she heard and did her own exam. She would be visiting Marie at home once a week until she went into labor. Charlie had been arrested at his usual haunt, she'd been told, after a bar fight. She knew it was at the hands of Brody. The police officer came to the house and told them he'd been taken in and Brody kept his face neutral as he spoke. Though she did notice that he squeezed her hand just a bit tighter while he spoke to the officer. Since then, he hadn't spoken about it and neither had she. But she noticed his bruised knuckles and the small bruise on his chin that was now only noticeable if the light hit it just right.

Grayson kicked her in her side and she winced. He was getting bigger, stronger and that was a good thing. Thinking about how she almost lost her baby made her terrified, but she put that behind her knowing that Charlie would be in jail for a very long time. He was charged with felony assault on her. Since the baby was a viable fetus that could survive out of the womb he was charged with assault on her unborn fetus. Plus felony breaking and entering, it would be awhile before he walked out of prison.

"Hey, babe, I'm done with the garden outside." Brody came in looking sweaty. The days were becoming warmer and longer and spring was on its way. He had decided to get outside to fix her flowerbeds and plant tulip bulbs before seeding the lawn. They had also spoken of wanting a nice, big vegetable garden this year and agreed to plant as many veggies as possible. He looked sexy as hell in faded jeans and a T-shirt that stretched tightly across his chest and shoulders. "I'm going to take a quick shower and then we can watch TV or something."

"Can we please go for a drive, go buy diapers, something, anything," she pleaded. "I'm going stir crazy. I can't lay here for another minute."

"But you're supposed to be resting." Brody frowned.

"Both the doctor and Jenny said I'm fine and the baby is fine. As long as I'm not lifting weights, I should be okay, Brody," she said. "Please, Daddy, let's go out."

She had started calling him daddy a few weeks back as a joke and now it stuck as an endearment she liked to use. He loved it. Every time she said it his chest would puff up and a slow grin would spread across his face, and today was no different.

And Baby Makes Three

"Okay, let me grab a shower and we can go," Brody said and then pointed a finger at her. "But you will push the cart only, no lifting, no bending, just the cart."

"Sir, yes, sir," Marie answered with a smile.

"You think you've got me whipped, but I'm on to your tricks," he called as he ran up the stairs.

"Yes, you are," she yelled and chuckled. Oh, she was going to marry that man just as soon as she could. The incident with Charlie made her realize just how much he really did care for her and that he was different, and that she no longer needed to be worried about their future together.

A few moments later, the doorbell rang. The last time that happened she ended up in the hospital so while she moved towards the door, apprehension made her wary. Charlie was in jail, but God knows who his friends were and what they would do.

"Who is it?" she called through the barrier.

A soft voice with a Texas twang answered. "Hello, I'm looking for my son, Brody Gillis."

His mother! Marie hurried to open the door. "Mrs. Gillis?"

"Why, look at you carrying so low!" His mother beamed. "You're going to be delivering soon."

"It will be a few more weeks," Marie said with a smile. She instantly liked his mother who had gentle eyes and a warm smile. Her hair was pulled up into a bun but some of the brown tresses fell loosely around her face and only a hint of gray was noticeable in the front. "Come in. Brody is upstairs taking a shower."

His mother stepped in and closed the door gently behind her while Marie walked over to the stairs and called, "Brody, your mom is here."

"What?" he yelled back and then cussed a blue streak. "Sorry, soap in my eyes, I'll be down in five."

Marie gave his mother an apologetic look and said, "He doesn't usually curse like that, ma'am."

"Call me Susan." His mother laughed. "He does sometimes. I've heard a few choice words come from that boy over the years." She reached out her hand to Marie's belly. "May I? I know some women do not like their bellies being rubbed when they're pregnant."

"You're Grandma. Go ahead," Marie said gently.

Susan placed her hand on Marie's belly and Grayson kicked as if to say, *Yes, I'm here.* Brody's mother laughed softly. "Oh, he's going to be wild like his father."

"Brody told you he is a boy?" Marie asked.

Susan nodded. "And his name. He's told me how much he loves you and I think you both are going to make fine parents."

Brody came bounding down the stairs, his hair still damp from the shower. "Mom, what are you doing here?" He lifted her in a hug and took her off her feet, causing her to laugh. "I thought Dad ordered you not to see me and my illicit family?"

"Your father is an asshole, pardon my French,"

his mother said primly. "I've decided to leave that man who keeps talking trash about my son, his choice of a partner, and my grandchild."

"Mom, are you serious?" Brody led her to the sofa and Marie followed. "What happened?"

"Your father's hate against everyone who isn't white is one thing." She looked at Marie apologetically. "I'm sorry to say that in your home, honey, but I taught Brody that people should be judged by what they are on the inside, not by the color of their skin. Trust me, it was difficult with a man like that in all of our lives. But no more, I cannot abide by him calling my grandchild a zebra or saying my son should have been aborted." His mother sighed. "I've been unhappy for way too long. He said awful things one too many times, so while he was at church spouting hate, I packed my things and left. I bought a ticket at the airport and came here. I'll stay if you let me. Not with you. A young family does not need a mom in the mix mucking it up. I have savings, I'll get my own place and do things I want to do with my life."

"You can stay here with us until you figure out what you want to do," Marie said gently. "Plus, you can play with Grayson all you want when he's born."

"I want to open a little dress shop making Victorian and other era clothing." His mother smiled. "Woodward would never let me do it, called it heathen clothes, but I kept saving, hoping one day to live my dream." She slapped her hands on her thighs.

"So here is where I'll build it, a cute little store front and be able to see my grandchild to boot."

"You sound so definite, Mom," Brody said softly. "Are you sure?"

"I've been sure a long time, sugar, I just needed motivation to take that step." His mother smiled. "When you told me you'd be moving in with Marie… All your life you've stood against your father's beliefs. You became a good man, not because of him but in spite of him. It's about time I find happiness as well. I plan on divorcing him."

"Good for you, Mom, good for you. But you may want to hold back on where you want to open that shop until you hear our news," Brody said and then grinned. "I'll have my two best girls in my life."

Marie's brow furrowed. "Our news? You and Rafe have been holding this secret over Ivy's and my head for the longest time. What is it?"

"Rafe called my cell while I was upstairs and I got the go ahead to finally tell you. We're moving the unit to a warmer climate. Like Hawaii warm. We're going to be training with the Navy SEAL team for unified missions."

"What about the house and…well, everything?" Marie asked. "Wait, Ivy and Rafe too, right?"

"Yes, them too. We won't be leaving until the end of the year, which gives us time to get the houses on the market and…" Brody took her hand. "That's only if you want to, baby, it is your decision too."

"Yes, I want to. The kids can grow up playing on

the beach." Marie smiled and looked at his mom. "How does that sound, Susan?"

"Opening a dress shop in the sunshine sounds fine to me." His mother winked. "I can make baby clothes too."

"Won't, um, Woodward come looking for you guys?" Marie had to ask. Everything seemed to be falling into place, but she had to voice what was bothering her.

Brody's mother answered. "No, he won't because he never cared to know where our son lived, never took the slightest interest in his life. I am sure he'll preach to his small congregation about how I was tempted away by evil and use me as an example to keep them in line. I really don't care what anyone in that town thinks of me. It stopped being a place I called home a long time ago."

"Then we're moving to Hawaii," Marie said, finally letting herself feel excited.

Brody took her hand. "Hawaii here we come."

Susan Gillis took Marie's and Brody's hands and winked. "I'm so excited I would say we jump around, but with the baby, we'll save that for later."

Marie laughed. "I like you, Susan, you have some serious spunk."

"I like you too, Marie, and thank you for inviting me into your home," his mother said. "Brody, my luggage is at the door. Can you get them in for me, please?"

"Yes, ma'am," Brody said and went to the door.

TO NURSE WITH LOVE

"You sit and rest, Marie, I'll make you some lunch. Do you like chicken salad?" his mother asked.

"Actually, we were going to do some baby shopping and grab some lunch while we were out. Come with us," Marie invited. "I want to get the baby room finished."

"Hmm, nesting, that means you are going to deliver soon, sugar," his mother said.

"The sooner the better," Marie replied, pulling her light blue zip up hoodie off the back of the recliner. She could no longer zip it up considering her ginormous belly, but it was still her favorite.

"Honey, I've learned that babies keep their own schedule rather than ours," his mother said. "If he is anything like his father, Mr. Grayson will be here early."

"Well, let's get to shopping in case he does," Brody said, as he brought his mother's suitcase into the house.

His hand was at Marie's back rubbing lightly as they stepped out into the sunshine. He leaned down to whisper *thank you* in her ear as he opened the passenger door for her. He didn't have to thank her for anything. His mother didn't strike her as a woman that was malevolent or mean in any way and Marie didn't mind having her in her home. It was just another piece in their family puzzle and when you love someone you accept every part of them. Marie loved Brody with everything in her.

* * * *

276

And Baby Makes Three

It seemed Brody's mom was right because two weeks later Marie was crying in bed and really didn't know why. She was uncomfortable, happy, sad, angry, miserable and more all at the same time. The baby's room was perfect and yet it still wasn't. She was hungry but nothing was appetizing. Finally, she gave up and went to bed for a good cry. Susan brought her up a cup of tea and some fresh, just-out-of-the-oven ginger snap cookies and sat with her while she sniffed. His mother had settled in well and would be making the move to Hawaii a couple of months ahead of them to get her shop together.

She and Brody had already found her an amazing condo as well as a little shop close to the beach and all in the area they had decided to live. Marie recalled the dinner event they had a week before where Rafe, Ivy and Rafe's parents came over and they had a major pow-wow about the move. Rafe's parents wouldn't be moving but planned to visit often, plus help with the move. They each picked houses and a time frame for moving everything they owned, which would be packed up and shipped by the military to make it easier when the time came. Thinking about it now made her cry harder. She was thrilled to be moving to a warmer climate, but it was still going to be hard to say goodbye. She saw Brody's shadow in the hallway, right outside the bedroom, hovering. She didn't know if it was sweet or if it irritated the hell out of her. She felt like a hot mess.

TO NURSE WITH LOVE

"I don't know what's the matter with me," she sobbed. "I'm so huge and…" She let the rest of her words trail off.

"And what, dear?" Susan asked sympathetically.

"My back has been hurting all day, like a dull throb and it just won't go away." Marie hiccupped.

"Honey, it sounds like you're in labor. What you are experiencing is back labor," Brody's mother explained. "I've seen this tons of times, the emotions and the achy back. You're going to have little Grayson soon."

Brody came into the room pale faced. "You're kidding, right, Mom?"

"But then he'll be too early." Marie suddenly felt afraid and that made a fresh wave of tears fall from her eyes. "It's too soon."

"You're over thirty-six weeks, honey, he'll be just fine," Susan encouraged. "It could be any day now. What you need to do is drink your tea and try and get some rest. Brody, you come over here and rub her back with those giant hands of yours. I knew they were meant for more than holding a football. Later, if you're up to it, you'll have some of my homemade red lentil soup."

Marie nodded. "Okay, but he's not ready to be born yet."

"Honey, babies know when they are finished cooking way before their mamas do," she said gently. "Now rest and I'll be in the kitchen making soup."

"Do you think she's right?" Marie asked when

278

And Baby Makes Three

Susan left the room and Brody came and sat next to her on the bed. He helped her lie on her side and began kneading her lower back gently. She moaned in delight as the pressure of his hand made her back feel instantly better.

"My mom knows a bunch of stuff about babies. She was actually one of the midwives for my father's church. They didn't believe in mainstream doctors and hospital births and so my mom has delivered a lot of babies," Brody explained. "If it wasn't for her, a lot of parents would have lost their children because of my dad's crazy cult. We'll just wait and see, darling. Don't worry."

She ended up drinking all her tea and was actually able to eat some soup later in the evening before falling asleep. It was after midnight when she awoke suddenly. It felt as if something inside her had popped and wetness pooled between her thighs. She shifted and more flowed out and Marie knew this was it. She was in labor and there was no mistaking that, not after your water broke.

Marie tapped Brody's shoulder. "Brody, wake up, my water broke."

He was up and out of bed instantly, like the bed had suddenly caught fire. "You're kidding. Shit, please say you're kidding?"

Marie shook her head. "Your mom seemed to have called it. I'm in labor."

He looked wildly around the room and ran his hand through his hair and Marie watched him. While she was surprisingly calm, he seemed to have become panic-crazed.

"Okay, where's your bag? Um, I know, we packed it… Shit, okay, I—"

"Brody," she said calmly.

He turned to face her. "Yes, baby, I'm sorry. I should be worrying about you, not the bag. What do you need? Anything, anything at all I will get it for you. I can go make you a hotdog sandwich if you need one. I may need to go get the hotdogs you like but it's okay, I can do this."

"No, thank you, honey. Can you please help me get into the shower and then go wake your mom, tell her what's going on," Marie explained. "Call Jenny, then Rafe and Ivy and we'll go to the hospital."

He nodded. "I can do that."

She held out her arms to him. "I know you can, that's why I love you."

He was kneeling next to her in an instant, kissing her over and over again. "I love you too, Marie. God, I love you so much." He cupped her face and stared into her eyes. "We're doing this, we're going to be parents."

She smiled and nodded. "Yes we are. Now help me into the shower because I think I'm having a contraction which means we need to hurry."

That propelled him to move and soon she was in the bathroom getting out of her wet things. He closed the door and she heard him yell, "Mom, this is it!" Marie laughed softly to herself as she got under the hot spray. She was dressed in loose sweatpants and sitting in the back seat of the suburban no more than a half an hour later. Brody kept glancing back at her every few minutes as she rubbed her tightening belly when each contraction hit. They were getting closer already and that worried her. Baby Grayson didn't seem to intend to make a slow entrance into the world. In no time, they were at the hospital and Jenny met them to head up to the maternity ward. Soon, she was in a wheelchair, being wheeled down the hall, with everyone she loved around her. Brody held her hand all the way while Ivy with her own burgeoning belly held the other. Rafe carried the bags and Brody's mother rounded out the group. Marie was checked in and settled in a birth suite in no time, and soon Jenny came in dressed in scrubs ready to check her dilation.

"What a big crowd to welcome Grayson into the world," Jenny commented with a smile. "I've met Rafe and Ivy, and who is this fine lady? Let me guess, I see some of Brody in your features. I'm thinking you are Mom."

Brody's mother laughed. "Yes, that would be me."

"Well, welcome, Grandma. Now, let's see how far along you are," Jenny said, coming over to Marie.

Marie felt her gently check her and a contraction hit at the same time making her moan in pain. "Well, damn, this really hurts."

"Breathe through it, sweetheart, just like in

Lamaze," Brody encouraged.

"You breathe through it. It's your fault I'm in this predicament," Marie muttered.

Jenny chuckled. "Well, Marie, you're already at five centimeters dilated and fully effaced. You can either try the doula and labor for a little while or you can get your epidural."

"Epidural. Two if I can order a second," Marie said firmly.

"No, only one." Jenny patted her leg and got up off the corner of her bed.

"Is he going to be okay being that it is early?" Marie asked worriedly. "It's only the middle of May."

"You're thirty-six weeks and healthy babies can be born between thirty-six and forty-two weeks," Jenny said gently. "I would have liked to see this bun bake a little longer, but he's ready to be born. We'll look for breathing problems and monitor him in neonatal but his heartbeat is very strong and honestly I think he'll be fine."

That lessened some of her worry and she looked over to the monitor where the little heart icon blinked in tune to his heartbeat. Brody leaned over and kissed her forehead gently. "He'll be fine, honey. I think you're having another contraction. The little squiggly line thing is jumping like crazy."

"Gee, thanks for pointing that out, I couldn't tell from the pain," she muttered and began to breathe through it.

"How bad is it?" Ivy asked worriedly. She was

sitting in a chair close by.

"It's okay. Really more uncomfortable than painful," Marie said, not wanting to scare Ivy who would be going through the same thing soon. Ivy gave her one of those *yeah, right* looks she was famous for and Marie laughed. "Okay, okay, it hurts like a mother...I mean bitch."

"I thought so. Rafe wants me to have a nurse with an epidural waiting at the door when the time comes," Ivy said.

"I don't think they will do that, honey." Rafe took her hand and kissed it, but Marie saw worry in his eyes.

"You guys will rock labor," Marie said through gritted teeth. "Oh, boy, these are getting fierce."

"Where's the damn anesthesiologist with the pain medication?" Brody asked irritably.

Marie gripped his hand as another contraction hit her and she spoke between breaths. "Can...someone go find...Jenny and tell...her I need to be...beaten over the head...until I'm unconscious?"

Rafe moved toward the door. "I'll go, Brody. You stay here. Your glowering is liable to scare the nurses."

Rafe left and returned with the message that she was making her way to them. Apparently, more than a few women were in labor and it was a busy night. The time ticked by with her laboring without medication.

After one really rough contraction, Marie looked up at Brody. "Let's get married."

"Okay, the license is still valid." Brody wiped her face with a cool washcloth.

"No, I mean now," she said firmly. "Before he's born."

Brody looked alarmed. "Honey, I don't think there is any possible way to do it now."

"Go find the chaplain. One is always in the hospital." She began to pant as another contraction began to surface. "Get him, pay him, and make a donation, I don't care. I want to get married before Grayson comes."

"Oh, Lord, woman, you are trying to kill me." Brody kissed her hard. "Okay, I'll find him and drag him here if I have to. Mom, take over."

"The marriage license, where is it? He needs t sign it!" She panted. "Oh god can you get home to get it before this baby makes an entrance?"

Brody smiled and patted his back pocket. "It's been with me since the day we got it, its my luck good luck charm."

"Ok go find the minister," His mother hurried him along. "Mister Grayson is very impatient to meet us."

Brody's mother took her hand and wiped her face. "Okay, sweetie, you keep breathing."

Rafe pulled out his cell. "I'll take floors one to six, you hit four to twelve. Whoever finds him first calls the other."

She watched them tear out of the room like fire was lapping at their heels. She watched the clock as twenty minutes passed with them not back yet. Her contractions were now five minutes apart and she knew his birth was closer with each round of pain. Finally, they rushed in with a frazzled-looking Brody and a smiling older man. He wore jeans and a black shirt with a collar.

"I hear we're getting married," he said.

"This is Father Griffith. He's going to marry us, sweetheart," Brody said.

"Okay." She gritted her teeth and began to pant. "We may need to hurry this, father, not that I don't want all the words, but this boy is also in a hurry to make an entrance."

"I'm on board. Take her hand," Father Griffith said to Brody. "Dearly beloved, we are gathered here in the sight of God—and the face of this company— to take part in the most time-honored celebration of the human family, to join this man and this woman in holy matrimony."

The father spoke and they answered at the appropriate times while her body went through the process of having a baby.

"Can we have the rings?" the chaplain said.

Brody smiled awkwardly. "Skip that part. We'll get those later."

"Okay. Do you, Marie Watson, take this man as your lawfully wedded husband?" Father Griffith asked.

"Yes, I do," she said and leaned her head back as another contraction hit. "Where in the hell is that medication? I need numbing!"

"Do you, Lieutenant Brody Gillis, take this woman to be your wife?" Father Griffith posed the question to him.

"Yes, sir, with all my heart," Brody said.

"By the power vested in me by God and the State of Maryland, I now pronounce you man and wife." Father Griffith smiled widely. "You may kiss the bride."

Brody leaned over and kissed her before she pushed him away. "Oh, God, here comes another one."

Finally, the anesthesiologist came in. The woman doctor was too perky for Marie's taste and she shuffled everyone except Brody out of the room. After about ten minutes she was blissfully numb from the belly down and decided the doctor wasn't that bad after all. Each contraction came and she felt nothing except the tightening of her stomach. Three more hours of contractions came and went before it was time for her to begin pushing. Ivy helped hold one leg while Brody held the other so she could have some support while she bore down to push Grayson from her body. Even with the medication could feel her body stretching as he moved downward.

"Come on, honey, you're doing it. I can see his hair," Brody said excitedly.

"One more will do it, Marie. You're doing great," Jenny said.

"One more, baby, push," Brody encouraged.

She gripped his hand and brought her head to her

chest, bearing down with all her might.

"Reach down and pull your baby out," Jenny encouraged.

Marie reached between her legs and Jenny put her hands around the baby's small body and she gently tugged. With a cry, she felt her baby slip from her body and then blessed emptiness as he lay on her chest.

"We have a boy," Jenny said happily. She suctioned his mouth and nose before tapping his little feet lightly.

Marie laughed between her tears when the baby gave a small cry and then a louder one and then a belting sound that filled the room.

"Nothing is wrong with those lungs," Jenny said. "Dad, cut the cord, and let's get him in the warmer."

After Brody cut the cord, the nurse took the baby while Jenny helped her expel the afterbirth. Brody's mother was openly crying and so was Ivy. Rafe's grin was wide and he held Ivy's hand tightly. The nursed handed the baby to Brody who cradled the tiny child in his hands.

"Hey, Grayson, welcome to the world. I'm your dad." His voice was husky. "And you have the most awesome mommy in the world."

"Let your mom hold him," Marie said.

Marie heard the little cooing noise Susan made when she took baby Grayson in her arms. She cuddled him and then met Marie's gaze with her tear-filled eyes. "Thank you for letting me be here for this.

I have needed this kind of joy in my life for a long time."

Susan handed the baby to Marie gently and she kissed those soft baby cheeks. "Hi, my darling boy, you are early but you are so very loved."

Everyone was escorted out of the room so she could be moved to a private room. There, Rafe and Ivy held their godson and when Marie started to doze off everyone quietly crept from the room. It was around 7:00 a.m. when she opened her eyes and Brody was sitting in the comfy daddy's chair across the room with Grayson held against his chest and a small bottle on the coffee table next to the chair.

"Hey, Daddy, what's going on? Bonding without me?" she asked sleepily.

Brody chuckled softly. "The nurse brought him in for a feeding and you were asleep, so she said he could have a bottle and you could breastfeed next time around."

"God, I'm hungry," she said with a smile. She could feel the ache of her body from giving birth but the emptiness as well and kind of missed the full, round feeling of Grayson being inside.

"Breakfast is at 8:00 a.m. and they promised me a tray as well." Brody grinned.

Marie rolled her eyes. "Charming the nurses, huh? You are a married man, Brody Gillis."

He held the baby close to his chest and came over to sit on the bed next to her. "I know that, Mrs. Gillis, and I wouldn't have it any other way."

And Baby Makes Three

He placed Grayson in her arms and gave her a kiss before leaning his head against hers as they looked down at their newborn son. Marie ran a finger down his open palm and even in sleep he wrapped his tiny fingers around hers and she laughed softly.

"Look at what we made," she whispered in wonder. "He's so perfect, six pounds and two ounces of precious little boy."

"He is, and strong too. Even though he was a few weeks early there is not a thing wrong with him." Brody fixed the little cap on his head. "My son. Thank you so much for this gift."

"He's our gift, one that brought us together and showed me what true love really is and what it feels like." Marie looked up at Brody. "I do love you, Brody, so much, you don't even know. No matter how much I fought it or said we were just having a good time, you were always in my heart and now that's where you're going to stay. You got me, Marine?"

Brody nodded. "Ma'am, yes, ma'am. I love you more than one man should be able to and no matter what, I'll make sure you know that you are treasured, every single day."

"That sounds good to me," she whispered and they shared a lingering kiss.

Her stomach growled and it made them both laugh. He got up and walked toward the door. "I'll go see about your breakfast, honey."

"Okay," she answered.

TO NURSE WITH LOVE

She watched the man she loved walk out the door with the knowledge that he was coming back to her. She looked down at Grayson who opened his eyes and yawned before staring up at her. She knew they said babies couldn't really see for the first two weeks or so, but Marie was sure that he focused on her face, looking into her eyes. This was the new love of her life and he shared that special place in her heart with his father.

"Oh, my sweet boy, you changed me for the better and made us a family," Marie said softly and kissed his head. She could smell the sweet baby scent of him and that was the balm that healed any and all scars and doubts she ever had in her life. All she had gone through was on that path that led directly to this perfect moment in time. With the man she loved and the baby in her arms.

Epilogue

In Kaneohe Bay, where the Marine Corp Base sat in Hawaii, two things happened. One, the Corp welcomed the Light Attack Helicopter unit aptly named Scarface to the base. Second, Brody and Rafe moved their families to Hawaii.

Marie sat on the beach on a large blanket with the sun warming her face. Beside her Ivy sat with her four month old twins Nicholas and Nicola in their double bouncy seat. Rafe was swinging Bonnie high over the surf and her squeals of happiness filled the air. Brody was in the middle of a beach football game with some of the men of their unit and the mood was light. Marie made sure that Grayson's hat covered his head and that the two umbrellas they had stuck in the sand kept the sun off the children. It was all so beautiful one could almost forget how harsh the sun could be, especially on children's skin.

The air smelled sweet of exotic plants and fertile soil. In the distance, you could hear the drums and music from a luau. Their homes were close enough to a resort that on their first week there, Grandma watched the kids while they danced the night away. Marie knew it was a good choice to move to Hawaii.

TO NURSE WITH LOVE

It could have been easy for the men in their lives to move back and forth between the sun and surf to Maryland, but Brody and Rafe both wanted their families close by. It worked out so well that both Ivy and Marie were able to transfer to Naval Health Clinic. They started work only a few weeks after arriving, even though they had thought there might be a few months waiting until positions opened up. All in all, things were blissful and they were content.

Brody ran up to them, shirtless and his feet covered in sand and sat beside Marie, smacking a kiss on her cheek. "How are my two favorite people in the world?"

Grayson let out a happy squeal and held out his chubby hands to his daddy. Brody scooped him out of his mother's arms and lay back in the sand, lifting Grayson over his head.

"He wants to play football too. Don't you, big boy?" Brody said.

"No, he gets to sit here with mom for a while longer until he can walk and talk," Marie said with a laugh.

"Hey, can you watch the twins for a minute? I want to go get my feet wet in the surf with Bonnie and Rafe," Ivy said.

"Sure, go ahead, the twins are both sleeping. I'll wave if they wake up and want something to eat," Marie said.

She watched Ivy run down the beach and Rafe wrapped one hand around her waist while he had

Bonnie lifted in the other. He kissed Ivy as they walked into the surf.

"Are you happy?" Brody kissed her shoulder and bit the string of her bikini. "I so want to take this off you."

"Later you can be as bad as you want," Marie purred. "To answer your question, yes, I am so happy I could burst for it. I love you, I love our home and this place."

"Good, now let's go home and make another baby." Brody give her a sexy grin.

She gave him a look. "How about not until he is potty trained and old enough to feed himself?"

"I guy can hope," he said.

"There's no hope necessary. We'll have more kids eventually and enjoy making each one," Marie replied.

"Did I mention I love the heck out of you?" Brody said.

"I'll never get tired of hearing it." Marie kissed him gently. "Now, take your son and sit in the surf with him, let him get his feet wet."

"Okay, honey."

She smiled, watching Brody walk off down the beach with Grayson in his arms. Those were her boys, her life, and her dreams all wrapped up in one. Ivy's twins made a sound and she looked over at the wonderfully cute sleeping cherubs. *Maybe one or two more,* she mused with a smile. There was so much love between her and Brody, it was more than enough to share.

The End

Made in the USA
Lexington, KY
17 July 2016